DEAD STREAM CURSE

A NORTHERN MICHIGAN ASYLUM NOVEL

J.R. ERICKSON

AUTHOR'S NOTE

Thanks so much for picking up a Northern Michigan Asylum Novel. I want to offer a disclaimer before you dive into the story. This is an entirely fictional novel. Although there was once a real place known as The Northern Michigan Asylum - which inspired me to write these books - it is in no way depicted within them. Although my story takes place there, the characters in this story are not based on any real people who worked at this asylum or were patients; any resemblance to individuals, living or dead, is entirely coincidental. Likewise, the events which take place in the novel are not based on real events, and any resemblance to real events is also coincidental.

In truth, nearly every book I have read about the asylum, later known as the Traverse City State Hospital, was positive. This holds true for the stories of many of the staff who worked there as well. I live in the Traverse City area and regularly visit the grounds of the former asylum. It's now known as The Village at Grand Traverse Commons. It was purchased in 2000 by Ray Minervini and the Minervini Group who have been restoring it since that time. Today, it's a mixed-use space of boutiques, restaurants and condominiums. If you ever visit the area, I encourage you to visit

The Village at Grand Traverse Commons. You can experience first-hand the asylums - both old and new - and walk the sprawling grounds.

DEDICATION

For my dad, Jack, the man who inspired me to read.

PROLOGUE

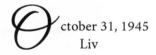

October 31, 1945
Liv

LIV TRIPPED DOWN THE STAIRS, her satin gown tangled in her mother's shoes. At the last step, plunging toward the open door and the lawn beyond, she kicked the shoes off, her breath pluming in the cold night air like little explosions. At the tree line, she fell, landing hard on her outstretched hands. She glanced down. In the moonlight she saw the dark flecks splattered across her chest. It was too dark to see their color, and yet she knew: deep crimson, blood.

She hiccupped and let the sob curdling in her belly rush into the night. It was swallowed by the heavy foliage. The wet, matted leaves took her cries and extinguished them as quickly as her halo of breaths.

She stood and looked at the soaring peaks of the Victorian house deep in the woods.

Candlelight still flickered from the windows. People moved inside, laughing, drinking, and oblivious to the horrors committed only two floors above them.

A curtain shuttered in the third-story window and for a

moment, Liv saw a shape there. The silhouette of a young man in a horned goat mask. The rounded spirals of his horns ended in points as sharp as knives.

Liv closed her eyes against the memory of blood splashing across the polished golden floor.

Her stomach turned and she retched in the grass, vomiting the champagne she'd drank that evening.

When she found the strength to move, she walked numbly into the forest.

CHAPTER 1

July 1945
Liv

"I'M HOT," Arlene complained, tugging on Liv's hand.

The girl wore a yellow smock. Two yellow bows captured her light brown hair in pigtails. Liv never understood why their mother insisted on making Arlene presentable when the seven-year-old dirtied her dress within five minutes of putting it on.

"Me too," Liv grumbled. "But we're almost there, peanut," she assured her little sister as they trudged down the dusty road.

The fast, cool water of the Dead Stream was not far away.

The summer had started early and furiously hot, with temperatures reaching seventy degrees in May. Now in July, ninety-degree days were common.

"This way," Liv urged Arlene, who dawdled, her feet dragging as they plunged through tall grass into the woods.

Beneath the canopy of trees, the temperature was five degrees cooler.

Arlene plopped on the ground, stretching her legs out on a bed of pine needles.

"I'm tired."

Liv leaned against a tree.

"Okay, we'll take a little break, then."

Liv looked into the high pine above her. Sharp green branches fanned out, offering respite from the stifling heat.

Liv pulled a jar from her leather bag and scooped pine pitch from the tree.

"Pine sap?" Arlene asked wrinkling her nose. "It's so sticky."

"It's also great for burns and sores. We can put some on those blisters of yours." Liv pointed at an angry red blister on Arlene's little toe.

Their mother had been given a pair of hand-me-down dance shoes for her youngest daughter, and Arlene had worn them for a week even though they pinched her toes.

"They don't hurt anymore," Arlene said pushing a finger into one of the blisters.

"But they're also not healed. "We'll put some pitch on when we get home." Liv tucked the jar into her bag. "Ready?" Liv extended a hand to her little sister.

Arlene nodded and took Liv's hand. Thick foliage shaded the last quarter-mile of their journey.

When they broke through the trees to the steep bank of the river, Arlene clapped her hands and laughed.

"Wait for me," Liv told her.

Liv stripped out of her shorts and t-shirt and spotted a good branch to drape them on. She slung them over the branch and turned back just as Arlene stepped from the sand into the water.

"Livvy, watch," she called, bending to scoop a handful of water.

Her green eyes opened wide in surprise as her feet slipped from beneath her and the river swallowed her.

Liv let out a shocked scream and jumped over the embankment. As she raced into the water, she saw Arlene's small, tanned arm reach up. Her head popped up and then the undertow pulled her beneath the surface.

The icy water took Liv's breath away, and the current's strong hands clutched and pulled her down.

George had taught her years ago how to handle fast-moving currents, but she ignored his advice to float on her back, legs in front of her. She'd never get to Arlene that way. She let the current take her, paddling only to keep her head above the water while searching for her sister.

Liv dunked under, rose up for a breath, and spotted a flash of movement at the water's edge.

Had Arlene made it out?

Liv watched a young man plunging into the water just as Arlene's head bobbed up and disappeared again.

The boy splashed into the river, his hands reaching for Arlene.

Liv knew her sister was panicking. She'd be thrashing her arms and legs, pushing herself beneath the water, unable to surrender to the flow.

That's how people drowned, but it was too late to tell her that now.

The man dove forward, arms outstretched as Arlene's hand shot above the water. Liv saw the man reach out and clasp the little girl.

Liv slipped beneath the water, struggling back up as the man hauled her sister against his chest. He reached for a branch that stuck out from a dead tree at the river's edge.

He caught it, and Liv cried out in triumph, allowing a flood of water to fill her mouth. She hacked and spit the water out, choking, but relieved as she saw the man pulling Arlene toward the shore.

Liv tried to direct herself to the same tree, but the current surged as she neared them, and it pushed her by.

Beneath her, a tangle of branches caught Liv's foot, and she felt herself jerked to a stop and thrust underwater. The stream rushed around her, but the branch held firm to her shoe. She tried to bend and release her foot, kicking her leg in the thick, rapidly moving stream.

She couldn't reach back. The water shoved and pushed and forced her away from her ensnared foot. Her shoe seemed suctioned to her foot and Liv could not wriggle out of it.

Her lungs burned as she struggled upward, but she couldn't get her head above the water.

Seconds ticked by. The cold stole her breath.

She gazed into the green, murky bottom, trying to continue her fight, but her limbs felt heavy and limp.

Soon she'd have to open her mouth and allow the water in.

She tilted her face to where the sun slanted through the green water. It was so close, and yet she couldn't lift up, couldn't catch even a breath.

Her head would burst if she didn't open her mouth. She released her clenched teeth and let the water pour in, filling her, but no relief came. The bright rays of the sun seemed to shift and darken. The river receded and blinked out.

IT WAS morning and Liv's mother was shaking her awake.

"I'm up," Liv grumbled. "I'm up." But as she spoke, a terrible burning seized her throat.

She coughed and a spurt of water shot from her mouth and splattered the face of the young man gazing down at her. He smiled, not bothering to wipe the water dripping from his chin.

"Livvy, Livvy," her little sister cried, wrapping her in a wet hug and plastering her soaking braids against Liv's cheek.

As Liv breathed, the heavenly intake of air both painful and exhilarating, she remembered Arlene washing down the Dead Stream, and then her own foot caught in the branches.

"You saved us," Liv breathed, wincing at the pain in her throat.

Her eyes welled with tears as she patted her little sister's slick back.

The boy gazed at her, his eyes as pale and sparkly as the quartz rock she sometimes found in the quarry behind the Kenworths' farm.

He nodded, let loose a shaky laugh as if he too had been holding his breath for a very long time, and ran a hand through his black hair. Little rivulets of water ran down his forehead. He sat back on his heels and patted Arlene on the head.

"Yeah, that was..." He shook his head, as if he hadn't figured out what it was yet. "That was alive."

"Alive?" Liv asked, puzzled. She gently pushed Arlene away and rolled to her side before sitting up.

Arlene hiccupped, her face red and splotchy. Liv tugged one of her pigtails.

"Come here, peanut," she told her, letting Arlene crawl into her lap. At seven, the girl was too big to be held, and yet Liv wanted nothing more than to cradle her sister and thank the gods for the man they'd seen fit to plant at the river, at the moment death arrived to take them.

"Yeah, alive," he repeated.

"Thank you," Liv murmured, resting her chin on her sister's head and smoothing away the goosebumps coating her folded legs.

"Thank you," Arlene squeaked.

The man smiled and looked toward the river, a mystified expression on his handsome face.

"Now that I owe you a mortal debt, I should introduce myself," Liv told him. "I'm Liv. This is my little sister, Arlene."

"A mortal debt," he murmured, as if that too baffled him. "I'm Stephen Kaiser. Pleased to meet you."

Liv closed her eyes and breathed in Arlene's scent.

Her thoughts were jumbled, and each time she looked at the river, she saw their deaths laid out and waiting for them, but they had not died that day. Stephen Kaiser had saved them.

Eventually, Liv felt ready to put some distance between herself and the river. Stephen helped Liv to her feet and they headed back the way they'd come.

The three walked through the woods, stopping frequently for Liv to lean against a tree and catch her breath. Her lungs ached and her limbs felt heavy and sodden, as if the water had seeped through her skin and caused her blood to thicken and freeze.

Arlene, in true child form, had bounced back quickly from the near-drowning. She hummed songs as they walked, stopping to point out flowers and pluck caterpillars off trees.

"Are you okay?" Stephen asked after they'd stopped for the third time.

Liv nodded.

"I think so. I keep wondering if there were signs, and I missed them."

"Signs?" Stephen asked. "About the current?"

Liv shook her head.

"Signs that we were walking toward our death. Signs to ward us off."

Stephen looked at her sidelong, and Liv saw the curious expression on his face.

She laughed and reached back for a handful of her long blonde hair, wringing it out. It was thick and tangled, wavy hair that didn't seem to know if it wanted to be curly or straight.

"I didn't have a dream. I had no idea." Liv searched the previous night's dreams but found nothing out of the ordinary, no foreboding of what lay ahead.

"A dream?" he asked, offering another curious glance. "You're a strange girl."

Liv blushed and wished he'd shift his pale blue eyes away from her face.

When he did, she tried to think of normal things to talk about. She didn't have many friends and had spent so much of her life with George; she'd forgotten that ordinary people did not speak of prophetic dreams.

"I've never seen you in school," Liv blurted, because she hadn't, and school was something normal people talked about.

"Do you go to Gaylord High?" he asked.

"Yeah. I moved here with my mom and stepdad last year." She didn't mention that they'd moved into the shacks on the south side of town, where civilization melted into the forest. The shacks were rundown and as likely to be filled with vagabonds as poor families such as Liv's.

"I go to a private school. Or I did," he amended. "I graduated in the spring. I'm moving to Ann Arbor in the fall to go to the University of Michigan."

"Wow," Liv breathed.

She'd never met anyone who went attended a private school. The only college-educated man she could think of was the town's doctor, who looked at Liv and her family like lice-infested rats that had scurried through the back door.

She touched her snarled hair self-consciously and wished she hadn't worn her summer clothes, which consisted of a ragged t-shirt and shorts not worth mending, since they'd just get torn again anyhow. "I have another year of high school left. I hate it," she added.

Arlene stopped by a tall prickly plant.

"Nettles." She pointed to Liv.

Liv nodded and silently willed her sister not to say more.

"Don't we want to pick them?"

"I don't have my bag," Liv told her, grabbing Arlene's hand and pulling her along.

"Why would you pick nettles?" Stephen asked, giving the sharp-looking plant a wide berth.

"Livvy uses them to heal mama's hands," Arlene announced proudly.

Liv felt the flush creeping back up her neck and turned to point at the big oak tree with the strange round protrusion in its trunk.

"Better go touch the boob tree for luck," she told Arlene, realizing her comment sounded as strange as the nettles remark.

Arlene skipped to the tree and pressed both palms on the knobby growth.

Stephen followed her, putting his hands on the place where Arlene's had been.

He looked back at Liv and smiled.

"We can all use a little luck."

CHAPTER 2

July 1945
Liv

LIV WAS HUNGRY. Not a new feeling by any means, but walking through town, she caught a whiff of Miller's Bakery, where something hot and cinnamony drifted from the windows. Her stomach knotted with longing, but instead of moving closer, she crossed the street and averted her gaze.

Her mother would cook boiled cabbage again for dinner, and even those servings would be meager, barely enough to satisfy a single person, let alone a family. Of course, Liv's two older brothers had left home several years earlier, so the mouths were less than they'd once been.

A white flower drifted in front of Liv's face. She reached out and caught it in her palm. It was an apple blossom with a pale pink center. As she tilted her head to seek the source of the flower, a dozen more rained down, blotting the sky with white petals.

Beyond them, she saw a man sitting on the parapet of the building that housed the hardware store. His legs dangled over the side, and he grinned down at her.

It was Stephen Kaiser. The boy who'd rescued her from the river.

Liv laughed and turned down the alley beside the building. A steel ladder clung to the brick, and she climbed it, finding Stephen at the top. He didn't turn when she approached.

"I thought the world had gone mad, and it was raining flowers," Liv told him.

The roof was hot. It seeped through her thin shoes.

Stephen sat on the raised brick ledge. He patted the space beside him.

Sitting on the hot brick, she noticed a Hollywood bar in his hand. He popped a piece of the chocolate bar into his mouth, and Liv experienced a desire so rapid and overwhelming, she almost snatched the candy and ran for the ladder.

"Are you rich?" she breathed. She couldn't remember the last time she'd eaten chocolate.

He looked up at her with those pale, snow-blue eyes. Without answering, he broke off a hunk and handed it to her.

Liv lifted it to her nose, inhaled the sweetness, and then placed the whole piece on her tongue. She should have saved it, taken a tiny bite and squirreled the rest away. She hadn't eaten sweets in ages. Sugar was rationed, but here stood Stephen Kaiser eating chocolate with not a care in the world.

"Thank you," she said as she swallowed the last traces of the smooth chocolate. It lingered in the back of her throat, and she wished the taste would last, but it didn't.

"Where's your pigtailed sidekick?" Stephen asked, taking another bite of the candy bar.

"She spends her days with her Grandma Kit, my stepdad's mom, or she goes to the little schoolhouse for summer lessons," Liv told him, leaning over and watching people amble down the sidewalk below. "How come you're up here?" she asked.

"I rarely come into town," he admitted. "When I do, it all seems so small. I hate standing on the street surrounded by buildings. Up here, I can see the whole world. Or more of it, anyway." He held his arms out wide.

Liv gazed across the town. She could see the little schoolhouse Arlene attended. The bigger school where she spent her days ducking into classrooms and avoiding eye contact with the other students.

From the rooftop, the town looked small and drab.

"Not much to look at, is it?" he asked.

"I moved here from Kalkaska last year," she murmured. "I miss my friends, not that I had very many, but the ones I did. I miss them, and I miss George. I miss fishing in the lake and going out on the boats. This place won't ever be my home."

"Is George your boyfriend?"

"Eww, no. He's my… uncle." She hadn't told the lie in such a long time, it seemed to stick on the back of her tongue.

"I've always lived here," Stephen muttered, bringing his heel down hard against the side of the building. A bit of brick flaked off and rained down to the sidewalk. "And yet I've never lived here at all."

Liv tried to see herself in the town that stretched out before them, but knew she didn't fit. Her family was still poor in Kalkaska, but they had a community around them. George lived in the Stoneroot Forest not far from their little house. He regularly brought Liv fresh meat and food foraged from the Stoneroot Forest. They didn't eat like the wealthy, but they always ate and they never had to beg.

After her mother married Roy, their family shifted. Liv's stepfather resented the charity from George. He didn't know the truth of Liv's birth father. He, like many others, had been told a story of an old family friend, but he sensed a deeper connection between his wife and the man who lived in the forest.

When he insisted the family move further north to the hometown of his own mother, Liv's mother complied. The adjustment was hard. They now occupied a small shack in the most derelict part of town. Both Roy and her mother worked six days a week just to stay in clothes and food.

Liv thought of the tally-lists in each of the shops. The little scratches that marked how many loafs of bread her family had eaten, how many cans of beans they'd taken without payment.

No, Liv would never be a part of her new town.

"What now?" Stephen asked. "Shall we rob a bank? Search for buried treasure? I mean, you've got a second chance at life. I think I should jump on that wagon and ride with you."

Liv widened her eyes, gazing at the boy who was revealing himself to be the most unlikely friend in this strange town. He wore shined loafers and a striped t-shirt tucked into stiff khaki shorts. His black hair was combed away from his forehead. Everything about him told a story of privilege, and yet he seemed interested in her. He wanted to be her friend.

Liv cocked her head, licked her finger and held it up before shaking her hand.

"The wind's not right for a bank robbery. Fancy a walk in the woods?" she asked.

He cocked his head, seemed to mull it over.

"Yes. My last walk in the woods ended strangely indeed. I got to jump into a frigid river and rescue not one, but two damsels in distress."

~

"YOUR SISTER SAID you used nettles to heal your mother's hands. How?" he asked.

He jumped up and grabbed the thick bough of an oak tree, swinging back and forth.

"Do you really want to know?" she asked, feeling her usual discomfort.

The modern world scoffed at George's beliefs. He told her to disregard the opinions of others. Easy enough for him. He lived in a cabin deep in the Stoneroot Forest. Liv was a seventeen-year-old attending high school. It was hard enough being poor without adding a penchant for plant healing and other forest magic.

Stephen dropped with a thud.

"I wouldn't ask if I didn't. I took an anthropology class last year, and we studied Native American tribes that used peyote. It's a cactus they consumed in religious rituals. Some tribes called it the divine messenger. Ever heard of it?"

Liv nodded.

George had taught her all about hallucinogenic plants. In Norway, his people had consumed certain fungi during their spiritual rituals, but he had never introduced them to Liv.

"The nettles stimulate blood flow. My mom has arthritis. It's not the most pleasant remedy, but it works."

"How about this?" He peeled a layer of white bark off a large birch tree.

"We can use birch bark on open wounds to encourage healing. Or make it into a tea for a liver tonic. It has a lot of healing properties."

Liv brushed her fingers over a leafy plant poking from the rocky embankment of the river.

"Mugwort," she said. "Induces sweating, soothes the rash from a poison oak, and creates prophetic dreams."

Stephen stopped, peering closer at the plant.

"Prophetic dreams? How?" He ripped a handful from the ground.

"Well, now you're likely to have nightmares."

"Why?"

"Because those plants are alive, Stephen. Intention is everything in magic. When you take a plant, communicate with it first. Get permission. And then cut gently. If possible, leave the roots so more can grow."

Stephen dropped the handful of mugwort.

"Might'a been nice if you told me that first," he muttered.

She laughed and bent close to another sprig of mugwort.

"You didn't exactly give me time," she retorted.

She touched the leaves, allowed her fingers to trail over the stalk and rest on the soil. Warmth seeped into her palm. After a moment, she dug into the dirt and, leaving the roots intact, pulled a stem of the plant from the ground. She wrapped it loosely in cloth and handed it to Stephen.

"Do I eat it?" he asked.

She smiled.

"I'd go for a satchel under your pillow, unless you're dealing with some digestive issues."

"Thanks," he said. "You know, since I met you, the woods have changed. They seem… alive now."

She smiled and stood, brushing dirt from the seat of her shorts.

"They are alive."

CHAPTER 3

September 1965
Mack

"I NEED a few days to think, is all. That's what men do at the cabin; they think."

Tina snorted and glanced up from her breakfast, a half grapefruit and a cup of green tea. Same breakfast every morning. The most god-awful, not to mention meager, breakfast that Mack had ever seen in his life.

After their first night in bed, he'd tried to make her pancakes for breakfast, and she looked at him like he'd offered to serve up the back leg of his dog, Misty. Apparently, pancakes belonged on the side of Tina's food book labelled BAD in large red letters.

"And here I thought you men sat down there looking at girlie magazines and chugging beer," she quipped, poking at her grapefruit with a fork. She lifted a tiny pink chunk to her mouth.

Mack frowned. Sure, they did that too, but he wasn't about to tell Tina that.

"Well, don't think too long, Mackey. I'm not exactly hard pressed for a date," she added.

He gritted his teeth, bit back 'the name's Mack,' and offered her a one-handed salute.

She twitched her long red fingernails in a half-wave, and he tried not to think of them digging into his shoulders as she cried out in bed. At the heart of things, Tina in bed was the reason he'd ignored the good, long think that had been coming for six months. Ever since the first night he took her home.

He'd met her just weeks shy of the one-year anniversary of his divorce, during a drunken night of bowling. She waited tables on the restaurant side of Marv's Bowling Alley.

As he walked by, Tina dropped her pen on the worn patch of red carpet that ran the line between the rows of tables.

Mack, oblivious that Tina had intentionally dropped her pen, flung himself to the ground to save the poor waitress with the tiny yellow skirt the effort of bending over to retrieve it.

He'd bedded her that night, shutting himself in the bathroom after the deed to stifle the cries bubbling in his gut. He was a big man, not the kind you'd expect to cry, but he blubbered like a baby that night.

"Pull it together, you dipshit," he'd whispered into the smoky glass mirror above his sink. A mirror his former wife Diane had bought at an estate sale. Diane used to leave him lipstick notes on the glass when she snuck out early for work.

Despite a year's passage since his divorce, and a handful of one-night stands, Mack still felt sick to his stomach every time he made it with another woman.

He missed his wife — ex-wife, he silently chastised himself.

"Did ya fall in?" Tina had called from the bed, and when he went out, he found her propped on her side, naked and ready for seconds.

Sex muddled a man's mind, probably more than anything else - especially if you added booze.

He fell into a Tina addiction and didn't come up for air for two months. Rather than return to his big Diane-less farmhouse, he moved into Tina's little Cape Cod on Harper Road, stuffing his duffel bag in the sliver of space he found not crammed with dresses in her walk-in closet.

For a while, he believed he'd moved on. But disillusion, like alcohol, was a creeper. And disillusion wore no more beautiful mask than lust.

The lust wrapped him in shimmery gauze. It set up a quaint little apartment in his brain, replete with satin sheets and lace underwear.

Then one morning, he looked over, and the gauze had faded. It looked more like a tatter of burlap full of holes and prickly spots. That beautiful apartment had grown dark, and a little ugly.

He wanted to move out, but the shimmery lust-turned-burlap-sack was hiding something nasty, something slobbering and flashing its pointed fangs.

The only way to escape was to kill it, and the death would be a slow one.

There'd be harsh words, more like screams, broken dishes, possibly a keyed pickup truck. He dreaded the confrontation.

Despite his size and girth, Mack was a peaceful man. He didn't want a scene with Tina. He wanted to slip out of their dark little dream as if he'd never been there at all.

But he knew better.

"TINA LET you out without a leash? Or did you jump over the fence again, you bad dog, you?" Mack's friend David asked when he opened his front door.

"Very funny," Mack told him. "I'm here for the fish, baby, nothing but the fish."

"Ah, damn," David grumbled, hanging his head. "I meant to call you. I'm out for the cabin. My sister's planned a fortieth wedding anniversary for my parents, and she's guilted me into hosting."

"Here?" Mack pulled a face, but as he gazed around David's living room, he realized it looked clean. The usual stack of magazines that littered the coffee table were nowhere in sight. The beer can pyramid had been wiped from the top of the bookshelf and replaced with sturdy paperbacks butted by two Abraham Lincoln bookends. Even the ever-growing pile of laundry outside the utility room had vanished.

David, a self-proclaimed bachelor for life who cleaned for the first date only, had succumbed to his sister's badgering.

Having grown up down the street from David and Nancy, Mack knew she was a worthy opponent. Nancy never lost an argument, and she used all that God gave her to get her way, whether that be tears or fingernails.

"Why isn't Nancy hosting? I thought her and Leon bought one of those Victorian monsters downtown?" Mack asked.

David nodded.

"They did and promptly unleashed a gang of construction guys who are tearing up floors and walls as we speak. They're staying in an apartment until spring, when hopefully, the house will meet my sister's highfalutin standards."

"Wow, poor Leon. Can you imagine five months in an apartment with Nancy? She probably vacuums over his feet when he's watching TV," Mack sympathized.

David laughed and cocked an eyebrow.

"You think she lets Leon watch TV?"

Mack shook his head in commiserate misery, thinking of his own better half, who at that moment was likely sifting through her closet for a hot dress to wear out with her girlfriends that night.

When Mack returned on Monday - if he returned - he'd likely find a scattering of men's phone numbers displayed on her bedside table.

Tina liked her men angry, possessive, and ready to fight for her. Mack could only imagine her perpetual disappointment at his unwillingness to take the bait. In truth, he hoped she'd call one of those guys, and he'd come home with a cooler of fish to find his bags packed on her front porch.

Mack grabbed a beer from David's refrigerator and plopped on the couch.

"If you put your feet on that table, my sister will drive down to the Stoneroot Forest to chew your ass."

Mack kicked off his shoes and hoisted his socked, size-fifteen feet onto the table.

"Now she'll never know."

David grabbed a beer and listened as Mack detailed Tina's latest series of hints about buying a ring. David surprised them both by carrying their cans to the waste basket after they finished.

"What?" David demanded as he dropped them in. "If you had a sister with a handgun, you'd probably bury your cans in the back yard to avoid her wrath."

"I do that anyway. Full ones, so I can send my friends on beer treasure hunts in the summer."

David grinned.

"That's not half bad. Think Nancy would go for that as an anniversary party game?"

Mack chuckled and leaned forward, bracing his elbows on his knees.

"Absolutely. I'm sure Nancy would love nothing more than crawling around on her knees for warm beer. It will remind her of college."

David guffawed. "My God, if she had a sense of humor, I'd suggest it." David's laughter trailed off, and he looked at Mack seriously. "You're coming back, right? I don't want my best friend to become a hermit in the Stoneroot Forest to avoid telling Tina you guys aren't headed for the altar."

"Ugh," Mack groaned, and leaned back on the couch, banging his head against the cushions a few times. "How did I get here?"

David sat down.

"You didn't. Your hard-on did. Unfortunately, he's not very good at breaking up either."

Mack looked down at his pants.

"Little bastard," he muttered.

"Damn, now you're insulting him too. I don't blame ya, though. If I woke up next to Tina, I'd have half a mind to whack mine right off."

Mack snorted and flipped him the finger.

David held up his hands.

"Don't get me wrong. She's a fox, but the rabid kind that most men can tell a mile off the fur ain't worth the bite."

Mack glared at him.

"How about some friendly advice, then?"

David's mouth dropped open. "Mack, how long have I been single? That'd be like a prostitute giving advice to a priest."

"Thanks," Mack grumbled.

"Okay, you want my advice? Go home, enjoy one last ride, and when she heads out on the town, pack your bag, leave her a note and some cash to buy a new dress, and hit the road."

"And then what? Ride off into the sunset? We live in the same damn town. I'll see her at bowling league, I'll run into her at Frank's market. Shit, she buys her gas the same place as me."

David shrugged.

"Join the senior league and bowl at 9 a.m. They'll take pity on you when they hear your troubles."

~

THE STONEROOT FOREST lay forty miles south of Grayling. Mack's cabin was off a grassy two-track deep in the woods.

Misty reared up excitedly, putting both paws on the passenger window as the cabin slid into view.

"Calm down, girl," he told her, scratching her red-brown head. Misty was a mixed breed with fox lineage. Some days she looked more fox than dog.

She followed him out the driver's door, bounding into the trees with her tail wagging her entire backside. She raced around the cabin twice, nipping at Mack's bag as he hauled it into the little two-story log cabin. He deposited his bag on the table and headed back out.

A few of the trees had shifted from green to gold. Twigs crunched underfoot as Mack and Misty lumbered through the forest.

The cabin roused nostalgic memories of hunting with his Uncle Byron, and less fond memories of watching his dad slam beers and shoot the cans off tree stumps.

Mack had honeymooned with Diane for a week at the cabin after their wedding. They slow-danced by the bonfire. 'I Only Have Eyes for You' by the Flamingos played on the record player next to the sitting-room window. They ate dinner by candlelight and took long walks in the woods, watching Misty run after squirrels and birds.

Those were the best days; Mack had realized later. The year before the wedding and the year after. Those were the best days.

But then life took its inevitable toll. Mack's drinking shifted from casual to constant. Diane's stubbornness grew cement legs. The hardship of finances, the endless work of the big farmhouse, losing two babies before Diane ever had a belly. Things they would have turned their noses up at in those first two years. A love like that doesn't falter, doesn't die beneath the weight of ordinary things. But oh, it does, it's the ordinary things that kill us all.

Misty barked and pivoted, running south. Mack followed without complaint. He'd left his fishing pole in the truck. He didn't much feel like fishing, preferring to walk and think and forget about the stillness of fishing, not to mention the backache of sitting on the little lopsided dock. With his luck, the damn thing would swallow the hook and he wouldn't even get the satisfaction of throwing it back alive.

"Maybe we can find some worms, Misty Girl."

He hadn't bothered to stop at the bait shop. There were enough rubber worms in his tackle box if he really felt like fishing, and he didn't - simple as that.

He kicked over logs and dug into the moist dirt, finding a centipede and popping it into the little metal cannister in the pack on his back.

Misty disappeared into a pile of brush and burst out a moment later, hackles raised, barking wildly.

"Just wait a minute," he called, trotting over to her.

The last thing he needed was Misty stuck with a face full of porcupine quills.

He grabbed hold of her collar and held her back as she barked and lunged at the pile of brush.

Holding her steady, Mack walked closer, squinting through sticks and dried leaves where a bit of fabric appeared, nestled deep in the overgrowth.

He frowned and squatted low, tugging the fabric, but it was stuck good. Looked like it had been red before the weather bleached it a pale pink.

As he tugged, Misty snarled and jumped back and forth at the thing. When Mack looked at her, he saw a terror in her eyes that made him drop the fabric and stand back up.

He looked across the expanse of woods, thick boughs of golden leaves and the red-brown that had already fallen.

The skin on the back of his neck crawled, and he felt as if someone watched them.

Misty paused too, head cocked, ears perked, and then she lowered on her haunches and bared her teeth at whatever lay beneath the brush.

Mack found a long, sturdy stick. He whacked at the brush and kicked with his heavy boots. The shirt was half-buried. He reached down and brushed away wet leaves before sinking both hands into the dirt around the fabric. His finger struck something hard. As he dug deeper, throwing handfuls of dirt behind him, the shirt came into view, and a trickle of ice slid down Mack's spine.

He peered at the skull of a human being, the bones of the spine disappearing into the pink fabric.

"Sweet mother of Jesus," he muttered, standing and taking two long strides away from the body, hauling Misty with him.

Now that he'd exposed the thing, the corpse, Misty appeared reluctant to go near it.

The sensation of being watched returned, and Mack shuddered, trying to still his agitated dog. He squinted further into the forest, even tilted his head to look up into the trees, half expecting to see a madman perched there like a man-sized hawk. But the branches stood empty save for a few crows.

"Damn," he muttered.

The cabin didn't have a phone. He'd have to drive to the police department. A ten-mile trek into Kalkaska.

"Stay back, girl," Mack ordered Misty as he returned to the body. He gazed into the shallow grave, hunching for a closer look. A small leather pouch rested in the dirt near the body.

Mack picked it up, but as he drew it away, it caught on the skeleton's neck.

Without thinking, Mack took out his pocketknife and sliced the leather strap.

Misty crept closer, emitting her low growl.

"Shh… just taking a look here," he told her, prising open the little bag. A series of flat white stones lay within the pouch.

Behind Mack, a twig cracked and he jumped, whirling around as two squirrels chased each other between the trees. Misty took off after them.

"Misty, no," he shouted, running to catch up with her.

She followed them a few more yards, but they darted up an oak and out of sight.

He caught up to his dog and grabbed her collar.

"Best if we get to a cop shop," he said, leading her back toward the cabin.

He was halfway back when he realized he still held the satchel in his hands. He paused, considered returning to drop it in the grave, and decided against it. He could just hand it over to the police - easier that way.

CHAPTER 4

September 1965
Liv

It was strange how time shifted. One morning, Liv gazed at a bright-eyed eighteen-year-old in the mirror, and the next a woman of nearly forty stared back at her. Through her eyes, not much had changed. The same brown eyes watched her from beneath unruly blonde hair that she'd never so much as trimmed.

She might have left George that fall in 1945, left everything, as it were; but she'd held onto his stories, and his magic.

Most people thought her young. She'd never married or had children, the things she now attributed to aging a woman. All those years carrying babies and then bearing them into the world. Cleaning, scrubbing, ironing, fretting, fearing for their safety.

Though it was more than that, she thought. The magic that had made George look young years beyond his prime flowed in her blood.

She'd never borne children, and yet they'd become the center her life. She was fast approaching seventeen years at Helping Hands Orphanage. Several years before, they'd offered her the position of Head Mother. She'd turned it down. The Head Mother did not hold the children or chase them in the play-yard. She didn't nurse the sick ones and soothe the fearful. Liv's purpose was to heal. George had told her as much when she was but a tiny girl, helping him collect wild rose for tea.

She took the bus as she did every morning to the stop on Tenth Street. From there, she ducked into the bakery and bought a bun and a box of cookies for the little ones.

When she arrived at the orphanage, the children ran from the breakfast room to greet her. They swarmed her legs, tugging on her skirt to tell her of their dreams and to beg for cookies.

"Miss Livvy, I dreamed last night I rode on a giant pink balloon," a little girl with white-blonde hair squealed.

Tanner, a swarthy boy with thick auburn curls, called out that he'd dreamed of a cockroach as big as a bus.

Lucas, her favorite of the children — though she'd never tell them that — stood in the back of the pack, his cheeks sunken in his angular face. Large, watery blue eyes stared up at her from beneath a sheaf of coal black hair.

"And what did you dream, Lucas?"

The seven-year-old dreamed every night. Sometimes they were nightmares of the train car he'd lived in before Helping Hands found him. Except it was not Helping Hands that found him, but Liv.

Liv knew where the wayward children dwelled. She sensed them from miles away. On her days off, she walked the city for hours, visiting the abandoned children and trying to draw them to the warmth and safety of her orphanage.

"I dreamed of George," he murmured, eyes cast toward the floor.

Liv's head shot up at the name.

She nudged the other children aside and squatted in front of Lucas.

"What did you say?"

Lucas looked up at her, his little mouth turned down.

"The man with the stones. Like yours."

Lucas pointed at the single hag stone that hung on a length of leather around Liv's neck.

Her fingers trembled as she brushed the dark hair from his eyes.

"What was George doing in the dream?" she asked. Her head had grown light, and she shifted from squatting to sitting on her knees.

"He was trying to get out of the hole in the ground."

Liv blinked at the little boy.

"Here, honey." She pressed a shortbread cookie into his hand and stood shakily.

Rather than pass the cookies out as she usually did, she handed the tin to Paulette, the oldest girl in the orphanage at fifteen, and allowed her to give each child a treat.

Liv retreated to the hall closet and hung her coat. As she stood at the rack, she put a hand to the stone at her chest.

She searched for George. She rarely reached out for him.

Energy is instant, George used to say. He knew when she thought of him, longed for him, dreamed of him. He taught her to attune to those sensations as well, but like everything else, she'd shut it off when she fled Michigan all those years ago. She'd rarely sought George in the intervening years, believing it better not to reignite that connection. She didn't want to give him access to her, for fear of what he'd see.

As she stood in the black, cramped closet, a void met her searching heart.

She could not feel him in the world.

~

LIV REACHED into the crib and lifted the wailing baby out.

His diaper was wet. Sad brown eyes gazed up at her from his round, red face.

"Shh… hush now, little sweet. I've got you."

She walked him to the changing table and unclasped the safety pin on his diaper. Lifting his legs to pull the damp cloth away, she blew on his face. He paused for a moment in his crying to gaze at the stone dangling from her neck.

Liv reached for the baby powder.

Barney grabbed hold of her necklace. Ferociously, he jerked her toward the table. Liv's head smacked the rail as the leather on the necklace snapped.

"Ouch," she cried, jumping back and putting a hand to her brow.

She stared at the baby. His eyes had gone black and empty. He held the stone clutched in his pudgy hand, the broken leather dangling below it.

As quickly as the change had come, the darkness fled from him. He was Barney once more. Big brown eyes, tiny pink lips blowing a bubble. He waved the stone around before dropping it to clutch his toes, which he stretched up and stuck in his mouth.

Liv took a tentative step back to the changing table, reaching out to retrieve the necklace. She tucked it into the pocket of her skirt and returned Barney to his crib.

~

IT WAS near dark when Liv left the orphanage to catch the bus home. As she stepped onto the front walkway, she paused, her heart skipping a beat.

Hundreds of flowers lay scattered in the grass.

Liv's eyes flicked to the graveyard that butted the property of the orphanage. The headstones were empty of their flowers. They had all blown onto the grounds of the orphanage, and yet Liv did not remember ever hearing a wind that day as she cared for the children. Just the opposite, in fact; it had been an abnormally quiet day. Even the children seemed subdued.

As Liv walked, a flower crunched beneath her. She looked down to see a dark purple dahlia flattened beneath her shoe.

That night she dreamed for the first time in nearly twenty years.

Liv walked through a familiar forest. Maple trees glittered gold in autumn. Beech, birch, oaks. She whispered the names as she walked.

George had taught her the names. They had foraged together, sipped nettle tea, ate the greens of dandelions, dug for wild onions in spring.

But this day, she was not in the Stoneroot Forest with George.

Instead, she walked near the Dead Stream toward the big house filled with beautiful, untouchable things.

The house loomed before her. A curtain in an upstairs window billowed out, but there was no breeze. Behind the sheer curtain, Liv could see a figure, a dark shape. She stopped, heart racing, her body awash in goosebumps. The figure watched her. She felt its eyes boring into her, beckoning her forward.

"No," Liv whispered.

But suddenly she was there, at the base of the grand staircase. Candles glittered, just as they had that Halloween night. Six-foot-high candelabras stood positioned on either side of the staircase. Red wax dripped and pooled on the gleaming wood floor.

The purple dahlias were thick, and their floral aroma concealed a smell of decay.

At the top of the stairs, the figure stood in the shadows.

Liv tried to back away, but the figure rushed toward her. A black blur streaked down the stairs.

Liv woke, sticky and heaving for breath. She fought the blankets from her waist and sat up in bed. Her hands shook as she turned on the little bedside lamp.

A yellow glow cast away the darkness, but not the dream. The dream remained, sharp and solid. It did not waver and slip away.

The second dream besieged her seconds after she closed her eyes.

She stood at the train station in Gaylord, Michigan, her single brown suitcase clutched in her hand. A man stopped beside her, and when she turned, she saw George.

Elation swept over her, swallowed by guilt. She burst into tears.

"There now, Volva." He patted her back and wiped the tears from her cheeks. "It's time to come home."

SHE WOKE for the second time in her little bed and gazed at the ceiling, feeling the warmth of her father's hand on her back.

She did not say goodbye to the children in the orphanage. Their clinging hands and cheeks shiny with tears would have crippled her.

For too long, she had run from her mistakes, and it was time to make amends.

She took the bus to the train station at midnight and boarded a train for Michigan.

CHAPTER 5

September 1965
Jesse

JESSE HITCHED a ride into Gaylord on a rainy afternoon in early September.

The heat of the day radiated up from the pavement, and Jesse felt it through the soles of his worn shoes.

The man in the truck had dropped him at an intersection, and Jesse gazed for a long time down the road that the man said led to town. He'd been travelling for two days. His eyes were red-rimmed, he stank of his own filth, and something deep inside him was rumbling for a fierce howl.

He needed to be alone.

He turned away from town and plunged into the trees. The bit of light from the gray sky disappeared.

When he'd walked a half-mile, he dropped to his knees and buried his face in the wet grass and bellowed. The sound erupted from his body like a mighty roar. Tears poured from his tired eyes into the mossy earth beneath his face.

He babbled through his cries. Mostly he said their names, Nell and Gabriel, but sometimes he called out for his father or even his old dog, Bruno.

After a while, he slumped forward and slept.

~

He woke to a crow pecking at his coat pocket.

"Scat," he shouted, rolling away from the bird.

He sat up, his back damp with sweat.

The bird did not fly away, but stood a few paces back, watching him.

"I don't have anything for you. See?" he shouted.

He turned out the pockets of his coat. A box of matches fell out, but nothing else.

Still the bird remained.

When Jesse stood, the bird flew into a tree just over his head. He huffed, considered which way to turn. When the bird flew deeper into the forest, Jesse followed it.

He was a stranger in a strange wood. The bird's direction was as good as any other.

Jesse had been walking for a long time when he spotted the house.

In the darkness, the moon only a whisper between drifting clouds, he gazed at the silhouette. Pitched roofs and tall black windows reminded him of an enormous slumbering creature rather than a deserted house. Thick overgrowth from bushes and trees crawled onto eaves and trickled across the long, wide porch that encircled the lower level.

No light burned in the house, and as he walked closer, Jesse smelled the air of abandonment. Everything had a scent — the air when a storm was brewing, a woman preparing for her first date, a place left and forgotten. He'd come to rely on his smell to know a bit about a man. Violent men smelled like fire, the sharp soot of the match striking flint. A kind man gave off an odor of freshly tilled soil.

Jesse put his hand on the bannister, sturdy wood with paint

flaking away, and crept slowly up the steps. He perked his ears and waited, counting the seconds, and then minutes.

He knocked on the heavy wooden door. The sound rang hollow, muted by the dense summer foliage. It was an odd place for such a grand house, tucked deep in the woods. Made stranger by the foreboding silence that blanketed it.

He tried the knob and found it locked. Of course it was locked. It might be empty, but it was a big house, a wealthy man's house.

Jesse was not a thief nor a criminal, but he hadn't slept beneath a roof in half a month. Rain was on its way, and he didn't want to greet the morning with his pants soaked through.

Walking the perimeter, he found a window low enough to reach if he stood on the cellar doors. He clambered up the diagonal red-brown doors and attempted to raise the window.

It stuck.

Climbing back down, he surveyed the house, sure that he should walk away. If the owners appeared in the night, they'd call the police. He'd be carted off to jail. Though jail offered a cot and a tray of food at sunrise.

"Nobody lives here," he told the night.

In its silence, the house seemed to confirm his statement.

Jesse considered breaking the glass, but dismissed it when he realized no lock and chain snaked through the cellar doors.

He reached down and pulled, surprised when the door opened on its rusted hinge. The screech made his flesh crawl, and his apprehension deepened when he gazed into the yawning black hole of the cellar.

Ignoring his knee-jerk desire to avoid dark, unknown places, he plunged down the stairs, leaving the doors wide behind him to let a dribble of moonlight through.

Once in the cellar, the blackness grew impenetrable.

Jesse blinked, shuffling his feet and holding his arms out in front of him. By sheer dumb luck, his shin smacked into a hard wood lip.

The stairs.

He leaned forward, finding the stairs with his hands and

monkey-walking up the dark staircase. The stairs were not hard and splintery, but softened by a layer of filth that revealed the house had been abandoned for a long time, indeed.

On the first level, a shimmer of moonlight through half-open curtains lit his way to a large sitting room thick with furniture.

Exhausted, he lay on the floor and drifted into sleep.

~

A THUD STARTLED Jesse from his dreams, and he jumped from lying on his back to standing crouched in the dark parlor.

A creak of a floorboard, and another.

Someone was upstairs.

Jesse considered his options. If he ran from the house, he'd be back in the night wandering through unfamiliar woods.

He waited, tensed, but the sound did not come again. After several minutes, he slid his hands over the furniture until he found a candlestick. He reached into the inner pocket of his coat, hoping the matches he carried were not wet.

They weren't. He lit a match and held the flame to the wick of a long black candle.

As he lifted the candle before him, he studied the room.

Heavily carved furniture upholstered in burgundy and dark fabrics crowded the space. It was not the style of the times, but a decor that Jesse imagined belonged to women in long puffy dresses and men who wore white powdered wigs.

He moved into the hallway, placing his feet gingerly and pausing at every step.

When he reached the staircase, an uncontrollable shiver rolled down his spine and left a trail of goosebumps in its wake.

He was not afraid of encountering a man in the house. Perhaps another person like himself, down on his luck, who'd sought refuge.

No, fear lived in the dark corners and shadowy back rooms. Fear's power came from the unknown things.

Jesse's father had laughed at fear. If Jesse woke in the night scared, his father would burst through the room like a madman waving a lantern, gleeful as he flung open the closet door and peered beneath the bed. There had been no mother in Jesse's life. She'd died giving birth to her only son. Jesse's father was a good man, kind and funny, better than many of the fathers Jesse had met along his journeys. But the man supported a son during a time when poverty and war were rampant. It was not an easy time to raise a child, and Jesse spent more than a few months in orphanages in Michigan, Minnesota, and even a spell on the east coast - Boston, New York, and the like.

He hadn't minded the orphanages until he got older. His father always retrieved him after a few weeks or months. Except the last time.

Jesse flinched when another creak sounded above him. He crept down the long hall and peeled back the curtain, expecting — no, hoping — to see wind bending the trees. The night appeared calm and still.

He'd seen large rats on a few trains, but found it unlikely they'd be wandering the old house. At least not the type large enough to make so much noise. But a house in a forest likely invited all sorts of vermin to seek refuge. A raccoon could make the noise. Especially when they were hunting for food or building a nest.

As he ascended to the third floor, he stared into the pocket of light cast by the candle. The faces on the walls gazed at him. A layer of gray dust coated the ornate frames, and the absurdity of such a house teeming with treasure, left abandoned in a northern Michigan forest, struck him anew.

Another creak sounded, but now it was on the floor beneath him - the second floor.

Nervous, Jesse blew out the candle and listened. He was now sure someone else shared the house. Whether they'd been there since he arrived, he couldn't say.

He crept back down the stairs.

A shaft of moonlight filtered through a door he thought had been closed when he passed the hall only moments before. He padded along the hall carpet; grateful that the rug muffled his movements.

As he peered through the half-open door, he saw a chaise lounge in front of a large window.

The curtains hung partially open, the moon splashing light across the room.

On the chaise, Jesse saw a woman's long, slender legs.

He stared at the legs, which ended in small, delicate feet.

Rubbing his eyes, he took a step away, not sure what to do.

Would a woman have come into the house alone?

Unlikely.

Her large, unforgiving husband was probably lurking somewhere close by.

The hairs on the back of Jesse's neck prickled.

He spun, ready to slash out with the candle, though it would do little against his attacker.

Behind him, the hall stood empty.

His heart thumped hard and fast.

He realized he'd been ready to fight.

His desire to survive came as a surprise. He'd greeted each day of the previous year with an expectation, even a hope, that death would come for him that day. Maybe an angry stowaway on a train he hopped on would sink a blade into his heart as he slept, to steal the worn shoes that had carried him so many miles. Perhaps he'd miss one of those trains, fall on the tracks, and be crushed by the merciless rail wheels.

Never happened. Men with more to live for died by the thousands, but Jesse Kaminski traveled on.

He turned back to the chaise, but the woman's legs had disappeared.

She'd heard him.

"Hello?" he called, his voice hollow and tinny in the quiet. The house seemed to swallow the sound.

He poked his foot forward and pushed the door in. It swung open and bumped gently against the wall.

He searched for her among the furnishings. Had she ducked behind the bed? Slipped into the closet?

"I won't hurt you. My name's Jesse. I just needed a place to sleep. I thought the house was empty," he explained, stepping into the room.

"I don't have a weapon. Just say the word, and I'll leave," he continued.

He walked toward the bed, surprised to find the woman had not ducked behind it.

Unsure how to proceed, Jesse continued to talk as he walked around the room.

"I'm harmless. I swear it." He moved to the window and peered behind the shimmery pale fabric.

After he checked behind every piece of furniture and in the closet, he returned to the center of the room. Beneath the bed was the only place he hadn't checked. As he considered laying on his belly to peek beneath the ruffled bed skirt, the flicker of disquiet in his mind grew louder.

He could hear the laughter of his father: *balk-balk*, he would cry out, imitating a chicken and ruffling Jesse's hair affectionately. He wouldn't have hesitated to drop onto his belly and look under the bed. Had Gabriel lived, Jesse would have done something similar for his own son.

He sank to his knees, and then his stomach. Inching toward the bed, he reached out a hand, dismayed to see his trembling fingers.

Lifting the dust ruffle, he stared into the black cavity beneath the frame.

As his eyes adjusted, he realized a masked face stared back at him. Dark eyes peered out from the cat-like mask.

Jesse sputtered and pushed away from the bed, dropping his candle, which extinguished.

He bounded to his feet, tensed and ready for the person to follow him, but she didn't. The room remained eerily quiet.

Jesse left the room and walked down the stairs. He opened the front door, and the damp of the night swirled around him

He could go. Slip into those woods and never look back.

A cool mist seeped from the forest grass. Fireflies lit the night, blinking in and out from the darkness of the trees.

After several breaths, Jesse stepped back into the house, gazing at the staircase.

Reluctantly, he lit another candle and returned to the bedroom.

This time when he lifted the bed skirt, he saw the mask resting on a heap of dark fabric. He reached beneath the bed and pulled out an evening gown with a frilly satin skirt. The black mask had sat atop it, merely an illusion in the dark.

And yet, he'd seen dark eyes peering out from the holes in the mask, hadn't he? And where had the woman gone?

He suspected he would not sleep that night, but when he lay down on the rug in the parlor, his breath grew long and deep and he slipped away.

CHAPTER 6

July 1945
Liv

"WHAT ARE YOU DOING?"

Stephen looked appalled as Liv shrugged off her trousers and blouse. She flung them onto a low tree branch.

"What?" she asked, following the line of his gaze to her undergarments. Her bra was a bit worn and her britches frayed at the edges, but it wasn't as if she'd stripped naked.

Stephen's face had gone red.

Liv stuck a hand on her hip.

"Don't blow your wig, Stephen. It's only underwear."

He continued to gaze at her with a stupid expression, so she rolled her eyes and ran to the water, flinging herself off the little dock jutting into the pond.

The cool water swallowed her in its sumptuous, clammy mouth and she dove deep, trailing her fingers over seaweed before bursting back to the surface.

Stephen had finally closed his mouth and set about removing his own clothing, folding them neatly on a flattened patch of grass.

His underwear looked white and crisp, and Liv noticed for the first time the shape of him. He stood long and lean, with hard patches of muscle rippling beneath his chest and arms.

She kicked her legs and felt a little tremor of curiosity. She'd seen half-naked men before. Her own brothers had spent most of their summers in tattered shorts, bare-chested and not the least modest. But as she watched Stephen, she noticed his body in a way her brothers' had been invisible to her. She'd never had a boyfriend, never really wanted one, though at times the girls in school wearing their boyfriends' letter jackets and showing off their promise rings had triggered something deep in her gut. She called it loathing, but envy might have been closer to the truth.

Stephen did not jump in, but walked out on the little dock and sat on the edge, dipping his feet in the water.

"Come on! It's like jumping in an icebox," she called before diving under again.

When she popped above the pond, he hadn't moved.

"How deep is it?" he asked.

She swam closer and splashed him.

He recoiled at the spray of water, and Liv noticed that his hands clutched the edge of the dock as if he were a cat getting shoved in.

"What's wrong?"

"Nothing," he snapped. "I just don't feel like it, is all."

Liv paddled her legs and watched him. She didn't believe for a minute he didn't feel like it. The sun bore down, angry and sweltering.

Through the haze, Liv watched Stephen take a deep breath, as if gathering his strength before slipping off the dock and into the water. He stayed close to the dock treading water and slowly paddled away, moving closer to where she dove in and out of the cool lake.

After they toweled off, Liv regarded Stephen, who sat on the dock, his legs pulled to his chest.

"You jumped in and saved us. You can't be scared of the water," she murmured.

He turned and glared at her.

"I wasn't scared," he snapped.

She closed her mouth.

Stephen didn't speak again until they were walking in the woods.

"I taught myself how to swim," he told her, gazing steadily at the ground as they walked. "My mother forbade me from swimming. Her baby brother drowned when she was a teenager. She insisted if I never swam, I'd never be tempted to go near the water. My father tried to teach me once, and she caught him."

Liv listened, glancing at his profile, but his face remained unreadable.

"What did she do?" Liv asked.

Stephen's cheek twitched.

"He never tried again," Stephen said. "But when I was thirteen, some guys at my boarding school started going out to this lake and jumping off the cliffs into the water. They talked about it all the time. The exhilaration of the fall, and then the sensation of disappearing into the cold, black water. They invited me a few times, and I made up excuses. I wanted to go so bad. I started to follow them. I checked out books on swimming from the library."

He laughed, though the sound echoed hollow and empty in the forest.

"One night, I jumped in. I climbed up to the highest cliff and stared at the moonlit water and just jumped."

Liv stopped, gazing at Stephen.

"You didn't know how to swim, but you jumped off a cliff?"

He put his hand to his chest, as if recalling the sensation.

"Yeah. Those seconds as I was falling…" He shook his head and turned to her with wide, almost bewildered eyes. "Were the most alive I've ever felt."

"And then what?" Liv breathed, imagining Stephen vanishing into the dark lake, the surface only a spread of ripples where he'd gone in.

"And then I swam. Or flailed might better describe it. I swallowed a gallon or so of water. It took me ten minutes to reach an outcropping of rocks, but when I pulled myself up on those rocks, I was a different person. I realized I could do anything I wanted. Anything."

"THIS IS YOUR HOUSE?" Liv gaped at the enormous house flanked with high, unruly bushes. "It's huge."

Stephen squared off against the house, hands planted on his hips as if he stared down a ferocious adversary rather than his own home.

"And you live here alone with your mom?"

"Yeah, come on." Stephen led her up the wide wooden steps and pushed in the heavy oak door. The door creaked and swung in, revealing a long, dusky hallway. Paintings with gilded frames lined the walls. Liv glanced up at the sallow, unsmiling faces, their dark eyes seeming to watch her mistrustfully as she followed Stephen down the hall.

"Is your mother here?" she asked.

He shook his head.

"You couldn't come over if she was. No one is allowed in the house."

"Why?" Liv asked, following Stephen up a polished wooden staircase. Long, fringed rugs lay along the hallway. They walked another hallway thick with paintings, and then up another set of stairs.

"How many levels are there?" she whispered as they ascended.

"Four, including the attic. My room's on the third floor." He stopped at a black door and pulled out a skeleton key.

"You lock it?"

Stephen nodded and slid the key into the brass keyhole. He wiggled it until it popped open, and they slipped inside.

A claw-footed bed, sheathed in a dark satin coverlet, stood in the center of the room.

A polished bookshelf held rows of books. Liv leaned down and smelled them, running her hand over the leather bindings. Gold-embossed titles read *The Ingoldsby Legends, Worship of the Serpent* and

Lives of Necromancers. The titles reminded her of George's books, though George's were worn, with pages ripped and stained. Stephen's books looked untouched.

"I've never brought anyone here before," Stephen admitted, sitting on a velvet bench at the foot of his bed.

Liv looked up, surprised.

"Why not?"

"Have you read any of those?" Stephen changed the subject.

"I don't think so. I've read a lot of Nancy Drew."

Stephen grimaced.

"Nancy Drew?"

"I like to escape when I read," she admitted. "I get enough textbooks in school."

Liv stood and flicked a tasseled lamp near the window. The little black strands shimmered in the yellow light.

"It's a beautiful day. Why don't we open the curtains?"

Liv started to pull back the heavy blue drapes, and Stephen jumped from his seat.

"No," he shouted, quickly wrenching them closed.

Liv backed away.

"Why not?"

"Because my mom might come home."

"She really doesn't let you have friends over?"

Stephen stood at the curtains, peeking between them for another moment.

"No, she doesn't."

"You're eighteen. You're a man-" Liv started, but Stephen cut her off.

"I don't want to talk about this," he muttered. "Okay?"

"Sure, fine."

"Let's go back into the woods."

"Okay."

Liv followed him down the two sets of stairs, still marveling at the opulence surrounding them. Liv had never been in a rich person's house before. Everything seemed heavy and expensive-looking. Even the doorknobs appeared precious and untouchable, though Stephen yanked on them as if he hoped to rip them from the heavy wood doors they protruded from.

In the forest, Liv breathed easier, and she noticed Stephen too seemed to calm.

"You don't like your house?" she asked after they'd walked for several minutes.

"I can't wait to get out of there," he muttered.

Liv puzzled at his answer. She couldn't imagine wanting to escape the beautiful house.

"I'm leaving town tomorrow for a few days," Liv told him. She didn't know why she told him. It wasn't as if he'd asked.

"You are? Where are you going?"

"To stay with my Uncle George."

Stephen nodded but looked away from her.

When he looked back, his eyes were troubled.

"Guess I'll have to swim on my own," he told her.

CHAPTER 7

August 1945
Liv

"GEORGE, how did you meet my mother?" Liv asked. She lay stretched out on the rug near the hearth in George's cabin, inhaling the sweet scent of pears roasting over the fire. She'd heard the story a hundred times, maybe more, but she never tired of the tale.

"Fate brought your mother and I together, Volva. The manipulations of man are helpless against it."

"But why does she say you seduced her?" Liv's mother rarely spoke of the one night she'd spent with George, but the handful of times Liv had begged her to share, she implied that the devil's song lured her to the Stoneroot Forest.

"Because your mother was raised in the fires of the church and among the furies of western men. How do we question our creator? It is difficult, and your mother is a good and pious woman. She believes she committed a mortal sin. Not you. You are pure in the eyes of her God, but she... she is not."

"But that's not true."

George held up a hand.

"I know that, and you know that. But only your mother can unburden herself of such ideas. The morning I met her; I woke to a pale blue flower drifting down to my bed. The flower landed on my chest. I picked it up, strapped on my boots and walked into the forest. I knew the place where the blue flowers grew. I found your mother there, wailing into the blossoms as if her dead beloved might be hidden amongst them. We talked for many hours. When I left, she followed me back here to this cabin, where we ate roasted hare by firelight. I'm sure it is the only night in your mother's life where she experienced magic. Not me," George laughed. "But in the world. She gazed into the fire and saw a girl running through the woods with long, billowing hair and fierce brown eyes. She saw you, Volva. We created you that night and, in the morning, I returned her to the blue flowers. You were her pathway out of the darkness, child. You do not realize it now, but as you grew, as she returned to her mother-self, she shirked off the burden of her grief and lived once more."

"She cried for years," Liv murmured.

"She still cries," George agreed. "We all cry. There is much pain in these lives. But you are wrong in why she cried. She cried because she longed for the freedom she saw in her only daughter. Even before you arrived, she knew you would not suffer her fate. You would be born free."

LIV WOKE on the little straw bed in the corner of George's cabin.

Someone pounded on the door.

"Volva, open up," George called.

Bleary-eyed, Liv stood and fumbled the door open.

George stood outside with a boy, no more than eleven or twelve, hoisted in his arms. The boy's eyes were closed and his lips purple. His wet, reddish hair hung across his ashen forehead.

"He was fishing. He must have fallen in the lake..." the woman babbled, following George into the cabin.

George laid the boy on the rug in front of the hearth.

The boy's mother followed; her eyes bloodshot from crying. Liv saw a darkening purple bruise on the woman's cheek.

Liv said nothing, but watched as George moved his hands over the boy's head, and then to his neck, and finally to his belly. As he pressed into the soft places on the boy's abdomen, George frowned. He opened his mouth and peered inside.

"Volva," he said to Liv. "Gather some dandelion root."

George turned to the boy's mother.

"He did not drown. He consumed nightshade."

Liv stepped from bed and slipped on her shoes, hurrying out the door.

In early summer, the dandelions were plentiful. She dug with her bare hands, since she had prepared no tools, and George insisted an unfortified tool could do more harm than good.

When she returned to the cabin, the boy's mother sat on a wooden chair, moaning and rocking back and forth. George did not shush her. He took the root from Liv's hand and added it to a jar of other herbs.

"Volva, put your hand here." He took Liv's hand and pressed it to the boy's soft belly.

George stood and went into the kitchen. He scooped water from a large drum into the jar.

As Liv sat, she felt a pulsing beneath her fingers, as if something wanted to escape from the boy's body.

"Will he die?" the mother asked, balling her hands into her skirt and squeezing.

George shook the jar and gazed at her.

"We will know soon, my dear."

Tears gushed down the woman's face, and she recommenced her rocking.

George returned to the boy, the jar in his hand, a hunk of smoky quartz in the other.

Liv pulled her hand away as George rested the quartz on the boy's throat.

"Get the drums, Volva."

Liv hurried to the cupboard by the bed and retrieved two oval-shaped drums. They were old drums that had traveled with George across seas. Reindeer hide worn smooth and stretched over a piece of wood, bent into a circular shape. Symbols decorated the hides. The twin ravens of Odin had always been her favorite of the images. She gazed at the two black birds locked together, more like one bird with two heads.

George tilted the jar over the boy's face, releasing several drops into his open mouth.

Satisfied, he sat back and took a drum. Liv held the other in her lap and, following George's hands, she began to pound the drum. The rhythm was slow at first, and then quickened. George murmured in the language of his ancestors. Liv barely heard him beneath the beating of the drums.

As they pounded, Liv slipped into a trance. She drifted from room and into sky. She soared over green-topped mountains and deep valleys filled with flowers.

The drum pounded in unison with her heartbeat. The rhythm of her blood matched the thrumming.

Voices called out from the blurry edges of her vision.

Another, clearer voice broke through her reverie.

"Come back, Volva," George whispered.

She blinked, her head lolling to the side, and the cabin slid into focus.

The boy no longer lay on the rug. His mother held him, though he was big and awkward in her arms. She crooned into the boy's ear.

He was awake, face sweaty and hands clutching his mother's arms as if he'd clawed his way back from the land of the dead.

And Liv knew, as she watched his sunken, haunted eyes, that he'd done just that.

~

THE FIRST TIME Liv saw Mrs. Kaiser, she gazed at the woman in awe. She seemed transported from the marquee posters. She looked like a Hollywood starlet, with silky black hair curled and fastened with a sparkling comb behind her ear. She wore an emerald green city dress with puffed shoulders and a pearl neckline. Her eyes were big and dark, and her lips painted red.

"What are you looking at?" Stephen asked, stepping to the window beside her.

He gasped when he saw his mother climbing from the polished black car and yanked the curtains closed.

"What?" Liv asked at the alarmed look on his face.

"You have to leave. Come on. Hurry." He pushed her toward the door and down the hall, but as they neared the top of the staircase, the front door opened and they heard the woman's shoes on the polished floor.

He jerked her back, and Liv started to cry out, but Stephen clamped a hand over her mouth.

He threw open another door and shoved her inside just as his mother's feet pounded up the stairs.

Liv gazed at another narrow set of stairs. He'd pushed her into the doorway that led to the attic.

"What are you doing?" Stephen's mother asked, her voice cold and filled with suspicion.

Liv took a few steps up the stairs, watching the door.

"Nothing. I heard the door open, and I was coming to see..."

"To see me?" Mrs. Kaiser snapped. "I'm sure. Go make tea. I'm exhausted. Bring it to me in the parlor."

Liv heard the woman's hard shoes clack down the stairs.

Stephen cracked the door open.

"Shh..." He put a finger to his lips and led Liv down the stairs.

"Is she angry?" Liv asked, but Stephen's lips were pressed in a tight line. He shoved her out the front door, closing it quietly behind her.

Liv hurried down the porch steps and toward the tree line.

She paused and looked back, catching the smallest flick as a curtain fell back into place in one of the lower rooms. She hoped it had been Stephen watching, but she didn't think so.

STEPHEN ARRANGED a cup and saucer on a silver tray. He added a small bowl with cubes of sugar, a glass pitcher of milk, and a single piece of chocolate.

When he stepped into the room, his mother was draped across the burgundy crushed-velvet sofa in her slip. She'd loosened her hair from the clip, and a curl fell across her forehead.

He set the tray on the table and lifted her steaming cup of tea.

As he reached toward her, her hand shot out and caught his other arm, holding it firm. Her fingernails dug into the soft flesh of his wrist.

"Who is she?" his mother asked.

Stephen's hand started to shake. A drop of tea splashed from the cup and burned his finger. He winced and tried to steady his arm.

"I... she..."

"Drink it," she told him, releasing his hand. "Drink it, now."

He looked at the tea, tendrils of steam rising from the liquid.

"Drink it or you'll spend the night in the cellar."

"She lives in town. She's harmless, Mother," Stephen tried to explain.

"Drink it," his mother shrieked.

Stephen lifted the cup to his mouth and opened. The tea scalded his lips and tongue, and he choked as it burned the back of his throat. He didn't dare spit it out on her Persian rug. Tears streamed from his eyes as the hot tea blazed a scalding trail down his throat and into his stomach.

When he'd swallowed the last dredges, he returned the cup to the tray.

His mother watched him steadily, her eyes hard.

"Go make me another," she snapped. "And then get out of my sight."

That night, Stephen barely slept. His mouth and throat ached. He drank three cups of milk, but the burning did not subside. He fell asleep just as the morning sun crested over the trees beyond his window.

CHAPTER 8

September 1965
Mack

MACK WOKE to the sound of something hitting the floor with a thud. He sat up and squinted into the room, unable to make out any movement in the darkness. Fumbling the lamp on next to his bed, he gazed toward his door, still firmly closed.

Misty lay at the end of his bed, the fur on the back of her neck raised and a low growl emitting from her muzzle. Nothing in the room had been disturbed. He scanned the meager furnishings, a dresser with a little portable radio, a wooden chair he'd stacked his clothes on, before climbing into bed. No shadows stirred on the knotty pine walls.

"What do you think, Misty?" he asked, leaning down to stroke her red-brown fur.

He waited, listening, but heard nothing else.

Probably the wind, he figured, laying back down. He closed his eyes and heard another sound: the slow creak of footsteps in the room above him.

Misty let out a single loud bark and stood up on the bed.

Mack sat back up and listened. The footsteps had stopped, but now his heart had caught on to the noises and it thudded behind his breastbone. Mack was not prone to panic. He stood six feet four inches tall and weighed two hundred pounds. He could more than take care of himself. But his mind flashed on the corpse in the woods.

The sensation of being watched returned, but in the closed bedroom, nothing could see him. Unless they peeked through the tiny slit beneath the curtain, he reasoned, but the sounds he heard had not come from outside the cabin.

"Stay here, girl," he told Misty, shutting her in the bedroom. Other men would have sent the dog ahead of them, but Misty was pushing ten years and excitement could kill her as quick as anything else. He would need Misty in the days ahead. Leaving Tina would not be an easy task. The thought of doing it without his pup made his heart ache.

He eyed his rifle propped next to the couch and opted for a baseball bat instead.

The upper floor consisted of a single large room with slanted ceilings, and Mack had to duck as he walked up the stairs. He gazed across the room. The blinds on the single window were lowered, but as he studied the opposite wall, his breath caught.

A figure stood there, a man as tall as Mack himself. His back faced Mack, as if he stared at the wall.

Mack's hand shot out and flicked on the lights, raising the baseball bat in his left hand. He took an automatic step backward as light filled the room.

The man no longer stood at the opposite wall.

Cheap plastic blinds and a picture of a buck standing in a meadow were the only objects before Mack.

Mack's heart hammered in his ears, and he walked across the room. There was nowhere for a person to hide. Two twin beds stood against one wall, a long chest of drawers on the opposite. He stared at the shag carpet as if he expected to see footprints, but the fabric appeared undisturbed.

"Damn, Tina," he grumbled, returning to the stairs. When he'd told Tina about the cabin, she'd delighted in sharing a story about her cousin's friend Marty who went camping for a week and disappeared without a trace.

"They found his shoe a year later," she'd said, picking at her disgusting grapefruit and challenging him with her made-up eyes. "Nothing else, just a shoe."

Of course, it wasn't only Tina. It was the dead man in the woods. Who wouldn't be spooked after a thing like that?

He flipped off the light and hurried down the stairs, returning to his room and sitting on the edge of the bed for several minutes.

Misty licked his face, but he nudged her away, listening.

Only the quiet of the cabin surrounded him. He laid down and slept.

THE MORNING ARRIVED crisp and sunny. Misty bounced around the cabin like a dog half her age. Mack fed her a can of dog food before giving in to her persistent pawing at the door and letting her out. She bounded into the wet grass that sparkled in the early sun.

He brewed coffee and sipped it black at the little kitchen table by the window. He watched Misty crouch and spring and run wildly in circles. He wished he could tell her to slow down; her ticker wasn't built for a decade of racing, but even if she understood, her instincts would override his good sense.

He thought briefly of Tina eating her grapefruit and nursing her hangover with a glass of seltzer water. And then he thought, as he inevitably did, of Diane.

Diane had moved out on a Tuesday, taking the cracked leather bag that had belonged to her father stuffed with a week's worth of clothes and toiletries. It hadn't been the first time she'd left, and Mack had ignored her, scraping the burn off his frying pan and pretending not to watch as she climbed into her Buick and sped away.

Afterward, he'd sat at the table, drank his coffee, and insisted she'd be back just like every other time. Later, he realized she wasn't coming back, not for good, not even for a night this time. She did come back a week later with her brother's pickup truck. They loaded her stuff, and she handed Mack her house key with tears streaking a trail down her pale cheeks.

Mack had drawn her close and whispered in her ear.

"Don't go, Diane. I swear, I'll never buy another bottle. I mean it this time. I'm done."

She'd let out a sob, buried her head in his chest, and then, without a word, she ran to her brother's truck and climbed in.

Diane's brother Dennis had offered Mack a wave and a sympathetic smile. Mack liked Dennis. They'd shared an easy friendship over the years.

But Dennis knew the stories of Mack's drinking. Late nights stumbling in half-cocked, sometimes angry.

He never hit Diane, never had and never would. But he broke the little glass swan her father had bought her when she was eighteen. It was a cherished gift from a beloved, and dead, father. An irreplaceable gift, and it had been the last straw.

He'd broken plenty of other things before that: plates, coffee mugs. He'd even kicked a hole in the wall once. The morning after his drunken outbursts, he'd wake ashamed and swear to Diane he would join AA; he'd never take another drink.

Sober, Mack wouldn't even paddle his dog for pissing on the floor; but drunk, a dormant anger rose up and lashed out at anyone willing to get close enough to see it.

Diane wasn't perfect. She was a stubborn beast who dug in her feet about the most preposterous things, like replacing the leaky faucet in the kitchen. She preferred to let the old faucet run a steady drip into a grimy bowl beneath the sink because the faucet *had character and belonged in their old farmhouse*.

Her brother once described Diane as a saint with the common sense of a turkey who'll drown in the damn rain trying to get a drink of water when there's a perfectly good stream behind her.

Mack had laughed and forever after called Diane his little turkey, which some days she found endearing and other days ignited a rage that sent her flying out the door, spitting at him like an alley cat.

But for all their ups and downs, Mack had never wanted to lose Diane. He wanted to be a better man for her. He tried too, but the drink had been his home since childhood.

He remembered his first taste of beer, a taste his old man had forced on him. Any desire for booze should have died that day as Mack's father clutched his eight-year-old son's arm in a vice grip until he swallowed the entire can of beer. Mack had stumbled behind the shed and thrown up.

His dad laughed, called him a girlie-boy, and continued pounding beers until he fell over drunk next to his lawn chair. Mack's mother sometimes threw a blanket over him and left him to sleep it off in the yard, but she never said a word against him, partially because she still had a fresh bruise from the last time she spoke up. Though she didn't have to say a word to get the back of her husband's hand. A look would suffice.

Mack rubbed his jaw and drained his coffee. As he refilled it, he looked for Misty outside. She no longer pranced around the yard, but stood obediently at the door.

Mack walked out, grabbed an armful of wood, and piled it next to the wood-burning stove. The temperatures would rise throughout the day, but the chill of night lingered, and he wanted wood for the coming cold.

In an hour, the sun would thaw the cold ground. Mack could take Misty for a walk and maybe take his fishing pole to the lake.

He yawned and glanced at the coffee table where the leather satchel lay. He'd never handed it over to the police. He'd forgotten all about it until the evening before, when he spotted it while frying up a couple of hot dogs for him and Misty.

He sat on the couch and picked the pouch up. Misty looked up from her water bowl and let out a low growl.

"Don't like this thing, do ya?" he asked.

He poured the stones into his hand. The stones were mostly white, rubbed smooth, and each contained a hole in its center. The holes were not large, too small for Mack to slide a pinkie through.

He cupped the rocks, examining each one before returning them to the satchel.

Misty continued to growl and glare at the bag.

Mack looked at her thoughtfully.

"Okay, you win," he said. He took the bag to the kitchen and closed it in a drawer. "Better?" he asked her.

She gazed at him, shifted her eyes to the drawer, and then back to him. Apparently satisfied, she padded to the wood burner and lay on the rug, resting her head on her paws and watching him.

Mack cooked sausage and eggs, sharing with Misty, who never begged, but waited patiently at his feet for her portion.

Afterward, they walked the woods in the opposite direction of the corpse. They wandered the forest, Mack knocking over dead trees while Misty chased squirrels and birds.

As he walked, he mulled over how best to end things with Tina. He didn't want the tears or the mean words. A note seemed like the easiest choice. The coward's way out, Diane would have told him.

When the sun was high, a rumble started in Mack's belly.

"Lunch time," he said aloud.

Misty stood at the base of a birch tree, barking up at a squirrel who'd outsmarted her.

She dutifully followed Mack as he turned back toward the cabin.

They walked a good mile, and Mack had yet to spot the gnarled beech tree that lay at the edge of his property. When he gazed at the forest around him, he couldn't place their location.

"Did we get turned around?" he asked Misty.

She barked and licked his hand.

He glanced at the sun, confirming what he already knew. "We're heading west," he insisted.

They walked for ten minutes and still no beech tree.

Dark clouds accumulated, blotting the sun. A light rain began to fall, pattering the leaves.

After several minutes, Mack's heavy coat and pants grew sodden. A wet sheen covered Misty, and she seemed to realize they were lost as she ran ahead and circled back, only to head off in a different direction and repeat the process.

Mack stopped searching for the sun and followed his dog. He'd lost his bearings completely.

As the rain fell, a fog formed low to the ground, and they walked in obscurity. The trees reached stark and skeleton-like out of the white mist.

Mack shivered, his teeth chattering.

Don't say it, he thought. *If you don't say it, it's not true,* but whether he voiced it or not, the thought reverberated in his head: *We're lost.*

The Stoneroot Forest was not a good place to get lost. Miles of woods, and the cold could kill you in a night, especially when you added the rain. In September, the temperature shouldn't drop below forty, but only a moron staked his life on it.

Mack had never been lost in the Stoneroot Forest in his life. He'd grown up there, after all, spending weeks at the cabin with his Uncle Byron, hunting and fishing and escaping the rough hands of his father. He'd learned the woods as thoroughly as his own bedroom. He'd never gotten lost in them, not once in his life.

He dug through his pack but knew he wouldn't find a compass. He never carried one. He'd never needed one.

Misty barked and ran off again, vanishing into the fog.

"Misty," he yelled, but she didn't return.

Far off, he heard a bark, as if in a matter of seconds, she'd covered a mile of woods.

He tried to follow the sound, but already it had faded.

"Misty," he yelled again, uneasy at the panic edging his voice.

He took a deep breath and opened his pack, digging for the dried beef he'd dropped in that morning. He dug until his fingers hit something.

He frowned as he drew the object out.

He held the leather satchel full of stones.

"What the hell?" he grumbled. He stuffed it into another pouch, trying to shake off the quiver tugging at his spine. "I thought I grabbed the jerky, is all," he told no one.

But then his hand hit the small plastic bag that held the jerky. He refused to think about it. He opened the bag, popped a hunk of dried meat in his mouth, and trudged on, calling out for Misty.

As he walked, a branch snapped behind him. He spun, expecting to see his dog.

Instead, far in the distance, obscured by the fog, a tall man stood in the forest. He was a black silhouette in a forest of equally dark trees, but the shape of the man was clear.

Mack waved, started to walk toward him, and then paused. Something about the man felt wrong.

Mack's mind flashed to the figure he'd imagined the night before. But of course, there'd been no man, merely a trick of his troubled mind.

He watched the man, waited to see if he waved back.

When he didn't, Mack turned and continued the way he'd been going. He walked for several minutes, listening, growing desperate in his search for a familiar tree.

Mack twisted around. The man had gained on him.

His heart gave a little skip.

He turned and picked up his pace. He ran a few yards before looking back.

Again, the man stood closer, tall, dark, and faceless in the fog.

"Just punch the son of a bitch," Mack chastised himself. "Ask him what he wants." But as he started forward, a crippling fear washed over him, as if someone had poured a cup of ice water over his head. He faltered, and looked up to see the man closer still.

Mack turned and bolted into the trees. His breath hitched and his legs burned, but he didn't stop.

Suddenly the thing was on him, leaves and twigs snapping, and Mack tried to run harder, but it was gaining on him. He felt the man touch his back.

He remembered the knife in the skeleton's ribs and waited for the hot slash across his exposed neck.

He cried out and flinched away, but then Misty's growl filled the quiet.

Mack dove to the ground and rolled, ready to face the man who pursued him, but the forest stood empty save for his dog, who jumped on him and licked his face wildly.

Mack lay, elbows propped beneath him, staring into the receding mist.

The man had vanished.

When Mack stood, he spotted the beech tree and dropped to his knees.

"Thank you, thank you," he murmured, imagining not a God guiding him home, but his mother somewhere up in the gray sky watching over him.

Misty nudged him as if she preferred they keep moving, and he agreed. He scrambled back to his feet, and he and Misty trotted back to the cabin.

CHAPTER 9

September 1965
Liv

"STEPHEN." When he looked up at her, his eyes revealed only confusion. But Liv's heart gave a little jump. He looked older, sure. But the same pale blue eyes gazed from his handsome face. He'd lost the smoothness of his youth. The bones of his face created depth to his jaw and brow-line.

"Liv?" He sounded curious, not excited or disappointed. He turned to a woman in a white smock. "Go ahead without me. I'll be in shortly."

The woman nodded and hurried away.

Liv took a step closer. Conflicting emotions raged within her. She'd missed Stephen, missed the closest friend she'd ever known, longed for him during some of those lonely years when she went home from the orphanage night after night, read a few pages of a book, and drifted off to sleep.

But she'd loathed him too. Hated how she'd followed his strange obsessions, hated that she'd committed the ultimate sin on his behalf.

He didn't hug her, but when she stopped before him, he took her hand and squeezed.

"How are you, Liv? It's been..."

"Twenty years," she whispered.

Twenty years to the day, soon. Twenty years since that fateful All Hallows' Eve, the costume party... Liv could still smell the purple dahlias, and the blood.

She shook her head and cleared the memory.

"Your mother said you moved west..." he started, studying her face.

So, he had asked about her.

Sometimes she'd wondered in those intervening years if he'd simply walked the other way from which she ran.

"I did, for a few years. And then I ended up in Boston. I've been there for almost seventeen years."

"Are you married? Children?"

Liv shook her head.

"There are children in my life. But none are my own." Because I'm barren, she thought. I paid for our treachery with the lives of the children I'll never have.

She didn't know where such thoughts came from. How could she possibly know? But then she thought of George and all the things he'd told her about wisdom rooted deep in the belly. How a person could access all the secrets of the universe if they merely traveled into themselves and grew very still and silent.

'The womb of the world lives inside of you, Volva, inside of us all. Ask her and she will tell you.' Liv could see George as he said the words, daring her to look deep enough to know it all.

"Do you have children, Stephen?" she asked, breaking from his gaze.

He recoiled as if the suggestion disgusted him. He shook his head.

"No. I'm married to my work." He gestured to the asylum.

"You're a doctor? You followed your dream."

He nodded.

"It wasn't easy, but yes. It's been very fulfilling." His voice shifted on the word *fulfilling*, and Liv took a step back. She wondered what sorts of things he did as a psychiatrist, how long his reach had become.

As she studied the soaring asylum, her breath grew shallow. Gazing at the high spires rising from the brick buildings made her unsteady on her feet, and she looked to the ground to escape the dizziness.

"Magnificent, isn't it? I can't give you a tour. It's a sanitarium, after all. But if you'd like, I can show you the offices."

Liv sighed.

"Not today. There are things we need to talk about. Meet me later?"

A crinkle of worry creased his brow, but he nodded.

"Yes. It would be lovely to catch up."

"I think somewhere private is best," she went on.

"Come to my house." He pulled a small notebook and pen from the pocket of his white coat. He wrote an address and directions from the asylum. "I leave here at six o'clock. Come by around seven?"

"Yes. Thank you," she told him stiffly.

She took the paper and walked away.

The familiarity of their youthful friendship had died. Had she expected anything else? And yet, she could not deny the shred of hope that had carried her to the train and kept her feet moving as she stepped off in Traverse City, Michigan.

'Once fractured, a bone will never be the same,' George had told her one morning while setting the wing of a crow they had found injured in the woods. *'He may fly again, but the crack will remain. All of life is that way, Volva. We are broken, torn down, sometimes ruined in this long walk to the grave, and every wound, every bruise and heartbreak changes us. Remember that. What once was will never be again.'*

Liv watched Stephen walk away. His gait had changed, his hair showed bits of gray at his temples, but something more had shifted in Stephen Kaiser. A blankness surrounded him. He stole light from the sky and gave off only darkness.

"THANK YOU. THIS IS FINE," Liv told the man who'd offered her a ride from town.

She stepped from his car and walked down the long driveway to Stephen's home. A black wrought-iron fence protected the sprawling property.

As the house slid into view, Liv stopped abruptly.

It was a large Victorian house, eerily similar to the house Stephen had grown up in. The rounded second floor room made her breath catch as she remembered the dark figure from her dream.

Stephen opened the door before she knocked.

"Liv." He beamed. "Come in," he told her, backing into the dim hallway and opening his arms in a wide, welcoming gesture that only added to Liv's unease.

Antique sconces held dim yellow bulbs. Oil paintings much like his childhood home covered the walls, but these were not drab family photos. Instead, Stephen decorated his walls with death and depravity. Images of humans chasing animals with spears hung in gilded frames. She saw a picture of a man, his neck broken, dangling from a hangman's noose. Another painting depicted a pile of bodies heaped in a barren field.

Liv blinked and almost commented on the paintings, but dread blanketed her in a kind of speech paralysis. Numbly, she followed him to a sitting room.

"I'm surprised you don't live at the asylum," she commented after he'd handed her a glass of sherry.

He shook his head and sat in a black velvet chair, stretching his long legs in front of him.

He'd changed from his doctor's coat and wore blue slacks with a black sweater. His pale face looked bloodless against the dark fabric.

"I lived at the hospital in the beginning, in a modest little apartment that I rather liked. But after a few years, I realized I longed for the creaks of an old house. Funny, isn't it? I hated that house on

Spellway Road, and now here I am." He waved at the room. "Of course, this one is mine and mine alone."

"It certainly is large," Liv told him, unable to fake a compliment. The house was ugly, and it was… unpleasant. She felt on edge just sitting within its walls.

"Tell me about you, Liv. You just disappeared. I wondered if you followed George's wishes and went to Norway."

Liv offered a sad smile and shook her head.

"I haven't seen George since I left. I fled, Stephen. I was terrified."

Stephen studied her.

"And you chose Boston?"

She shifted uncomfortably on the satin sofa.

"California, and then Boston, yes."

She recalled her final night in Gaylord, walking dazed into her bedroom. She had packed a bag and slipped into the night. She knew how to hop a train, but that night she couldn't. She had no courage left. She remembered wishing she'd eaten the boar's heart. Such a foolish thought, and yet she wondered if it might have changed everything. Instead, she bought a bus ticket, with money she stole from her mother's can behind the potatoes, to California.

The memories of her first days in California were like peering through a fogged window. She had walked catatonic for three days around San Francisco. She slept in sips during the day, in a woman's powder room or at the picture show.

When she had met an old man tilling a garden outside his little house, he invited her in for lemonade. She lived with him for two years. When he died, she bought another train ticket and travelled back across the country.

Again, she wandered the streets, but this time she had a bit of money. She stayed at the YMCA. There she met a young pregnant mother soon to give up her child. Liv accompanied the woman, Meredith, to the hospital, where she gave birth to a healthy baby girl.

When Frannie, the head mother from the orphanage, arrived to take the child, Liv promised Meredith she would see the baby settled. After a day of sitting vigil with the baby girl, Liv never left Helping Hands.

The children loved her. They flocked to her in droves. They ran to her with their colored pictures, their stubbed toes, their favorite toys.

In Liv, they found the parent they'd never had. Here was a person who saw them, who not only looked but truly saw them. And in the children, Liv found purpose in an existence that for several years had been empty and unbearable.

Liv occupied the moment before her and no other. She had learned the practice of presence from George many years before, but after her final night with Stephen, it had saved her life.

In the moment, she never had to visit the past. She could almost believe it never happened at all.

"I work at an orphanage in Boston. The children are my home now. Or they were."

Stephen's face fell, as if disappointed.

"You work in an orphanage? Caring for children?"

Liv nodded.

He frowned and shrugged.

"To each their own, as they say. I had rather imagined you as a sorceress on the islands of Scandinavia, directing the wind, but here you are…" He trailed off.

Twenty years earlier, the comment would have bruised her, but she no longer cared for Stephen's approval.

"Liv, I'm delighted to see you. But why are you here?" he continued, swirling the dark liquid in his crystal glass.

Liv crushed her hands in her lap. The courage of the previous days had been battered by the travel, and more so, by the memories. Memories that beat against the doors of her mind as she rode on the train to northern Michigan.

"It's time to make amends," she told Stephen, looking into his eyes. "George always said the past circles around. We've no idea how long it will take, but eventually it returns."

"Have you seen George?" Stephen asked, sipping his drink.

Something in his tone put Liv on edge.

"No." Though she had seen him in her dreams.

He nodded, finished his drink and stood.

"Stephen." He stopped and turned back to her. "We have to go to the police. We have to tell-" Liv insisted.

"You're right," he interrupted her.

She watched him. His jaw was set, as if he held his cheek clamped between his teeth.

"I hate to do it. It's the end of our lives, after all. But of course, you're right," he conceded.

He slipped from the room, and she loosened her twined fingers, though her heart continued to thump against her breastbone.

She tried to relax, invite a sigh into her constricted diaphragm, but her body remained tense.

'Your body knows, Volva,' George used to tell her. *'Your body knows what the mind can't see.'*

She realized she did not believe Stephen.

She had expected him to resist, to be angry. His compliance troubled her. But why should it? Perhaps he too had been plagued all these years. How could he not have been?

She watched the doorway he'd disappeared into when a small creak sounded behind her.

Twisting around, she saw him from the corner of her eye. He had slipped into the sitting room through another door.

She hitched forward and tried to jerk away, but he sank his hand into her long hair and yanked her head back. He jabbed something sharp into her neck.

Liv cried out and hurled her body forward. He released her hair, and she catapulted from the couch, out of control, and into the coffee table. She landed on the wood, and one of the legs splintered. Her glass of sherry tumbled to the floor, staining the rug.

Stephen watched her, making no move to catch Liv as she scrambled away.

The drug moved swiftly through her veins. She felt the icy current fanning down her legs, pumping toward her heart.

'Block it,' George whispered in her ear.

She gazed at the floor as if he would be sitting there, but saw only the fine particles of dust drifting in the lamplight.

She crawled on her hands and knees toward the hallway.

Drawing in a shaky breath, she tried to imagine how she might stop the poison in her blood. Only the panicked emptiness of her mind returned. She didn't know.

Her hand grew numb, and when she went to put weight on it, she crashed onto her face instead. She lay in Stephen's hallway, face down, the toes on her left foot twitching.

Focusing on her breath, she counted to ten.

"One, two, theer, no thwee, no." But she couldn't say it. Her tongue lay thick and heavy on the floor of her mouth.

Stephen's feet moved into her line of sight, but her eyelids had grown too heavy.

She wanted to grab him, demand that he stop, but the darkness reached up and pulled her in.

CHAPTER 10

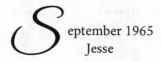

September 1965
Jesse

JESSE WOKE AT DAWN, refreshed as he hadn't been in months. He sat up and gazed around the room.

The walls were papered in scrolling foliage that ended in a dark velvet border topped by crown molding. A heavy gold chandelier dangled in the center of the room.

Jesse watched cobwebs swaying beneath the chunky fixture, light filtering through the gauzy tendrils.

Remembering the woman, Jesse searched the house. He opened curtains, peeked in closets and beneath furniture.

The search took on a feverish quality when he reached the attic, but he maintained his composure, carefully returning furniture to its exact location rather than flinging it aside in his frenzy to find some evidence the woman had been there.

There was no woman, and the more he thought about it, the more absurd the idea of a woman became. What woman in her right mind would arrive at that house in the dead of night?

No car had pulled into the driveway. He would have awoken to a splash of headlights, a car door slamming, something.

He'd imagined her.

Strangely, he could still see her long, pale legs stretched on the chaise.

Jesse was no stranger to hallucinations.

In the months after Nell and Gabriel died, he saw them everywhere. He once grabbed a woman at the train station who so resembled Nell that his heart nearly leapt from his chest. The woman had turned wide, terrified eyes on him, clutched her purse, and ran toward the conductor as if Jesse had attacked her.

Eventually, the visions faded. Even in his dreams, he rarely saw his departed wife and son.

Perhaps had they had gone on. To where, he didn't quite know.

Jesse's father had been a man of faith, but not a man of the church. They never attended a single service.

Jesse's understanding of the bible came through the harsh declarations made by the nuns in various orphanages he'd occupied in his youth. When he could not quote scripture, they beat him. In that cruel way, he learned the words of God — some of them, anyhow — but they did little to comfort him in the days after the death of his family.

Instead, he grieved Nell and Gabriel as if they'd gone into the ground to darkness.

After his search, Jesse returned to the kitchen.

He flicked on the faucet. It groaned and spat rust-colored sludge into the sink, but after several seconds, the water ran clear.

Jesse found an old cannister of coffee. As he waited for water to boil in the kettle, he opened cupboards, marveling at the stacks of porcelain dishes and the sparkling goblets.

Drinking his coffee from a delicate white and silver cup, he toured the house a second time, more slowly, no longer hunting for a phantom woman.

The house appeared as if the owners woke up one morning and walked out. Clothes hung in the closets. A hairbrush lay by the sink in the upstairs bathroom. The beds were made.

In the largest bedroom, where he'd imagined the woman, pink satin slippers lay next to the bed as if their owner had taken them off one night, climbed into bed, and disappeared.

The third floor contained a bedroom he imagined belonged to a young man. The clothes were about Jesse's size, but included school uniforms. A stack of high school textbooks lay scattered on a dresser top.

When he returned to the kitchen, Jesse found the remains of a half-eaten cake in the icebox. The cupboard held jars of apples and blueberries, and he gorged himself on the oversweet pie fillings.

He bathed quickly, unable to shake the sense of eyes gazing at him from the cracked bathroom door. He would have liked to savor the shower. Like so many other things, a proper shower had been a luxury of the past, but his paranoia got the better of him.

When he opened the door, the long hall stood empty - save the hundreds of eyes staring out from the portraits on the walls.

~

JESSE CLEANED the kettle and returned it the cupboard. He rinsed his cup and put it away. He even smoothed the fibers of the rug he'd slept on the night before.

Convinced that the house looked exactly as it had when he entered it, he left through the cellar.

The daylight through the open cellar doors washed away the darkness from the night before. He observed bottles of wine and stacks of empty crates.

He closed the cellar doors behind him and wandered into the woods, deep in contemplation.

He'd never been a thief.

A year before, when he'd lost his wife and child, he walked out on his life. He left their little house, surely now cleaned and rented to someone else.

He'd abandoned his job without so much as a note to his boss.

He'd just left - left it all. Packed his bag and walked out of town.

He still wore the same pair of shoes. He'd brought one change of clothes, a booklet of photographs, Gabriel's stuffed Mickey Mouse, and all the money he'd had to his name, which after the funeral expenses had been little.

Since then, he'd slept beneath bridges, or tucked between boxes on the railroad cars. The soles of his feet were hard, his face was tanned, and the youthful appearance he'd had for the first forty years of his life had been replaced with grooves of sorrow.

For two hours, Jesse walked the woods around the big, abandoned house, considering his options. He paused at the train tracks that would take him to another town.

The thought of walking away from the house caused an ache in his gut.

"Why?" he wondered out loud.

Birds and crickets and the breeze in the leaves offered their own replies, but none told him the answer he sought.

Maybe his achy body needed a rest, or he longed for another morning or two with running water. Whatever the reason, he would stay a few more days.

And why not fill the coffers first, his father would say?

With a few bucks, Jesse could buy a new pair of shoes. He could easily pilfer a few items that would never be missed.

He walked back to the house.

The house was desolate and, Jesse paused at the thought, almost hostile. Even the midday sun did little to warm its dark façade. Patches of moss coated the once black shingles on the roof. The porch looked rotted in spots, paint peeling from its rails and beams.

Perhaps most of all, Jesse noticed the overgrowth. Vines crawled up the house's exterior as if trying to squirm into the tightly shut windows. Bushes, likely once manicured, were heaping and bushy. They rolled out from the house in prickly waves.

Yes, the house had been abandoned, and Jesse wanted to know why.

~

THE THIRD-FLOOR BEDROOM held clothes in a size just about perfect for Jesse. They were dated items, but good quality. Tailored jackets and pressed white shirts hung from satin-covered hangers.

The boy who'd worn them clearly lived a life of privilege. Jesse doubted a few pairs of trousers would be missed.

He grabbed a clean leather suitcase and headed for the dining room, selecting four silver candlesticks and a handful of sterling silver cutlery. He added an antique-looking mantel clock, which he wrapped in a towel.

Wearing the young man's clothes, Jesse walked into town and, using the last few dollars to his name, he bought a train ticket for Harrison.

"Jesse K., what brings you to these parts?" The man eyed him up and down with fast, dark eyes that reminded Jesse of a watchful owl.

"I need to move a few things, Rockie," Jesse murmured, glancing toward the other men sitting at tables drinking hooch and playing cards. The man's name was not actually Rockie. Jesse didn't know his true name, but he knew how Rockie used to chisel holes in rocks and slip papers inside to smuggle them into the prison during his ten long years at the Southern Michigan State Prison.

"Come into some inheritance?" Rockie smirked.

"Seems so." Jesse tilted the suitcase so Rockie could see the candlesticks and silverware.

"Come on back." Rockie led Jesse into the back room.

The room held only a single wooden table. Beyond the first back room stood two more, one with merchandise and the last with a safe. Rockie had drunkenly showed Jesse the interior rooms after a long poker game several months before. Jesse doubted that Rockie remembered. The man had passed out, face pressed against a full house, and not woken. Jesse had joined him in sleep, happy to be indoors, opting to stretch out on the sticky floor rather than suffer the backache of sleeping over the table.

Rockie gave him a handful of bills and slapped him on the back.

"Guys are fixin' to start a game. Care to join us? Sees how you got some cash to work with." Rockie winked at the money, but Jesse shook his head.

"I'm fixing to travel south."

Jesse slipped out the door and down the alley, heading to catch his return bus.

By the time he reached Gaylord, the storm had come.

He stepped from the bus and hurried out of town.

Somehow in the downpour, Jesse could breathe again. As if the oxygen from all that water bled into the air, and he gulped it like an alcoholic who'd almost made it, but then found the bottle again and relieved a thirst that felt thousands of years in the making.

He rushed beneath canopies of willows and maples, ash and pine. Some held the water high, nature's way of scrimping and saving for the big drought. Others just let it go, and it poured onto his head and flattened his carefully parted hair. It roared over his face and soaked the lapels of his stiff jacket.

He paused beneath a willow. It was like standing inside a waterfall. Miserably, he remembered one such moment, years before, when he stood beneath a waterfall in the Upper Peninsula with his wife. She had leaned into him, her breath moist against his ear, and whispered that he was going to be a father.

Sorrow stole the joy from his memory.

Jesse ran, and soon his slacks and socks were soaked to his skin and his shining shoes had gone from black to muddy brown. He ripped off the stranger's jacket and left it laying in a tangle of brush.

After a while, he found a river. He sat on a sledge of rock, flat and dulled by the sun. The water ran off its edges, and he clenched his eyes against the rain that continued to pour.

He wished to close his brain as tightly as his eyelids, but it fluttered and thrashed until the images he'd run so hard to escape began to slip back in.

Gabriel, his child, in his dark suit with his face a white mask of indifference bedded in the satin-lined casket Jesse had chosen. *Gabriel, God is my strength*. His name had been his wife's choice, and Jesse complied. He hardly counted himself devoted to God, but in Nell and Gabriel, he had found his elusive creator.

And almost as quickly lost him again.

Jesse laid back and let the rain wash over him. If it picked up, it might sweep him into the river.

An appropriate death, he thought. Nell and Gabriel had both drowned. Not on a rainy, gloomy day, but in the peak of summer, when death crept in without a whisper of warning.

Who noticed the angel of death on a sunny Monday afternoon at a little lake in the woods?

The rain slowed to a drizzle.

Jesse stared into the overcast sky, the gray of sodden clay, and wished he could fill the emptiness inside him. If he gulped the river until he was near to exploding, he wondered if he might find a moment of relief from the constant hollow within.

He returned to the house and emptied the money he'd tucked into the pocket of another man's pants.

Jesse looked at the wet bills spread across the table and considered lighting a fire in one of the home's three fireplaces and burning them.

Objects that once held value, that ruled his life, had become obsolete. The bills conjured no joy, no dread, no anything. They merely represented his likelihood of surviving, eating, getting a bath. If he selected a few more items, he'd have a grubstake. He could buy a train ticket south, land somewhere warm before winter returned to Michigan.

He could head for Mississippi or to the Florida Keys.

No, not there.

Nell loved to dream of Florida. *Mangoes that grow in your backyard,* she used to whisper. *Oranges the size of melons.* But they'd never had more than a few pennies to rub together between them. They'd both grown up poor, his father a drunk and hers a farmer.

Jesse didn't dream the way Nell had. He'd watched his father do so for years, but his dreams never came true. Not even the small ones, such as winning the poker game so they could get a motel for the night.

Sometimes Jesse wondered if they weren't the lucky ones - Nell and Gabriel. They got out early.

In his forty-one years, Jesse had seen mostly disappointment and despair. His seven years with Nell, two that included Gabriel, had been the only years of happiness he'd known. But their happiness had not included wealth. They lived in an old farmhouse with a big garden out back that they rented from an old man who'd moved in with his children years before. Jesse worked long hours drilling and servicing oil refineries. Before Gabe came along, Nell worked four days a week cleaning rooms at the Doherty Hotel.

They made ends meet, never went hungry, and for the two years they had their boy, they saved enough for big Christmas celebrations and a red tricycle on his second birthday.

Jesse imagined the tricycle on the farmhouse lawn. It had been his final image of the house that June day when he'd walked away from it all. He'd buried his wife and son two days before.

He stripped off his wet clothes and plodded up the stairs, forgoing his intention to leave the furniture untouched. He crawled into bed and pleaded for sleep to take him.

CHAPTER 11

August 1945
Liv

"WHAT IS THAT?" Stephen asked, startling Liv as she sat on a rock near the lake.

She pulled the stone from her eye and held it up to reveal the small round hole in the center.

"It's called a hag stone."

"A hag stone?" He crinkled his forehead and held out a hand.

"Can I see it?"

Liv hesitated. George had been very clear when she found the stone, she must never share its magic. *The stone chose the seer,* he said. Liv had only one stone, but George had six. They hung in a small leather satchel around his neck.

"Sure." She handed Stephen the stone. It wasn't as if he'd know what to do with it, anyway.

He turned the stone over several times, rubbing his hand over the smooth edge.

"What's a hag stone, then?" he asked, handing it back to her and already shrugging out of his clothes.

They'd met at the pond every day for a week now, and Stephen no longer blushed when she stripped down to her undergarments.

Liv considered how to explain it.

"Some people believe they're magic."

He perked up at the comment and leaned in for a second look at the stone.

"Magic, how?"

Liv shrugged.

"Sometimes when people look through them, they can see things."

"May I?" He held out his hand again, and Liv pulled the stone away.

"You have to catch me first."

She jumped off the rock and ran down the dock, diving into the pond and swimming fast. She heard Stephen's dive follow her own.

Suddenly a hand grabbed her ankle and pulled her beneath the water. She almost kicked out, but instead spun and put both hands on Stephen's shoulders. She popped above the water and leveraged up, pushing him down. He thrashed away from her, and she realized he was panicking. When his head shot above the surface, his eyes were filled with terror, and he coughed and hacked as if he'd taken in a mouthful of water.

"What'd you do that for?" he yelled, kicking away from her. He climbed from the pond and kneeled on the bank, continuing to cough.

She followed, putting a hand on his shoulder.

"I'm sorry," she gasped, remembering his story of jumping off the cliff. She should have known better.

He rubbed his throat, and when he looked at her, she saw red blisters inflamed on his lips.

She put a finger to his lower lip, but he jerked his head away.

The blisters had not been there the day before.

"What happened?" she asked.

"Nothing. I'm fine."

Liv thought back to the previous day and the angry tone of his mother.

"She saw me, didn't she? You mother?"

He didn't look at her but nodded.

"Does she hurt you, Stephen?"

He glared at her and then stood.

"I don't feel like swimming today."

He stalked back to his clothes and grabbed them before disappearing into the trees.

She almost let him go. Years later, she would reflect on all those chances to turn the other way and let their friendship dissolve as quickly as it took shape.

Instead, she followed him.

"Wait," she called. "I'll show you how to use it."

He continued walking — stomping, really — and then slowed, turning back.

"How to use what?"

She held up the hag stone.

His eyes narrowed on the stone. The ugly blisters on his lips had paled, but when he bit his lip, he winced.

"Okay, yeah, sure." He strode back to her and held out his hand.

She dropped the stone in his palm, ignoring George's voice in the back of her head.

"I need a drum," she told him.

"A drum? And you think we might find one lying around in the woods?"

She smiled and shook her head before walking to a tall, leafy fern. She pulled the largest leaf from the bunch.

"Now, something hollow," she murmured, walking around the forest and kicking at downed trees. She walked back to the lake and pulled branches from a weeping willow. Weaving several branches together, she made a frame, and then stretched the leaf over the branches, securing it by tucking the leaf's edges into the braided wood. When she bounced her finger on it, a barely audible ping reverberated out.

Stephen stood back, watching with interest.

"Not much of a drum," he murmured.

"The best kind are born of necessity," she told him, repeating words George had told her more times than she could count.

She paused and gazed toward the lake, and then back into the forest.

"I think right here beneath this willow," she said. "This is the best spot."

"For what?"

"To call in the spirits."

He gaped at her and then gazed beyond her, as if he expected to see one such spirit gliding across the lake toward them.

"As in dead people? Ghosts?"

She laughed.

"As in ancestors. They lived once, but it was a very long time ago."

Liv settled on a patch of grass and placed the makeshift drum in her lap.

"What should I do?"

"Sit." She patted the space beside her. "And look through the stone."

Stephen held the stone up to his eye, and Liv began to drum her fingers on the leaf. The sound was small and seemed swallowed by the crickets and birds, but slowly the resonance seeped in.

She felt the drumming in her blood, in her heartbeat. The steady throbbing pulse as it pulled her deeper, until her eyes drifted closed and she swayed with the sound. The voices of the spirits rose in a steady hum.

Beside her, Stephen let out a little gasp.

She tried to open her eyes, to ask him what he saw, but the drumbeat pulled her down and down. She did not fly, but sank. The voices rocked her, lulled her, but soon they shifted, their tones no longer warm and comforting. They seemed to be shrieking at her.

"Go away, go away, go away..." the words flowed together, stretched long and angry.

It took her a moment to understand. The spirits didn't want her there.

Her eyes popped open, and she saw that Stephen had shifted to his knees, the hag stone pressed so tightly against his eye, the surrounding skin bulged. She could see the pale blue of his eye peering through.

He gasped and fell back, throwing the stone away.

Liv watched him, dazed. The thick, murky darkness she'd been plunged into had not fully released her.

For a moment, they both sat unmoving, lost in their separate reveries.

"What did you see?" Liv asked him.

She pushed the drum off her lap, and then wrenched the leaf free of the branches.

He swallowed and touched a finger to his blistered lips before shaking his head, as if banishing the images.

"I don't know… I-"

"Never mind," Liv said quickly. She realized she didn't want to know what was responsible for the haunted look in Stephen's eyes.

He said nothing, and then a grin slid over his face.

"That was amazing," he breathed. He gazed into the distant sky, again lifting his fingers to his lips. "You're magic."

Liv smiled, no longer scared by the angry voices of the spirits. Stephen's giddiness enveloped her.

"You don't think it's weird?" she asked, gesturing to the stone and the bent sticks from the drum she'd already destroyed.

"It's incredible. You're incredible."

A little tremor passed through her at his words.

"I'd like you to meet someone," she told him.

CHAPTER 12

August 1945
Liv

"HURRY," Liv called as the train started to pull away. "We've got to catch it on the fly."

They waited in the trees, and then ran together toward the last car on the freight train.

Liv jumped onto the little ladder that clung to the back and shoved the door open. She swung inside. Stephen ran along behind the train, his face determined as he sprang onto the ladder.

He hurtled into the dusky interior, grinning.

"Hot damn! We just jumped on a train. We're like stowaways," he laughed.

Liv grinned and leaned back against a bag of corn.

"No bulls on this line of freights, either, so we don't have to keep a lookout," she told him.

"What are bulls?" he asked, settling on a sack of corn beside her.

"They're guards who throw people without tickets off the trains. Sometimes they club ya, too."

Stephen grimaced and glanced toward the open door.

"Has that ever happened to you?"

She shook her head.

"I know which ones to ride. George taught me years ago. We didn't ride much, but when we did, we steered clear of any trains with bulls."

"Your uncle sounds sharp. I can't wait to meet him," Stephen said, leaning back and putting his hands behind his head.

"TIME TO JUMP," Liv announced. They walked to the edge of the train car. It was moving along, not fast, but quickly enough that she felt a little tremor of exhilaration as the ground passed by.

"On three," she said.

They counted together, "One, two, three!" They jumped, landing in a thicket of leaves at the edge of the forest.

"This way?" Stephen asked skeptically as Liv led him into the trees. "Your uncle lives in the boondocks."

Stephen jumped when a twig cracked nearby.

George stepped from the shadow of trees.

He was tall with dark hair and a dark beard and wore clothes he made himself from the hides of animals and the fabric Liv brought him a few times a year. A deerskin bag was slung across his chest.

"George," Liv beamed. She walked forward, and he embraced her, but Liv felt the rigidity in his shoulders.

"Listen, Völva," you must go home," he told her, pulling her away and looking into her face.

"But George, we hopped a train. We rode the rails to get here. I want you to meet my friend Stephen," she argued.

George frowned over her shoulder.

She glanced back at Stephen, who stood with his hands stuffed in his pockets, his face sooty and scraped.

"I'll walk you into town. There's a bus that leaves in an hour," George insisted.

"George-"

"Don't argue with me, Volva," he growled, and she clamped her mouth shut.

He rarely rose his voice, and her face grew red.

She walked back to Stephen and shrugged.

"I guess it's not a good day," she lied.

"Did he call you Vulva?" Stephen asked with a sneer.

Liv laughed and rolled her eyes.

"Volva. It's a Norse word."

"What does it mean?"

Liv paused and half-considered a lie.

"Witch," she admitted, realizing in that tiny confession how much she trusted Stephen.

George, apparently, did not.

As they walked into town, Liv and Stephen stuck out their thumbs, giggling and complaining when cars passed them by.

"You'd rather ride?" George asked, after several minutes of their antics.

"My feet are killing me," Stephen admitted.

George looked pointedly at Stephen's once shiny, now scuffed loafers.

George disappeared into the forest for several minutes. He emerged with a handful of fine green ferns. He held the plant near his face before tossing it on the road.

A truck ambled down the road, and Liv quickly stuck her thumb out. The driver pulled over.

"In the back," the driver called.

The three scrambled into the bed of the pickup.

"What was that?" Stephen asked, nodding toward the ferns the truck had run over just before stopping.

"Dill," Liv told him.

As they bounced along the road into town, Liv tried to fill the strained silence.

George's displeasure was plain, and Liv vacillated between angry and embarrassed at his poor treatment of Stephen.

"Stephen goes to a private school, George. He's going to the University of Michigan in the fall."

"And how did you find Liv?" George asked, directing his gaze steadily at Stephen, who seemed to shrink smaller within his skin.

"He rescued me," Liv announced, tilting her chin up. "He saved me and Arlene from drowning in the Dead Stream. If he hadn't shown up, we both would have drowned."

George flicked troubled eyes to her.

"When?" he asked.

"Last Saturday," Stephen offered.

George shifted his attention to the trees. Liv knew he was searching for his own signs of their misfortune, but like her, she thought he found none.

"Why didn't you tell me?" George asked.

Liv clutched the tailgate as the truck bounced over a bump in the road.

"I forgot," she told him, and she had.

The truck deposited them in front of the Kalkaska Tavern and drove off.

George fished some money out of his pocket.

"Go have a sandwich and a Coke. I will get your bus tickets," George told them. He stuffed a few quarters in Liv's hand and walked off without another word.

"I think it's safe to say he doesn't like me," Stephen said after their hamburgers arrived.

~

"Why can't we go to the cabin, George? I told Stephen I'd show him the bones."

George studied her, a worried look in his eyes.

"Volva, you shouldn't have brought him here."

"But why?" Liv demanded, growing frustrated at George's lack of kindness toward her new friend, her only friend. "He's my friend."

George shook his head.

"I won't speak about this right now. Go."

George inclined his head toward the bus, where Stephen stood with their tickets.

Liv stormed away, not looking back as she and Stephen climbed on the bus and pulled from the station.

CHAPTER 13

September 1965
Mack

MACK READ a few chapters of Peyton Place; a paperback abandoned by Diane during their last attempt at reconciliation. They'd gone to the cabin with a teaspoon of hope and a bucket full of resentments and bruised egos.

They squabbled over petty things for three days, until Diane finally threw up her hands and stormed into the summer woods, disappearing into the dense foliage moments after she walked out the door.

Mack thought of going after her. Misty barked and howled at him like she could hardly believe what a jackass he was being, but he had his own streak of stubbornness. He sat in a chair outside and waited until Diane wandered back two hours later, dirty, sweat-streaked, and puffy-eyed from crying.

They had driven home in silence.

A week later, Mack had gotten drunk and smashed Diane's glass swan under his boot.

When Diane left with her bag, Mack had still believed it wasn't the last, last time. People in denial never do. He'd seen it with his own drunken dad a dozen times, at least. His mother bruised, lips bleeding, insisted she was done, her husband could go to hell. She'd pack their things and rush her little family out the door.

Two weeks later, Mack, his little sister Kate, and their mom would move back in. His dad would have bought flowers, cleaned the house, and put on a white button-down shirt.

Two weeks after that, he'd stumble in, stinking of whiskey, with a mad gaze searching for someone or something to punch.

Mack's mom finally left after his father broke her arm. He grabbed her and snapped her wrist because she'd poured out a bottle of scotch she'd found in his sock drawer. Mack was fifteen by then, and despite his insistence he'd never be like his dad, the damage was done. Somewhere in his brain, wires had fused together, telling him just a little nip took the edge off.

His mom died five years after her flee to freedom in a car accident, and his father, dead now two years himself, had mourned her for a decade.

It was a sad story, and a confusing story that Mack never quite got the lesson out of. His mother, after finally liberating herself from the monster, died at the start of her new life, burned slowly in a heap of twisted metal as rescuers attempted to save her and failed.

Mack threw Peyton Place on the floor and went to the cupboard. Three half-bottles of booze stood inside. He selected the Johnnie Walker scotch and poured a glass to the brim, swallowing half in a single gulp. Fire roared through his belly. The loneliness rising up at the memories of Diane, and his mother, coiled back down and went to sleep.

He finished the bottle and walked with surprising steadiness to his bed, closing the door and not bothering with the lock. His drunkenness made the previous day's fears into a mirage of the mind, no greater terror than the terror itself. He laid in his bed, fully dressed, planting a foot on the floor to steady the swaying of the room. Misty hopped in the chair, curled her tail over her face, and they both fell asleep.

He couldn't say what woke him, but it wasn't the need to piss.

More like the strand of a dream jumping across the void into the here and now, rousing Mack from a deep, inebriated sleep.

"Huh?" he said, as if in answer to a question that hadn't been asked.

And then to his bleary dismay, a guttural whisper replied.

"Mine..." the voice rasped.

Misty growled from the corner, and Mack fought up from the abyss of sleep, eyes blinking in the darkness; his head was impossibly heavy on the pillow.

As his eyes adjusted, a figure took shape, and Mack froze.

The man towered over him, and in the pale light of the moon, Mack could make out portions of his shadowy face: skeletal, flesh hanging loose, sunken eyes in a bone-white skull.

"Mine..." the thing told him, and Mack knew that it was the dead man at his bedside.

The dead man from the woods.

Misty had not moved from her chair, but she stood, ears raised, emitting a deep growl.

Mack watched thread of saliva, silvery in the moon's glow, drip from her muzzle.

"Mine," the man hissed.

Mack smelled the dead man's decayed breath as it blew out icy cold from his lipless mouth.

He rolled from the bed and thudded to the floor.

Terror poked tiny holes in the veil of drunkenness that blanketed Mack as he crawled toward the door, jumped up, and wrenched it open.

Groggily, he ran to his bag and ripped the satchel from within.

Misty followed him, barking.

Mack hurled the pouch into the darkened bedroom.

Running forward, and not pausing to think, he reached out and yanked the bedroom door shut.

He stood, heart hammering and eyes fixed on the door. Misty stood beside him; eyes locked on that door too, waiting for it to open.

But it didn't open, and after several minutes, fatigue and the start of a hangover led Mack to the couch.

He laid on his side, legs awkwardly pulled up, and rested a hand on Misty's back as she curled on the floor beside him.

He watched and waited until his eyes turned gritty. When he could hold them open no longer, Mack fell asleep.

THE BRIGHT MORNING sun brought its usual wash of clarity. The night's events drifted surreal at the back of Mack's mind.

He didn't open the bedroom door.

His back and hips ached from sleeping on the couch, and Misty seemed slow-moving and weary.

He made coffee and bacon, mechanically forcing food into his mouth.

Without entering the bedroom, he packed his bag and walked to his truck, holding open the passenger door for Misty to jump inside.

He had intended to return the satchel to the police, but to do so, he had to open the door.

Instead, he left it.

Maybe he'd call and let them know where to find it.

He bypassed Tina's house and drove around town, filling his tank with gas, picking up a set of nails, and finally landing outside Henderson Excavating, where Diane worked as a receptionist for her brother.

He let the engine idle and watched the sun glint off the glass door, not sure why he'd driven there knowing he couldn't possibly go in.

A rap on his window startled him, and when he shrank away from the sound, he found Dennis grinning beside his driver's window. Mack rolled the window down.

"Mack Gallagher, yours was the last face I was expecting to see today. How ya doing?" Dennis held out his hand, and Mack shook it.

"I'm all right," Mack told him, heart still a pace above normal.

"How's the gig?" Dennis asked.

Mack nodded, gazed at the front door of the office and wondered if Diane was watching them.

"Still paying," Mack shrugged. "Don't ask for much more than that."

Mack owned a roofing and painting company. They roofed in summer and painted in winter. Business was steady, and Mack liked it well enough, but since his divorce, even the work had changed. He struggled to get through the hours, his foreman's bad jokes grating on his last nerve. If a homeowner so much as looked at him sideways, he left the job and went to the bar.

"How about you?" he asked Dennis.

"Sweet, real sweet. Big job coming up for the city next spring. Winding down now, but Rachel's overjoyed I'll be home more."

"And Rachel and the kids?"

"They're real good. Itchin' to drive to Florida for Christmas."

"And Diane?" Mack asked, trying to sound casual, knowing that Dennis could see right through him.

"Diane's good, happy. She's got a boyfriend and a beagle puppy called Snoopy. Is that why you're here, Mack? To see Diane?" Dennis's tone told Mack what he thought of the idea. He liked Mack, but he didn't like him messing things up for his baby sister.

"Nah, I don't know why," Mack laughed and brushed a hand through his red hair, already showing strands of silver at thirty-four years old. "I was at the cabin and... well, I'm trying not to go home."

Dennis studied him.

"I heard you found yourself a real wildcat. She givin' ya trouble?"

Mack grinned and leaned his head back.

"Diane knows? About Tina?"

Dennis cocked an eyebrow.

"In this town? Diane knew about Tina the night you met her. But don't let that get you down. What do you care if your ex-wife hears about your girlfriend?"

But of course, they both knew why he cared.

"I'll tell her you said hi," Dennis told him, clapping him on the shoulder.

Dennis walked toward the door, and Mack shifted into drive. As he started to pull from the parking lot, Diane walked from the office. Dennis held up a hand as if to stop her, but she brushed past him.

Mack slammed the brakes, and Misty went tumbling to the floor. She gave him an irritated look and jumped back on the seat.

"Sorry, girl," he said rubbing her head. "But look who's coming."

Misty's ears perked up and she let out a stream of excited barks, rearing up and pressing her paws against the window.

As Diane walked to the driver's side, Misty fumbled over Mack and stuck her head out.

Diane's silky dark hair was pulled back in a red headband and flipped out at the bottom. She wore a red pencil skirt and a black sweater.

She looked happy, and Mack withered a bit inside.

"Misty, you're messing up my makeup," she scolded, but hugged the dog around the neck.

Mack leaned from the window and kissed her cheek.

"How's Misty's slobber taste?" she asked him.

"Like good memories," he admitted. "You look beautiful, Diane."

She smiled, her red lips curving up and her dark eyes sparkling in the sun.

"You look tired," she told him honestly.

He scratched at his jaw, conscious of his unshaved chin and unclean shirt. He wondered if he smelled. He hadn't taken a shower once at the cabin.

"I haven't been piling up too many Z's lately," he admitted.

"Why is that?" she asked, taking a step back but continuing to rub Misty's head.

He imagined the figure of the dead man and shuddered.

Diane frowned.

"Did something happen, Mack? Is Kate all right?"

Mack swallowed, the need to unburden his story creeping in

and grabbing him by the throat. He'd never been big on talking emotion, but when he did go there, he only went with Diane.

"Kate's fine. I've been at the cabin for a few days. I found something while I was there… a body. I found a man's body in the woods."

Diane put a hand to her mouth, eyes growing wide.

"That's terrible, my God. Did he get lost in the woods?"

Mack shook his head, remembering the rusted knife poking from the faded shirt.

"I think he was murdered."

She shook her head in disbelief, pushing Misty back as she continued to struggle further through the driver's window.

"Who is he?"

"I don't know." Mack grabbed Misty's collar and pulled her back into the truck. "The police were going out there, but… who knows? It will probably take a while before they identify him."

"Mack." Diane put her hand on the door. "Why are you telling me this?"

"I just needed to get if off my chest, I guess."

"What I mean to say is, why aren't you home telling your girlfriend, Tina?"

Mack laughed uncomfortably.

"I can't talk to her, Diane. Not like this." He waved a hand between them. "The truth is, Tina and I were never — I mean, we're not… we're not you and me."

Diane looked away from him, gazing at the office where a man had stepped out and stood watching them. He was tall, not quite Mack's height but close, with light hair and tan skin. If Mack didn't hate him on sight, he might have called him handsome.

"That's Dale," Diane said.

"Dale's your boyfriend?"

Diane nodded.

"Diane and Dale," Mack muttered. "Has a nice ring to it."

"He works for Stephen. He moved here from Detroit last year. He wants to marry me," Diane spoke in an offhand, thoughtful way, as if she too was still trying to make sense of Dale.

"Is that what you want?" Mack asked, forcing the tremor out of his voice.

He wanted to reach out and take's Diane hand, but he clutched the steering wheel instead.

Diane watched Dale for another moment. He smiled and waved at her.

Mack's father would have called it a shit-eating grin, and the man himself a jockstrap.

"I have to go, Mack. I'm sorry about the man in the woods. I can't imagine." She gave Misty a final rub on the ears and kissed the dog on top of her head.

She gazed at him for a final moment, and Mack clutched the steering wheel to keep from throwing open his door and jumping out.

She waved and walked away.

IT TOOK the better part of an hour to work up the balls to bid Tina farewell.

When he finally turned onto Harper Road, his 'you're better off without me' speech swirling in his head like a bad tune you can't shake, he almost drove by.

But then he saw her empty driveway and slammed on the brakes, whipping his car to the left and barely missing her mailbox. That would have been a cherry on his shit-sundae of a weekend.

Mack slid his key in the lock and cracked the door, listening.

He wouldn't put it past Tina to park down the street and wait in the foyer to confront him while his guard was down.

The house stood quiet. Tina didn't like quiet. At any given moment, the radio, the television and some beauty appliance, usually a hair dryer, were all yelling at once. Some days, he sat in his truck to escape the ever-present noise.

"But not anymore," he said, more gleefully than he should have. He immediately turned, half-expecting to find her behind him, armed with a nail file.

She hadn't left him a note, but he figured she'd picked up an extra shift. Or maybe she had found a hot date a few nights earlier and decided to shack up with her new guy.

"Doubt it," he muttered, rushing up the stairs and into her bedroom. He stuffed his things into his bag and thundered down the stairs and out to his truck.

He drove to the edge of town, where the farmhouse he'd shared with Diane stood forlorn amongst the remnants of a once-garden. It was overgrown now. A tangle of weeds and wildflowers invited the bunnies he and Diane had worked so hard to chase from their meager vegetables.

Misty barked excitedly and leapt through the window before he'd even stopped the truck.

Diane hadn't wanted the house. After the divorce, she moved into an apartment in town.

Knocking around the empty house had been near-unbearable those first few months, and when Tina appeared, Mack fell over himself to put an end to the long nights listening to the creaks of his house, the snores of his dog, and the yawning emptiness in the bed beside him.

"And now that's over too," he muttered, slamming his truck door and following Misty onto the porch.

The house felt closed-up and musty. He walked from room to room, opening windows and welcoming the warm breeze. He hadn't been home in a month, and the groans of the house beneath his feet seemed especially loud, as if she wanted to communicate her bitterness at his absence.

Misty followed on his heels as he walked back outside and grabbed his bag from the truck, dropping it in the front hallway when he returned.

He searched the kitchen cupboards for food, settling on stewed tomatoes, jarred years earlier by Diane, and a can of ham.

He ate and then nodded off on the couch to the Twilight Zone. The episode involved a little boy who terrorized his small town with his mental powers.

When Mack woke, the television emitted a low static sound,

the picture replaced by a black and white haze. He stood and walked to the set, pausing when he heard a sound within the static.

"Mine," a deep, gritty voice said, as if the man spoke from within the buzzing television. The sounds merged and made it hard for Mack to distinguish one from the other. The humming grew louder. "Mine," the voice said.

Shaky, Mack flipped off the television. Silence fell over the room.

He looked for Misty and saw her space on the rug, empty. Walking slowly, he left the sitting room, and peered into the kitchen. His half-eaten can of ham sat near the sink. Warmth filled the room from the wood-fire, but Misty wasn't lounging on the rug before it.

As he started down the hall toward the front door, he spotted her. Erect, the fur on her back prickly, she stared at the door. Her ears stood at sharp points, and she released a low growl registering in her diaphragm.

Her legs were tense, as if preparing to attack.

Mack stopped, pulse jumping, and lifted his gaze to the closed door.

"What is it, girl? Somebody out there?" He tried to make his voice light, reduce the tremors starting in his brain and reverberating out through his hands and legs.

The knock on the door startled him so bad that Mack jumped backwards and hit a side table, sending his bag crashing to the ground. The contents spewed out, rolled across the scarred wood floor.

From the corner of his eye he saw an apple, a pair of socks and, to his horror, the little leather pouch. It lay on its side, the twine holding the strange rocks within it from spilling out.

Misty barked at the door. The knock had come only once, loud and clear, but nothing followed.

Mack walked to the door.

"Who's there?" he called, hand shaking as he reached for the knob.

Misty didn't move, her entire body taut as Mack jerked open the door.

Night greeted them - cold and sharp and desolate.

No one stood on the porch.

Mack didn't sleep that night, but walked to the kitchen, took out a bottle of Jim Beam and sat at the kitchen table.

CHAPTER 14

September 1965
Liv

"I'VE PREPARED a special room for you, Liv," Stephen told her.

She had come to in the back seat of his car. Her arms were bound against her body by thick fabric, and when she gazed down, she realized he'd secured her in a straitjacket.

The drug had not worn off, and she stumbled and nearly fell as he pulled her from the car.

The hospital rose against a backdrop of starry sky. Dense woods surrounded the buildings.

"But first," he went on. "I have a very special place to show you."

They walked into the forest, up a hill of tall grass and down into a shadowy valley of warped trees. A willow that seemed to brush the stars stood in the center of the space.

It might have been beautiful. The dark silhouette of trees against a starry sky. The sounds of the wild, except in the small basin of forest, there were no sounds.

The instant they'd moved down the hill, the crickets and owls ceased their cries. As if not a single living thing — bug, mammal or reptile — occupied the damp grove.

But that wasn't right either. Because Liv sensed that something alive did indeed reside there. The ground seemed to expand and contract, as if with breath. She felt hungry eyes upon her, and though no one spoke, in her mind she heard whispers. Not the whispers of the spirits she and George had contacted so many times, but cunning, insidious whispers.

She thought of a man she'd once encountered in Boston. He'd pulled to the curb, near the orphanage, in a sleek maroon Chevy and rolled down his window. On the sidewalk stood Virgil Tort, an eight-year-old with pop-bottle glasses. He'd been at the orphanage for two months because his mother had given birth to her sixth baby and couldn't handle her slow-learning child.

"Hey, little boy," the man in the car had called out. "Give ya a nickel if you help me find a fuel station. And I'll get ya an ice cream too."

Liv had been pushing a double stroller with two infants who'd just fallen asleep, but her head popped up at the man's voice.

He was a bad man and if he got Virgil Tort into his car, Liv knew they'd never see the boy again.

"Push the babies," she directed one of the older girls from the orphanage.

Virgil had just stepped off the curb as the man pushed open his passenger door.

"No!" Liv had shrieked, running to Virgil and yanking him by his arm away from the maroon car and the horrors that awaited him.

The driver hadn't said a word. He sped off, his passenger door hanging open, and disappeared around the corner.

Liv had held a crying Virgil for five minutes, reassuring him that he wasn't in trouble but that he should never, ever get into a car with a stranger.

As she stood, chilled in the dark forest, a similar voice seemed to be luring her to come closer, to take a peek at what lay in the dense trees.

"Stephen," she started, but a hole had opened in the brush before him, and he pulled her inside.

She wanted to dig in her heels and buck away from him, but with her arms pinned against her sides, she wouldn't get far.

"You feel it, Liv. You do." He wasn't asking, and yet he was. There was a note of desperation in his voice.

His pupils had grown large, washing the color from his eye. The gleam in Stephen's eyes was a familiar one. She'd witnessed it almost twenty years before, on Halloween night, 1945.

Yes, she did feel it. An aliveness permeated the damp, dark chamber they'd entered. A hunger.

The straightjacket squeezed Liv too tight, and she felt hot and short of breath.

"The eye," she murmured. "We're in the eye."

Stephen's eyes widened at her words.

"Yes," he hissed. "The eye."

He moved across the room to a wooden pedestal that held a huge book. A book of magic, she thought, though not the healing magic George had taught her. This was a book like those George hid beneath the floorboards, a dark book created by dark men.

"It's all real. All the things I read about as a boy. Witches and wizards, people who speak to the dead, even those who bring them back, Liv. It's all here. Those people have passed through this chamber. They sat in that chair. I've seen dozens with my own eyes."

He spoke now like the boy she'd known. His voice high and excited, as if they'd just left the picture show and he couldn't wait to gush about the film.

"Don't you ever get tired, Stephen? Tired of chasing this elusive force?"

He seemed not to hear her as he pressed his hands against the brick walls.

"I feel it. I feel you," he whispered.

Liv watched him and shuddered. She imagined just beyond those bricks, something waited; something with teeth.

"I want it," Stephen told her. "The power. You can help me get it, Liv. Destiny, that's what brought you here."

Stephen was silent on their walk back to the asylum.

At a large brick building, he fished out his keys and unlocked a door.

He led her up a dark, echoey stairway. Heavy white doors closed off each floor. They walked until Liv's legs burned, and then he stopped, pulling out another keyring.

She stood stiff, arms pressed against her sides, fearing if she moved too much, she might plummet down the cement stairs behind her.

When the door swung open, she gazed into a large attic with angled ceilings and wood beams cutting toward the floor. A single lamp sat on the floor near the door, casting long, dark on the walls.

A bird took flight from a rafter and soared away, disappearing into a shadowy crevice in the high-pointed ceiling.

In the center of the room, a little cot stood. She saw a bedpan, a glass pitcher of water, and a plate of bread.

"It's meager, to be sure," Stephen offered, "but under the circumstances, you must make do. I wasn't expecting you, Liv. But I hated to put you in the asylum with the other patients. They can be a rough lot."

"You're able to do this to me, Stephen? Lock me away?"

Stephen turned Liv to face him, his hands pressing hard into her numb arms.

His crystalline eyes searched hers, but they lacked the power they'd held in their youth. His eyes had grown empty. No light danced in the spheres of blue.

He led her to the bed and helped her sit. She considered kicking him. The door was still open, she might escape, but she didn't.

Her fate unfolded before her, and she could not run away from it - not this time.

"Liv, did you really think I'd let you turn us in? Destroy everything I've worked so hard to create?"

Liv shut her eyes.

"It's coming, Stephen," she whispered. "The end is coming for you."

Stephen's eyes darted sideways, his mouth turning down.

He took a strand of her thick blonde hair, unruly even when pinned back, and pushed it behind her ear.

"You are the only person I ever loved. Did you know that? The only person in my entire life." He gazed at her as if mystified, and then he laughed. "But puppy love is all that was, wasn't it, Liv? A summer romance."

"That ended in murder," she spat, glaring at him.

He chuckled and stood.

"Let the past go, Liv. Haven't you read the new books about living in the now? This," he gestured at the attic, "is all there is."

He undid the bind of her straightjacket but did not loosen it or pull her arms free. He stood and strode across the room, quickly, as if he feared she might wriggle free before he could escape through the door and lock it behind him.

Liv listened to his footsteps disappear down the stairs.

It took several minutes, but she freed her arms. She shoved the straightjacket to the floor and drank half the pitcher of water in two gulps.

"What now?" she asked the empty room.

The bird had returned to its roost. It watched her from its small black eye. It stretched its wings, ruffling its feathers. Liv watched the tremor move up the bird's body. When it shook its wings, a black feather drifted down and landed on the dusty wood floor.

Liv stood and retrieved it. She tucked it beneath her pillow and fell into a dream-filled sleep.

~

"I've been waiting for you," George said.

He stood in the doorway of the cabin, aged and yet the same.

Liv hung her head, tucking her long wavy hair behind her ears.

"Don't fret, Volva. You're home now."

He opened his arms, and she stepped into his solid chest. He smelled, as he always had, of a wood fire and chamomile with other heady scents like garlic and dill. In the hovel, she would find tea and soup simmering.

In autumn, George prepared for the long winter by making tonics, satchels of healing herbs, and divining the best remedies for the coming season of disease.

As she stepped across the threshold of her true home, the tension in Liv's shoulders melted away. She nearly fell as she stumbled to a chair near the fire and collapsed, dropping her head into her hands and sobbing.

She cried until her sinuses were fat and sore. Her face had grown puffy, and George had not spoken a word.

When she lifted her head, he placed a mug of tea in her shaking hands and sat opposite her.

She sipped the chamomile tea spiced with cinnamon.

George gazed at her, his eyes soft and misty. Liv had never seen George cry, and after a moment the sparkle cleared and his eyes were dry once more.

"I've missed you so much," Liv started. "I wrote you letters. Hundreds of letters, but I couldn't send them. I..."

"I know, child. I know. Do you think we haven't spoken in all that time? I've followed you in my dreams."

Liv swallowed and looked away.

Did he know? Did he know her secrets?

"We have little time, Volva, so listen to me carefully. A curse is most powerful at the beginning of another ten-year cycle. It is the weakest at the end. To unbind yourself, you must draw the spirit of the cursed back from her Eternity in Darkness. Do you understand me, Liv? You must reawaken the cursed?"

Liv blinked at George. He did know. He'd always known.

"But... I can't. The spirits have abandoned me, George. I've tried to call out to them..."

"Then you have asked the wrong questions, Volva. It is time to try again. The door has already been opened."

"The door?" Liv shook her head. "I don't understand."

"When a curse is contained, it grows strong. Open the doors and let the light in. Banish the darkness."

Liv tried to follow his words, but George often spoken in ambiguities that made little sense to her.

George slid from his chair and knelt, leaning toward a cast-iron pot suspended above the fire. He inhaled the steam before plucking a ladle from a wood block and stirring the contents.

"Garlic and leek stew?" she asked.

"The winter will be unseasonably cold. I fear the influenza will strike early and spread fast."

Liv sighed and thought of the children she'd left behind in Boston. Little Maggie Sue had been born premature. She regularly took a chill. Only Liv had been able to heal her when illness took hold, but now Liv had gone, and she wondered if she'd ever return.

"I'm sorry I left, George. I have so many regrets."

George did not respond, but merely sat stirring and stirring. The liquid bubbled and popped. Something rancid had replaced the garlic smell, and she wrinkled her nose.

When she peered closer at the pot, a bit of bone floated up to the surface, and she saw a skull peering out from the oily broth.

She jumped from her chair.

When George turned to look at her, she saw all the flesh from his face was gone. His black hair hung in tangles on his bleached scalp.

Without a word, George stood and slipped through the cabin door and disappeared into the forest.

Liv tried to follow him, but the forest closed in.

She'd never been lost in the Stoneroot Forest. She'd never been frightened. Now she was both.

She turned in circles, chest heaving, until she spotted a wisp of something. She ran after it.

A black crow soared between the trees. He dove at the forest floor and disappeared into a pile of brush.

Liv ran to the foliage and pulled at the tangled branches.

She gasped at George's skeletal face gazing up at her through the overgrowth.

Liv woke crying in the asylum attic. She touched her cheek, and then her damp pillow.

George was dead.

CHAPTER 15

September 1965
Jesse

HE'D BEEN at the house for three days when he started to look at things. Not merely glance in passing, but really look. A newspaper lay folded in the master bedroom.

He opened it and studied the date in disbelief.

October 31, 1945 - nearly twenty years before.

Who saved a newspaper for such a long time?

Or - and this was the question that niggled at him - had the occupants not returned since that day? Had October 31st, 1945, been their final day in the house?

He glanced around the room. A bottle of perfume sat on a glass mirror at the vanity. A mint-green silk robe lay draped over a luggage rack.

If an illness had come for the family, surely there would be signs. Beds sunken and stained, trays scattered with medicine, wash rags in basins.

Jesse had seen the rooms of the dying. He'd sat vigil with Nell at her mother's bedside when cancer stripped the flesh from her bones and left her hollow-eyed and impossibly frail. Pressed against her soiled sheets, she'd looked more like a stick-figure drawing than the flesh-and-blood woman whose laughter shook the floor of any room she stood in.

In the downstairs study, Jesse discovered a drawer containing the birth certificate of a child. Stephen James Kaiser, born on December 13, 1927. In another drawer he found a wedding certificate and a black-and-white photograph of a striking dark-haired woman in a long white gown. Her husband was tall with pale eyes and a half-smile as he gazed at his bride.

The more he searched; the more unnerved Jesse became.

Stock certificates, medical records, letters and photographs. Little by little, the study revealed the seemingly charmed life of the Kaiser family.

And every discovery posed the question: who left behind such things?

In the long, slim drawer in the center of the desk, his index finger jammed against something hard. He reached deeper and retrieved a small pistol. Behind the pistol, he felt a fat envelope.

The envelope contained a stack of twenty-dollar bills as thick as a deck of playing cards.

Jesse slid the envelope and gun back into the drawer, stood slowly, and walked out the front door. He sat on the top step of the house.

Paint peeled in curls off the porch. Vines crawled over the railing and onto the roof.

The Kaisers had left everything behind.

Gordon and Adele Kaiser, and their teenage son, Stephen, had simply vanished.

The money made Jesse uneasy.

Money, like all good things, seemed to invite bad luck. Anytime his father won a poker game or found a job with a decent wage, misfortune soon followed.

Jesse remembered the night his dad walked away from a game with fifty dollars, a veritable fortune for the father and son. They'd barely walked a block when two young men, one holding a pipe, jumped from behind a dumpster and demanded the cash.

Jesse's dad, too drunk to know better, took a swing at one of the guys. The second guy cracked Jesse's dad across the back with the pipe, snatched the money from his pocket, and both men disappeared. Jesse had been ten. He hadn't tried to fight for his dad. He'd stood and cried, snot and tears pouring down his face, until he found enough sense to run for help. Later, Jesse's dad would joke that they lost fifty bucks, but won two free nights at the Stick-em and Prick-em Motel with a pretty nurse named Mallory, who snagged extra puddings for Jesse.

Jesse learned not to trust money.

Nell poked fun at him for his superstitions. When she found a two-dollar bill on the sidewalk after they'd gone to see a picture show, he insisted she turn it into the ticket window. At first, she applauded his moral studiousness, but when he explained his fear that something bad would befall them, she'd only laughed and said, 'Yeah, we could have gotten fat on French fries and cokes.'

The money, coupled with the abandoned house, only confirmed his fears.

Something terrible had befallen the Kaiser family, who once upon a time, appeared to have it all.

~

AFTER A LONG WALK, Jesse returned to the house and showered.

He would take enough money to travel south, rent a room, and start pretending to be alive again. The money made his stomach knot, but he wouldn't take more than necessary.

So what if God punished him for his avarice? Let God's wrath come; Jesse wanted nothing more than to give him a piece of his mind.

He cringed at his thoughts.

"Sorry, Nell," he murmured. "But your God abandoned you, and I'm sick of prostrating myself before the bastard."

He toweled off and started up the stairs to the third-floor bedroom, the young man's room.

A rancid odor invaded his nostrils, and he flinched. It smelled like something dead and spoiled. Cupping a hand over his nose and mouth, Jesse hurried to the second floor.

An animal must have gotten into the house, maybe dragged a carcass in with it.

The smell seemed to come from the guest bedroom. He pushed the door in, and the odor overwhelmed him.

His eyes watered and he pulled the towel from his waist, stuffing it over his nose.

The room appeared empty, but Jesse looked beneath the bed anyway.

When the towel slipped down, Jesse sniffed.

The smell was gone.

He took a long inhalation through his nose, walking through the room and searching for the origin of the scent, but the room looked exactly as it had the day before when he'd napped on the bed.

He shook his head, puzzled, and returned to the hall to trek up to the third floor. As he stepped into the third-floor hall, the smell returned, worse than before, like something left to rot and decay in the hot sun.

Jesse gagged and turned for the bathroom. He plugged his nose and steadied his hand against the wall, willing his gag reflex down. When the desire to throw-up passed, he crept back toward the bedroom.

The animal was surely in there, and somehow the scent had seeped down into the room beneath it.

He kicked the door open with his naked foot, ready to hop back if an animal came barreling out.

The room was still and quiet. The only sound, the hinge creaking on the still-swinging door.

He stepped inside, eyes darting into the shadows.

He released his nose for an instant, recoiling at the overpowering stench.

It seemed to emanate from the closet, but the closet door was closed.

Jesse hurried to a window, wrenched back the curtains, and pulled the window up with a screech of protest.

He stuck his head through the open window and gulped the warm air.

Reluctantly, he ducked his head back inside, covering his nose and stepping to the closet.

He pulled the closet door open and waited.

Nothing scurried out. Nothing moved at all.

When Jesse released his nose again, the smell had vanished.

CHAPTER 16

August 1945
Liv

"GEORGE TAUGHT ME," Liv explained, closing her eyes and reaching deep into the cool mud at the pond's edge.

"Liv, who is George, really? I know you say he's your uncle, but I get the feeling that's not the whole truth," Stephen said.

She continued to sink her hands into the mud, allowing her fingers to brush over stones and twigs.

She cracked an eye open and grinned.

"Got one." She pulled out a long purple-black earthworm.

"A plump little fella," Stephen said, nodding his approval.

"George is my father," she told him, standing and wringing her hands to flick the mud off.

Stephen's mouth fell open.

"Your father? But I thought your father died."

"My brothers' father is dead. Everyone believed he was my father too. The timing was close enough, and people never asked questions." Liv told Stephen the secret as if she did it all the time. In truth, she'd never told another living soul. Her mother and George were the only two in the world who knew of her true parentage.

"So, your mom had an affair?" he asked.

Liv shook her head.

"Never. She loved Mark, her first husband, but he went away and got killed. She says that George seduced her. It happened only days after she discovered my dad had died. She met George in the Stoneroot Forest. She was crying, hiding from her young sons. He took her back to his cabin, and three months later she found out she was pregnant."

"Your mom told you all that?"

Liv nodded.

"She feels guilty. She thinks she ruined my life. Everyone in town believed I was Mark's child, and she never intended to tell George I existed, but a few months before my birth, he arrived at my mother's house. George knew she'd conceived a child. He knew when he found her in the forest that day that she would be the mother of his child. He didn't care what my mother told people, so long as he could see me and spend time with me. In the beginning she fought him, but he… he has a way with people."

"And how do you feel about George?" Stephen asked, reaching his hand into the mud she'd pulled the worm from.

Liv smiled and imagined the man who'd given her half of who she was.

"I don't know a world without him. He's not like most fathers."

Stephen nodded, drew his hand out empty and frowned.

"I gathered as much."

"He's more like a teacher," Liv continued. "He tells me stories of the old ways. His people came from Scandinavia. He says there's magic in our blood."

"And that's why you can do the drum thing?"

"I think so." Liv thought of the other things, countless things she'd experienced with George.

She held up the hag stone.

"I see things when I look through this that other people can't see. I also dream. Sometimes I dream the future. Other times, I dream as if I'm inside an animal. Though that usually comes after I eat a heart."

"After you eat a heart?" Stephen asked, eyebrow cocked.

Liv expected him to look disgusted. Instead, he appeared intrigued.

"Yeah, George kills his own meat. In his clan, they believed if you ate the heart of the animal, you absorbed its strength. After I've eaten the heart of a deer, I will dream that I am a deer moving through the forest. My ears and nose are so powerful. It's strange."

"You've dreamed the future? Things that haven't happened yet?"

Liv nodded.

"Dreams aren't always easy to decipher, though. Before my mother said we were moving to Gaylord from Kalkaska, I dreamed I was running to catch up with a train. My mother, my stepfather and Arlene were on it. They were surrounded by boxes and suitcases. George was standing behind me, waving goodbye. Three days after the dream, my mom said we were moving here to Gaylord."

Liv held the worm near her face.

"Did you just talk to that worm?" Stephen asked, wrinkling his nose.

Liv winked at him, threaded the worm on the hook and string she'd set aside, and then cast it into the water.

"Can you do other witch things?"

"I guess," she murmured, biting her lip as she made little patterns in the water with the worm. After a few seconds, a dark shadow appeared near the dock.

"What was that?" Stephen asked, jumping from his rock and running closer to the water's edge.

"A dog fish," she told him.

The line grew taut and Liv pulled, jerking the string and the dogfish from the lake.

Stephen jumped back, and then stepped closer, watching as Liv put a foot on the fish's wriggling body.

"What are you doing?" he asked, as she took the stick she'd sharpened to a point and plunged it through the fish's eye. It flopped once and lay still.

"It's the fastest death," she murmured.

"Now what? You'll eat it?"

"Yes," she admitted. "But that's not why I caught him. He's a gift for you."

Stephen stuck his hands in his pockets, as if he expected Liv to hoist the slimy fish into his arms.

"What do you mean? I wouldn't know what to do with it."

Liv smiled.

"You don't have to. Meet me back here tomorrow."

LIV CLEANED THE FISH, careful not to damage his spine.

Arlene jumped up and down at the smell of fish in the frying pan, and Liv's mother kissed her head before retiring to her room for a nap.

Her stepfather would work a double shift, not returning until the morning, which suited Liv just fine. Roy was nice enough, but no bond existed between he and Liv, and Liv knew that Roy longed for the day in the near-future when Liv would leave their little house and he could have her mother and his true daughter to himself.

She carried the spine to her room after dinner and wrapped it in a swath of fabric. She carved a dream stave on a piece of brown coal. The symbol consisted of a circle within a series of forked arms. The dream stave granted the sleeper dreams of the future. She added the coal to the fabric and closed it tightly, sliding the package beneath her bed.

George worked with many spells, but the dream stave with the dogfish spine had been one of the more common throughout her childhood. Each season, George place a stave and spine under his and Liv's pillows, so they could determine what the next season would bring.

She lay back on her bed and stared at the cracked ceiling, imagining Stephen's delight at the gift.

CHAPTER 17

August 1945
Liv

THREE DAYS PASSED without a sighting of Stephen. She didn't see him at the pond, and on the third day, she turned brusquely away from the woods and instead walked into town. She didn't want to go to town, but sitting at the shack mending clothes or reading her worn copies of Nancy Drew for the fiftieth time made her want to jump off the roof.

There were other young people who lived in the seedy little houses at the edge of town. Boys and girls with dirty knees and elbows, smoking cigarettes and drinking gin with their fathers. Sometimes the boys watched her with sharp, wolfish faces, but Liv steered clear of the lot.

The forest was her respite from the squalor of her home life, and she never complained — not to her mother and not even to George. Her mother worked too hard to carry her daughter's shame as well.

In town, Liv was merely a spectator. She didn't have money to spend and had grown weary of the shopkeepers who watched her with suspicious or pitying eyes.

Rather than look at people, she watched the sidewalk. Every few feet a weed poked from the hard surface, or much to her delight, a flower.

Step on a crack, break your mother's back, Arlene liked to sing as she skipped down the sidewalk after school.

Superstitiously, Liv found herself avoiding the hairline cracks in the pale cement.

"Psst..." a voice whispered just behind her.

Liv looked up, startled, and spun to find Stephen.

"You looked very purposeful just now," he said, lifting both eyebrows.

"Trying not to step on cracks," she admitted, feeling foolish and wishing she could tell the flush in her cheeks to get lost.

Stephen's eyes twinkled.

"Any truth to that? Step on a crack, break your mother's back?" he asked.

Before she could answer, he took a step and leaped into the air, landing both feet with a thwack on a series of fractures in the cement.

He looked at her expectantly, and then burst out laughing.

"Oh, come on," he said. "All our mothers would be dead if that were true."

Liv shrugged.

"You haven't been at the pond," she murmured.

"I couldn't," he said, his voice irritated. "My mom's been... sick."

"Sick?" Liv asked.

"I'm free now," he told her. "And *The Picture of Dorian Gray* is playing at the theatre. Will you go with me?"

Liv's heart gave a little leap. She'd only been to the movies twice in her life.

Stephen bought their tickets, two Cokes, and tub of popcorn.

As they shuffled into the dark theatre, Liv spotted several girls from her high school.

One of them, Veronica, their ringleader, glared at Liv.

Liv barely knew Veronica, but the girl had taken to bumping into her in the halls so that Liv dropped her books.

"Those girls hate me," Liv admitted as they took seats in the theatre.

Stephen craned around in his seat to stare at them.

"Don't look," Liv whispered, poking an elbow in his side.

"Why not?" he asked, still watching them. "Believe me, they're more uncomfortable right now than you are."

He continued staring at them for another moment, and when Liv turned, she saw all the girls' faces were red and they were looking pointedly away from Stephen.

"There, see?" He turned back around and offered her the popcorn.

She took a handful and munched it happily, surprised at the satisfaction she felt at the girls' discomfort.

~

AFTER THE MOVIE, Stephen and Liv walked out of town, following the train tracks.

"Wy don't they like you? The girls in the theatre?" Stephen asked.

Liv shrugged.

"Because I live in the shacks, because I'm new in town. I don't really know. Veronica, the one with the dark curls, seems to be the reason. My first day in school, I noticed her watching me, and she just had this expression like… like a cat gets when it's hunting a mouse. I knew she'd be trouble for me."

"We could kill her," Stephen said casually, balancing on the tracks.

Liv imagined Veronica, with her glossy brown hair perfectly curled in the popular style of the times. She wore pretty bright dresses and pleated skirts. Her lips were always painted red, her face pale and smooth as an egg.

"How would we do it?" Liv joked.

"Stabbing, shooting, hanging, burning. It all leads to the grave, but so unoriginal. I think we'd need your magic, Liv. We need the Volva on this one."

Liv rolled her eyes.

"My magic is only for good."

"Oh, come on. Play the game. What has George taught you about black magic?"

"He hasn't."

"Have you ever asked him? If the good magic exists, the bad does too. That's the balance of things."

"Your gift is at my house," Liv told him, changing the subject.

"My gift? Oh, the dogfish?"

"Wait here and I'll go get it."

"I'll come with you," he said, but she shook her head and ran off before he could argue.

When she returned, the dirt road they'd been walking stood empty. She held the wrapped dogfish spine and the carved coal, fighting down her disappointment. An acorn flew from the woods and landed at her feet, and then another.

She walked into the shadowy canopy of trees and spotted Stephen halfway up a fat oak tree, one hand filled with acorns.

"About time you came back. I was sweating like a pig out there."

Liv held up the gift.

Stephen climbed to a lower branch and leaped from the tree, landing and immediately folding into a somersault. He sprang to his feet and held out his arms as if he'd just performed a feat defying regular man.

Liv whistled.

"Very well done, Mr. Kaiser. And now for your prize."

Liv handed him the package.

He unwrapped the fabric and gazed at the spine of the dogfish. He picked up the coal and squinted at the design.

"It's a dream stave," she said. "Put it under your pillow tonight."

His eyes lit up, and he looked at the spine and coal with renewed interest.

"What will I dream?"

She smiled.

"You'll have to wait and see."

~

GEORGE FROWNED at Liv's mention of Stephen.

"Why don't you like him?" she asked.

She'd taken the bus the Stoneroot Forest the day before, arriving in time for the new moon. The new moon and full moon each month were their times for ritual, gathering herbs, and preparing tinctures. As a young girl, Liv had found the ceremonies fascinating, and she looked forward to the moon changes for days ahead. However, this visit she'd dragged her feet, packing her bag at the last minute and dreading two days without seeing Stephen.

George didn't respond, but continued to meticulously chip away at a piece of granite. He made runes on the new moon of each month.

"George?" she repeated.

He looked up, setting his hammer aside.

"It's not an issue of like, Volva. It's an issue of trust. I don't trust the young man you've indebted yourself to."

"I'd be dead without him, George. So would Arlene."

George looked away, staring out the window to the woods beyond.

"The fates always offer a fork in the road, a chance to make a choice. You will be faced with a choice regarding this young man. It will be troubling, and you will be tested."

"I've been faced with lots of choices. Have I failed yet?" Liv demanded.

George smiled; a small, sad smile.

"Failure is not what's at stake. It's the purity of our hearts. If we compromise that, we are lost." He returned to the granite.

Liv thought of continuing her quarrel. She wanted to argue with George until he came around to her side, choosing to accept and even like Stephen. But she knew better. George was unwavering in his beliefs. He saw something in Stephen he didn't approve of. There was no shifting him.

GEORGE KISSED HER HEAD, slung his leather bag over his shoulder, and walked out the door.

Liv watched the closed door for a long time. If George sensed something, which he often did, he would return.

She focused on things she'd normally do at the cabin. She peeled potatoes next to the wash basin and put them in a pot of water over the fire. Afterward, she swept the floor, carefully moving in an eastern direction to encourage not only dirt but evil spirits to leave the cabin. Pulling open the door, Liv gazed into the empty woods. She listened for the crunch of twigs underfoot.

Satisfied that George had indeed walked to town and would not return for several hours, she slipped back into the cabin. She grabbed the edges of George's straw bed and pulled it aside, revealing the rough-hewn floor beneath.

There were three loose floorboards. Liv had watched George retrieve items from beneath them before. She had never dared open them, though he had never given her a direct order not to do so. It was an unsaid thing between them. She knew it was forbidden, and as she pried up the first board, she experienced a little pang in her chest.

She squatted on the floor and inched the board up.

She had never lied to George. For most of her life, she believed it was impossible to lie to the man. He knew things. He sensed lies before they were even told.

She could drop the board back into place, tell Stephen she'd found nothing, and return to life as she knew it.

The dark crevice beneath the board seemed to glow with mystery. Finally, unable to will herself to push the board back down, she lifted further until the hole within was exposed.

It was anticlimactic. Beneath the floor lay a jumble of worn leather books. She got on her hands and knees and peered into the hole, looking for the magic it surely contained.

Disappointed, she pulled out one of the books. It was oddly clean. The cover was plain, not an image or title in sight. When she opened the book, she saw words written in another language. Old Norse, she figured, based on George's occasional use of the language. He had never tried to teach her the language of his ancestors. Few in the world still spoke it, he'd told her many times. His own mother had clung to the words, but George too had been more devoted to English than an ancient language that no longer offered much value.

Though all the books were in Old Norse, one of them was translated. Norse was written on the left page and the English translation on the right.

Halfway through the book, her eye caught on a spell to displace favor among the gods. She slipped a leaf between the pages and continued flipping. Near the back of the book, she paused and read a much more sinister spell.

"Eternity in Darkness," she read. The spell implied that the person who fell under it would bypass the afterlife and exist in perpetual nothingness. *A torment of the worst kind,* a note beneath the title stated.

The spell itself was disturbing, calling for the hide of a freshly skinned black cat for the template. It went on to describe that the spell must be written in menstrual blood.

Liv wrinkled her nose and shut the book.

She tilted her head and listened, but only the forest sounds filtered in.

Putting the book in her bag, she slipped on her shoes and shuffled into her coat before leaving the cabin. She didn't leave George a note. She rarely did. He understood the comings and goings and never expected word, one way or another.

As she walked, the book in her bag thudded against her side. Each nudge grew sharper, and the bag heavier. When she reached the train, it took all her effort to heave the bag into a moving car and haul herself in after it. She pushed the bag into a dark corner and fell asleep on a sack of wheat.

CHAPTER 18

September 1965
Mack

*M*ACK STOOD *before a Victorian mansion silhouetted against the starry sky. Lights blazed in the windows, and the sounds of music and laughter drifted out.*

A masked man in a tuxedo stumbled onto the porch, a waif-like woman in a silver dress hanging on his arm. They laughed and supported each other down the wide wooden stairs before climbing into a white car and driving down a driveway that disappeared into the trees.

In an upstairs window, Mack saw a young woman. He should not have been able to see her face, not from the lawn, and yet he could make out the 'O' of horror frozen on her mouth. Her big brown eyes were filled with tears.

"Mack, Mack."

He turned on the lawn, looking into the trees, seeking the voice who called out to him. But the trees had begun to fade.

Mack blinked.

A slimy tongue slid across his cheek, and he batted Misty's nose away from his own.

He looked through Misty's ears to find Diane, her eyes big and full of tears, not unlike those from the woman in his dream.

Diane gasped, put a hand to her chest and closed her eyes.

"Di?" Mack mumbled. He tried to sit up and his head spun.

He leaned over the side of the couch, bracing a hand on the wood floor and trying not to throw up. His head pounded and his mouth tasted sour and fuzzy.

"I thought you were dead," she breathed. "I knocked and knocked, and then when I walked in, I shook you and you didn't move." She sank into a plaid chair next to the television.

He struggled up and rubbed his eyes.

"Thought I was dreaming ya for a second there," he said, smiling.

"Mack, what's going on? You look…" She didn't continue, and Mack had a pretty good idea of what her next words might have been: drunk, exhausted, terrible.

Purple shadows hung beneath his bloodshot eyes. His copper-colored beard and mustache, which he'd been shaving for a decade, had grown in. He hadn't been to the barbershop in weeks.

He self-consciously patted at his face, and then glanced down at his coffee-stained shirt.

"Has it gotten so bad?" Diane asked, gesturing at the empty glass on the table.

"I've had a hard week," he said at last.

"Because of your break-up with Tina? Dennis told me," she admitted.

Word traveled fast in small towns, especially when you beat feet on a girl like Tina.

Mack let loose a harsh laugh, propping his elbows on his knees and resting his head in his hands.

"No, not because of Tina." Mack stayed quiet, massaging his face for several seconds before finally regarding her through watery eyes. "I've got to tell somebody," he said, more to himself than her.

"Tell somebody what?" Diane asked. "What's going on?"

Mack nodded. If he could tell anyone, it was Diane. .

"Give me a half-hour?" He stood and wobbled on his feet for a second before steadying.

Diane looked at her watch.

"I told Dale I'd meet him for lunch. I stopped by because Kate called me."

"Diane." He regarded her gravely. "I'm drowning here. I really need to get this off my chest, but I've got to get coffee in me first, and wash a layer of this grime off." He waved at himself.

Diane nodded.

"Okay, I'll call Dale, and make the coffee. You go have a shower," she told him.

~

STILL BEARDED, but smelling of ivory soap and wearing a white shirt opened at the collar, Mack felt better than he had in days.

He found Diane in the kitchen, and drank his first cup of coffee in silence.

He stood, poured a second cup, and walked to the hallway, returning a moment later with the small leather pouch. He dropped it on the table before her with a plunk.

She eyed it for a moment.

"What is it?" she asked finally.

He stared at the satchel as if it contained something truly disgusting.

After several seconds, he pulled at the twine wound through the top of the leather. His big hands shook as he opened it.

He dumped the contents of the bag onto the table.

She leaned closer, studying the six smooth white stones. A hole ran through the center of each stone.

She looked up. "What are they?"

Mack touched one, and then pulled his hand quickly away, shuddering.

"I haven't got a clue."

Diane sighed.

"Mack, speak sense, please. I stayed; I canceled my plans. Let's not play games now."

He didn't look at her, but puzzled at the stones for another moment.

"Do you remember when I stopped by your office last week? I'd just come home from the cabin."

Diane nodded.

"I told you I found the body of a man?"

"Yes, I remember."

Mack pointed at the stones.

"That pouch was hanging around the guy's neck, and I took it."

She grimaced.

"Why on earth would you do a thing like that?"

He threw up his hands.

"Beats me. I saw the thing in the grave and cut it loose. Misty took off, and I forgot I was holding it in my hand. I went back to the cabin, drove into town to the police station, and forgot all about it."

"And?"

He sighed, bent his head back to gaze at the ceiling.

"And now the dead man's after me. He wants this bag of rocks, but I can't give them back."

Diane frowned and glanced toward the garbage can. Mack knew she was looking to see how many empty bottles were stacked inside.

"Diane, I haven't told a soul about this. But you know me. Don't you? I'm not a lying man. I've got a lot of faults, but I've never been a liar."

Diane lifted her hands as Misty appeared and propped her head in Diane's lap. She rubbed the dog's ears.

"What do you mean, he's after you?" She stared at the stones as she spoke.

"He appeared in the cabin the night I found his body. I woke up and found him standing upstairs. When I turned on the light, he was gone. Then he followed me in the woods. I got all turned around and he was there, watching me. He's shown up every night,

Diane. Eight nights in a row, this guy has made himself known. After the first night, I started drinking. I mean, I never stopped, but I started drinking more. It was the only way to keep him at bay."

Diane leaned back and crossed her arms, glaring at Mack as if something had clicked into place.

"You're telling me you have to get loaded every night, so this ghost doesn't bother you," she demanded.

He braced his hands on the table.

"Diane, it's not like that. I'd love to never have a sip again, if this thing would go away. I'd make a deal with the devil to get rid of it. The drinking just… I pass out and I don't have to see it, feel it."

"Then how do you know it's still there? If you're spending every night in a drunken haze, what makes you think it's not gone?"

"Because it's getting worse. I still wake up to it, I just… I barely register it. But he's standing over me, clawing at me, shrieking. Misty goes nuts. Every single night, Diane."

Diane bit her lip. He could see her mind working behind her eyes, wanting to believe him.

"Have you tried to give it back?" She motioned at the satchel.

He nodded.

"I left it at the cabin, but when I got home, it was in my bag. I've thrown it out my front door. I've buried it the garden. I've driven out to the woods and chucked it in. Every night, it's back on the hall table."

"This all sounds very far-fetched, Mack," Diane told him, eyeing the rocks wearily.

"You think I don't know that?" he sputtered.

~

TWO DAYS LATER, Mack opened his door to find Diane standing on his porch. She wore a white scarf over her dark hair. Beyond her, a steady drizzle of rain cast the world in various shades of grey.

"I'm giving you the benefit of the doubt, Mack. Let me in."

She didn't wait for him to answer, hurrying across the threshold and wiping her muddy boots on the rug.

Misty jumped and licked at her, and Diane sank her hands into the dog's red coat.

They stood for a moment surveying one another in the foyer.

He had shaved, put on a sweater she'd bought him for Christmas years earlier, and dotted cologne on his neck.

"You look better," Diane said, handing him a jar with a ribbon on top.

"A present?" he asked.

She smiled.

"Raspberry jam. I jarred five quarts of it this summer. I know you always liked it."

He held the jar and remembered a Christmas when they spent a week decorating jars of Diane's raspberry preserves to give to family as gifts. They'd added maple syrup from the trees they'd tapped that spring, and fresh-baked cookies. It had been their first Christmas married. Diane was eight weeks pregnant. Four weeks later, they'd lost the baby.

"How did you sleep?" Diane asked, walking into the kitchen.

Mack followed her, gazing at the gold necklace around her slender pale neck. When she turned, he saw that a small gold heart lay at its center. She noticed him looking.

A flush lit her pale cheeks, and she touched the delicate charm.

"An early birthday present from Dale," she murmured.

He nodded, wondering if a ring would soon follow, and wishing he could wind back the years and do it all differently.

"How did you sleep?" she asked a second time.

He frowned, remembered the dead man watching him from the rocking chair across the room, the steady creak-creak-creak and the hiss of *Mine*.

He shook his head and banished the image.

"Not great."

"He's still coming?"

Mack nodded.

"Every night."

Diane squared her shoulders and drew a sheet of paper from her purse. She handed it to Mack.

He opened it and read: *George Corey*. Written beneath was the *name Wilma Burns*, followed by an address in Kalkaska.

"I don't understand," he said.

"George Corey is the dead man you found in the woods," Diane explained. "They haven't made a formal identification, but they're pretty sure. I called the sheriff in Kalkaska and bugged him until he gave me the name of one of Corey's friends. Apparently, the man didn't have any family. Wilma Burns grew up near the Stoneroot Forest. She knew Corey, and she'll talk to us."

"How?" Mack sputtered, holding up the piece of paper.

"I picked up the phone, Mack. It wasn't hard."

Mack sighed. He hadn't thought to call the Kalkaska police, to find out about the man who haunted him. In the few moments he'd sought a solution, his mind had wandered to priests and witch doctors.

"We have to leave now," Diane continued. "We're meeting Wilma in an hour."

"An hour? What if you'd found me passed out again?"

Diane smiled.

"I have more faith in you than that." She tugged on the sleeve of his sweater. "I remember this old thing. Still looks good on you."

Mack brushed a hand down the sweater, almost got sucked into a memory of Diane wearing it with only a pair of panties, and clapped his hands together to wipe the thought before it took hold.

Diane started.

"Sorry. My brain was trying to take me on a ride. You said, we. Are you coming with me, Diane?"

She nodded.

"I told Dale I had errands to run."

"You lied?" Mack could hardly believe it. Diane couldn't lie to save her life.

"I felt justified. He'd never understand, and… you need help, Mack. I want to help you."

Mack stepped toward her, ready to gather her in his arms. She gazed at him with clear, kind eyes, and he stopped. She was not his anymore. Another man went to bed with her every night.

Mack had his chance, and he blew it. He swallowed and sighed, looking away from her to break the spell.

"Thank you, Diane," he told her, though he couldn't imagine how anyone could help him get rid of a ghost.

~

WILMA LED Mack and Diane into a sitting room stuffed with worn, cozy chairs.

Mack shrugged off his coat and took Diane's, draping them over his arm.

"Hot cider? Or tea, perhaps?" the woman asked.

She looked to be approaching seventy, with white curls fluffed about her head. She wore a grayish-pink housecoat and thick wool socks.

Strewn about her sitting room floor, Mack saw dolls and doll clothes, including a tiny wooden bassinet.

"Those are my granddaughter Betsy's things. She'll be around," Wilma told them. "Have a seat."

Wilma returned with a tray, including a small teapot of cider and three cups on matching saucers. She poured them each a glass.

Mack took a sip. The cider was hot and spicy and warmed him instantly. He leaned back in the chair, at ease in the old woman's home. She reminded him of his own grandmother on his mother's side. Gran Mags, they called her, though her name was Magnolia.

"Such a pity to hear about George's passing," Wilma started. "You're the young man who found him?" She regarded Mack with sharp blue eyes.

He nodded.

"A little over a week ago. He was buried in the woods in the Stoneroot Forest."

"Sheriff Long's rather tight-lipped about the whole ordeal. I wonder if you might tell me, young man. Did George die a natural death?"

Mack glanced at Diane, startled.

"Um... no. No, I don't think so. The sheriff hasn't told the community it was a murder?"

Wilma lifted an eyebrow and took a sip of her cider.

"An old woman's questions are a bother to a man like that. But soon as I heard George had passed, I suspected malice was behind it."

"Why is that?" Diane asked. "Did George have enemies?"

Wilma regarded her.

"Everyone has enemies, my dear, whether or not we know it."

Diane frowned, but didn't push.

"Was George a good man, Mrs. Burns? In reputation?" Mack asked.

Wilma nodded.

"Yes, a good man, but not a man to trifle with. George was part of the Corey Clan, a bloodline you'd find in history if you were interested in Scandinavia."

"Known in history for what?" Diane asked.

Wilma flipped her hand back and forth.

"This and that. But if I had to give them a name, I'd call them healers. The more ignorant of our kind might have called them witches."

"Witches?" Mack asked, too quickly to suppress his distrust in the word.

"And that right there." She pointed at his face. "Is why I prefer the term healers."

"Was he a medicine man, then?" Diane asked.

"You could call him that," Wilma agreed. "He treated my ills more times than I can count. People visited him for all manner of ailments. Broken leg - see George; broken heart - see George. Course, he wasn't an easy man to see, living in the Stoneroot Forest, but George knew when you were looking for him."

"Where did he live?" Mack asked, confused. "I've been roaming that forest since I could walk. I've never heard of him."

"You're a hunter, young man. An outsider who visits the forest to pluck its bounty and take it home. George worked with the local folk, with his people."

"But where was his cabin?"

Wilma shrugged.

"I don't know."

"Who does?" Diane asked.

"He had a daughter," Wilma murmured, wistfully. "I remember seeing her a handful of times. She was a wild thing with wavy blonde hair that never got combed and dirty, bare feet. She and George would walk into town sometimes, both holding their walking sticks, grinning like they knew the secrets of the world." Wilma chuckled.

"Where is she now?" Mack asked.

"She came around less as she grew. Young women do that, you know? Even when you have a daddy like George, you drift away."

"Did she leave, or did something happen to her?" Mack asked, trying to reconcile his ghost with the man Wilma described.

Wilma shook her head.

"I asked George about it, and he said 'she moved on.' I never saw her again."

Mack jumped at the shrill ring of a telephone from the other room.

"Excuse me." Wilma stood and shuffled to the kitchen.

Mack looked at Diane, who stared back at him with an equal expression of puzzlement.

She started to open her mouth, but a little girl skipped into the room.

She stopped, looked back and forth between them, and then plopped on the floor, picking up one of her dolls. She had auburn hair that fell in curls over the collar of her pale blue sweater.

"You're here about Uncle George?" she asked, not looking at either of them.

Diane glanced at Mack, and then scooted off the chair to sit next to the girl.

"She's beautiful. What's her name?" Diane asked, patting the hair of the doll in Betsy's hand.

"This is Wilma. I named her after my grandma." Betsy picked up a tiny ribbon and tied it in the doll's hair.

"Wilma is a lovely name," Diane told her. "Was George really your uncle?"

Betsy giggled and shook her head, curls bobbing.

"All the kids called him Uncle George. He gave us honey from his bees."

"He kept bees?" Mack asked.

"Oh sure, bees and spiders and birds. He had all sort of creatures."

"Have you been to his cabin?" Diane asked, making eye contact with Mack, who glanced toward the kitchen where he could still hear Wilma on the phone.

"Yes, but don't tell Grandma." Betsy lowered her voice. "Only the kids could go."

Diane frowned.

"Why?"

Mack had an uneasy feeling.

"Because we're pure of heart," she said, as if the answer were obvious.

"What kinds of things did you do at George's cabin?" Diane asked.

Betsy shrugged, set the doll in the bassinet, and pulled a small, silk-lined blanket up to her chin.

"Listened to stories, ate honey, picked flowers. Sometimes Uncle George showed us the bones hanging in his shed. He put on the skin of animals who'd given themselves to him and spoke in their language."

"He never hurt the kids, did he?" Mack asked, feeling duty-bound to put the question forth.

"Oh, no," Betsey shook her head. "Uncle George did not believe in hurting others."

"But you said he wore animal skins and had bones? He hunted, then?" Diane asked.

Betsey looked at her as if she'd asked a fool's question.

"The animals came to him. They chose him to end their lives."

Mack looked at the kitchen. He no longer heard Wilma talking. Their time with the girl would soon be up.

"Betsy, how can we find George's cabin?" he asked.

"With the hag stones, silly. There's no other way."

"The what?" Diane asked, but Wilma cleared her voice from the doorway.

"What are you going on about, child?" Wilma asked, resting a hand on her hip and planting a stern eye on her granddaughter.

Betsy smiled.

"The hag stones, Grandma Wilma. I was just telling these people, it's the only way to find Uncle George's cabin."

Wilma did not relax into her seat, but sat perched on the edge. Her face looked drawn, as if she'd received bad news during her telephone call.

"I'm sorry to run you out after you've driven all this way, but my sister's had a fall, and it's best if Betsy and I go around to help her."

"We understand," Diane said politely, as Mack helped her into her coat.

"Mrs. Burns?" Mack asked from the doorway. "Do you know what Betsy means by hag stones?"

Wilma knotted her hands together, her thoughts clearly elsewhere.

She gestured at her neck.

"George carried a bag of stones around his neck. He called them hag stones. He showed them to me once. Each had a little hole right in the center. The kids said if you held the stone up to your eye, you could see his cabin. If you took it away, it disappeared. I once asked George what the stones were for, and he rattled on for a half-hour about their abilities. He claimed they offered protection, could heal or cast curses. Perhaps the most interesting of all, he said you could gaze through the hole in the stones and see the dead."

CHAPTER 19

September 1965
Liv

SMALL WINDOWS, near the attic floor, sat on opposite ends of the long room. Liv had to lie on her belly to gaze at the property below.

She watched orderlies, nurses, and doctors, all dressed in white, ushering patients between the buildings. Sometimes the patients walked freely.

She saw a young boy and longed for the children of the orphanage she'd left behind.

If she called out, would they come?

She thought so, but it would not be to release her. No, they would hand her over to Stephen Kaiser, and he would silence her.

For now, he kept her, his little pet in the attic of his new world, the place where he had absolute power.

She rolled onto her back and gazed at the crow perched on the rafters. Somehow, he moved in and out of the building. She'd searched for the hole that morning after dawn but had yet to find out how.

"The door is open," she murmured, trying to make sense of George's words in her dream.

He'd set things into motion. Of that she was sure, but how? Had his death allowed him to see what she'd done all those years ago? Or had he always known, and his death acted as the catalyst to draw her home?

Liv heard a clank of metal near the door.

She jumped to her feet, expecting the door to swing in. Instead, she saw a pair of hands slipping through a hole in the door's bottom. A metal grate slid back into place.

A bowl of stew and a small loaf of bread sat on a little metal tray. He'd also added a fresh pitcher of water.

Liv walked to the door but did not speak. She could see Stephen's shadow beyond the grate.

"Why didn't you just kill me last night, Stephen? Why have you brought me here?"

He didn't speak, but Liv listened to his breath.

"You know what scares me, Liv?" Stephen told her after several minutes of silence. "I'm scared that if you die, I'll lose it."

"Your mind?" she asked, sitting and pulling the tray across the floor with a dull scrape. She leaned close to the stew and smelled. No bitter aroma hovered beneath the spicy scent of onions and pepper.

He laughed.

"Oh, no, not my mind; not that at all. My sense of knowing things. Before I accepted the position at the Northern Michigan Asylum, I *knew* this place was special. I came here on a tour during my undergraduate work. I felt… the power hidden in this place. You feel it too, don't you, Liv? It breathes as we breathe. It sleeps and hungers. It reaches out into the world and draws us in. Do you know how many patients arrive at this hospital who can do special things? They can speak to the dead or discern your darkest secrets. There are asylums all over the world, but this place is unique. Extraordinary people are drawn here. There's a magnetism, Liv."

Liv nibbled the plain bread and wondered if she could prise the grate open. Even if she could, she'd never fit through the small hole.

"I'm working with a woman right now who sees the dead. She speaks to them," he continued, his voice rising excitedly.

"And what do the dead tell her, Stephen? Do they seek vengeance for your crimes?"

He was silent for a long moment.

"Pretend you're innocent, Liv. Deny your culpability, but that summer we were guided, driven. I was not alone in that room."

The bread stuck in the back of Liv's throat, and she struggled to swallow it. She remembered retching into the woods that Halloween night, the smell of her bile mixed with the dahlias and the blood, always the blood.

Liv hunched forward, bracing her elbows on her crossed legs. Tears slid from the sides of her eyes and into her hair.

"You're sick, Stephen. All those years ago it wasn't your fault, but now..."

His voice came again, closer, as if he'd pressed his mouth to the grate.

"You don't have to pretend with me, Liv. I'm the only person you could ever be real with. Not even George, because he needed you to be pure and good. You longed for that dark magic. It is inside of you. Liv, you're the only woman, the only person, I could ever have joined with. Think for a moment of the influence we'd have in the world if we gave ourselves over to this power? Let it act through us."

Liv sat up, understanding now why he'd kept her. Their heinous crime had not dashed his delusions from that summer, it had strengthened them.

CHAPTER 20

September 1965
Jesse

Jesse woke with a start, blinking into the dark parlor. He rolled to his side and fumbled for his matches and the candle he'd placed on the floor earlier that evening.

A long, terrified scream split the house, and Jesse froze, the match between his thumb and forefinger.

Footsteps pounded down the stairs.

Jesse didn't light the match, but jumped up, ready to face whatever hurtled from the darkness.

In the shaft of moonlight that illuminated the front hall, he saw a wisp of a woman as she raced down the stairs. Her eyes were large and terrified, and her dark curls were glossy in the opaque moon glow. Her slender neck disappeared into a pale purple dress, but her body seemed to grow more ethereal the lower his gaze moved.

And then she was gone.

The front door didn't open, and her footsteps didn't continue onto the porch.

Jesse swallowed, clutching the match and candle, and tiptoed to the hall.

It was empty.

The woman had vanished.

Jesse struck the match and lit the candle.

He turned to the darkened stairway, knowing the girl had not run back up them. She had not run at all.

He ascended the steps numbly.

When he glanced in a mirror in the second-floor hallway, Jesse jumped at his own reflection. His face looked sunken in the glass, his eyes black and hollow.

Beyond him in the reflection, he saw the slender fingers of a woman's hand clasping the frame to the bedroom door.

Frozen, he watched the fingers disappear into the dark doorway.

The door slammed behind him, and Jesse spun to face it.

His mind ran with possibilities, but he knew no explanation existed in the world of science.

He recalled the harsh words of Sister Anne, one of the crueler nuns at an orphanage he lived in for several months: *'As for the person who turns to mediums and to spiritists, to play the harlot after them, I will also set My face against that person and will cut him off from among his people,'* she had hissed, quoting scripture from the bible. *'They're in purgatory, Jesse, those spirits you court at night. Keep conversing and God will turn away from you. He will forsake you!'*

He'd woken to find her at his bedside, her hands curled around his thin wrists. He'd been having a nightmare and must have been talking in his sleep.

The nuns' opinions of ghosts and spirits had been clear. They were lost souls, punished by God to purgatory for their sins.

Jesse had found the words empty, but he'd not slept that night, and for many nights after, he woke afraid he'd open his eyes and find the nun's leering face above him.

Gritting his teeth, he walked to the bedroom and shoved the door open, thrusting the candle before him.

The room was empty, but he caught sight of the closet door

clicking shut.

He had to look in the closet. His only other choice was to walk out the front door and never look back.

He had to look.

He paused at the closed closet door, steadying his hand on the knob before pulling it open.

A rack of coats blocked the interior. Holding the candle back from the fabric, he shoved the coats aside.

The space was empty. As he studied the white plaster walls and the wood floor, he gazed at a large discoloration on the floorboards.

He hunched down and held the flame closer. The stain was long ago hardened. Little bubbles had formed in the brown-red mass.

He touched a finger to the hardened spatter.

Standing, Jesse tried to make sense of the stain. He glanced at the ceiling, and then held the candle high. A matching stain, darker in color, marred the white plaster.

Something had seeped through the floor from the room above. The boy's room.

Jesse didn't think. He took the stairs quickly and pushed into Stephen Kaiser's room before his daring left him.

He opened the closet, casting aside the hangers filled with the young man's jackets and shirts.

On the floor, at the back of the space, stood a large trunk with a padlock. A dark stain spread out from the chest, besmirching the polished floor surrounding it.

The stain matched the one from below. A red-brown color that was likely sticky at one time, but had grown hard. When Jesse leaned close, he saw tiny bugs trapped in the hardened ooze.

He searched for the padlock key on the bookshelf and the bedside table not expecting to find it, but still disappointed when it didn't easily reveal itself.

He sat on the bed and gazed at the trunk for several minutes.

The mystery of the trunk perplexed him, and he'd forgotten about the girl running down the stairs. But a movement in the corner of his eye startled him and brought the vision back.

He stood, waving his candle to the darkened corner of the room where he'd sensed movement. Nothing stood there, and yet he felt eyes watching him from the emptiness.

With a rush of breath, he left the room, briefly entertaining the thought of returning to the parlor to sleep.

He dismissed it the moment his feet hit the first floor. He bypassed the parlor and went to the washroom. He'd noticed a wooden box of tools in the room earlier that day. He grabbed a hammer from the box.

As he returned to the third floor, the air grew thick and stale. A bead of sweat rolled from Jesse's hair toward his eye, and he swiped it away.

He set the candle on the floor next to the chest and hammered the padlock. The sound rang loud and metallic in the silent room. The brass trim on the chest gleamed in the flame, and Jesse watched it as he slammed the hammer again and again into the lock.

By the time the lock snapped and fell away, Jesse's shirt clung to his body. His breath came out in fast, steady gulps.

He laid the hammer on the floor and sat on his butt, his legs bent to keep his feet from touching the stain.

Eyes fixed on the trunk, he mopped his face with his damp shirt.

He didn't want to look inside until his heart had slowed and he had control of his body once more.

When he reached for the chest, his hand shook.

He flung the lid open.

Dark fabric was bunched in the top of the trunk.

Jesse grabbed a corner and pulled it away. It clung to something inside.

As he jerked it free, Jesse saw with horror a mass of dark hair clinging to the blanket. Beneath it, more hair partially concealed a human skull.

Jesse staggered back, dropping the blanket and knocking his candle sideways.

Before the flame could light the fabric on fire, Jesse fell on it, slapping the flame out and casting the room into darkness.

CHAPTER 21

August 1945
Liv

"Eternity of Darkness," Stephen announced after he'd spent an hour buried in George's book, reading every curse it contained.

Liv arranged a circle of stones on a patch of hard sand.

"We can't do that one," she told him. "That's a death curse. We're not going to kill her, Stephen."

"I thought we *were* going to kill her," Stephen mused, the cunning twinkle back in his eye.

Liv looked up and frowned, unable to read if he was serious or not.

"I liked the sulphurous odor curse," Liv offered, completing the circle.

"You want to make her stink?" Stephen rolled his eyes.

Liv stood and walked to where Stephen sat on a stump.

She flipped the pages toward the front of the book.

"Or this one sounds interesting."

She pointed to a curse titled *Night Haunts.*

He read it, though Liv knew he'd already read all the curses, likely more than once.

"Mildly intriguing," he admitted.

"Then it's decided." She leaned over the book. "I'll get the bat poop; valerian has to be collected on the full moon. You can join me if you'd like. The curse bag needs to be made from a personal item that belongs to the recipient. You'll have to get something of Veronica's."

Stephen sat up, nodding as she talked.

"I've seen her around town. She always wears that ridiculous yellow scarf."

Liv shook her head.

"She'll recognize it. We have to make it from something personal she won't immediately recognize. Or we can dye the scarf with blueberries. Okay, yeah, get the scarf."

"Yes!" Stephen stood from the stump and paced away. "If this works, Liv. We could try other spells, we could..."

"Stephen, we've got to copy this spell down so I can get the book back to George. He may already know it's gone. He-"

"Let me take it home," Stephen insisted, picking up the book and holding it against his chest. "Please? I swear I'll bring it back tomorrow. I'll copy the spell tonight."

Liv looked at Stephen's pleading eyes, pale and sparkling. She bit her lip, knew she should say no, and nodded instead.

"Okay. But you have to bring it tomorrow. Don't forget."

"Cross my heart," he told her, slipping the book into his bag. "Now let's get on with this invoking Freya business.

~

Stephen

THEY WORKED in silence for an hour. Liv had told Stephen how to erect the pyre and where to place the herbs. She drew the symbols from memory, strange circles and arrows that he wished he understood.

"What?" Stephen had looked up to find Liv watching him across the clearing.

She smiled curiously and shook her head.

"I've never done anything like this with anyone other than George. And here you are in your tweed coat and polished loafers, building a pyre with me so we can invoke Freya." She laughed.

"I'm bored with the ordinary world," he told her.

Stephen had courted the extraordinary his whole life. It started with a book given to him by his grandfather, his mother's father. The man tucked the book into Stephen's hands, the one and only time they met.

It was the day of his father's funeral. They had laid Stephen's father out in the parlor. Family and friends Stephen had never met arrived to pay their respects. His mother's parents, he was surprised to see, were modest people with drab clothes and lined faces. His grandfather had tired but soft, inviting eyes. He spoke in a slow, soothing voice, and when Stephen went to shake his hand, the man squatted down and pulled the boy into a hug. Stephen had seen the look of distaste on his mother's face across the room.

The book his grandfather gave him, The Magus by Francis Barrett, had fractured Stephen's world. He realized that another force existed in the world embedded in the stones, the water, and the bones of man. The book had ignited in Stephen an obsession with the supernatural, and he'd searched for it ever since.

"Tell me about your prophetic dreams," Liv prodded.

Stephen shuddered, imagining the gnarled bone-fish spine he'd placed beneath his pillow and the carved coal beside it.

He knelt by the circle of rocks Liv had arranged, adding the jumble of sticks she'd tied together with twine.

The dreams disturbed him, and though he wanted to confide them to Liv, he feared she would see deeper into their meanings and know things about him he'd rather not reveal.

"I dreamed of a black cat with yellow eyes and a trunk floating down a river," he confessed, leaving out the sense in the dream that a black veil was falling over the world. The dreams had been vivid and unsettling.

On the third night, he'd woken crying and wet the bed. Rather than an eighteen-year-old man, he'd woken feeling like a five-year-old child, disoriented and terrified of the darkness in his room.

He'd ripped off his sheets and ran into the dewy early morning forest to bury them. Later, it had seemed foolish. He should have washed them, but he couldn't bring himself to see the yellow stain on the cream fabric.

He was a man. He hadn't wet the bed in years.

Though in the months after his father died, there'd been an accident or two. Stephen's mother made sure he never forgot those.

He felt Liv's eyes on him.

"I threw the dream stave away. The spine and the coal. My mom almost found it, so I threw it away."

Liv didn't respond, but returned to her digging, and Stephen wished he'd never mentioned dreams. Why had he wanted prophetic dreams? It wasn't as if they revealed anything useful.

How could a black cat and a trunk possibly foretell his future?

Liv

"WHO WAS FREYA AGAIN?" Stephen asked when they'd completed the pyre.

"Freya was the Norse Goddess of love and fertility, beauty, sexuality, and even war. When I was a child, George prayed to Odin, and I prayed to Freya. He told me she was the true embodiment of the Volva, and I was made in her image." Liv blushed as Stephen watched her. The sun had set, and a violet sky gazed upon them. "I used to see her in this sky," Liv murmured, gesturing above. "Pink and violet. I imagined her riding in the heavens on her chariot pulled by her two Skogkatts."

"What are Skogkatts?" he asked.

Liv grinned.

"They're cats."

"Cats! What an awful choice. Didn't the Norse men who wrote the history books think they should give the Goddess of Love a better beast than a cat?"

"Where's your faith, Stephen Kaiser? Freya was a Volva. She could have instilled a butterfly with the power to pull her chariot."

He shrugged.

"I still think a tiger would have sounded better."

"A tiger in Scandinavia?"

"Okay, fine. A bear, then, or some mythical beast with the head of a mountain goat and the body of a bear."

"Who do you pray to, Stephen?" Liv asked. She had never doubted George's stories of the Norse Gods, but she was suddenly curious who Stephen worshiped.

"Your question implies I pray at all. I've never suffered that common affliction."

Liv looked up, startled.

"You don't believe in any gods?"

Stephen did not return her stare.

"I don't believe in the God of the church. I went to Catholic school, Liv. Do you know what God is? Eternal damnation if you covet your neighbor's wife?" He chuckled. "Hell must be packed."

Liv laughed despite herself. She too did not believe in a Catholic God, but she believed in the old Gods, she believed in the balancing of good and evil, and she'd never been around anyone who openly mocked the common faith. George disagreed with most religions, but he deferred to a need for belief in a higher power. His ancestors came from Norway. Thus, he worshiped those Gods, but worship them he did.

Liv's mother followed a Christian faith. A crucified Jesus hung above the bed she shared with Roy. Simple wooden crosses hung in every room in their small house.

When Arlene had gotten pneumonia, Liv's mother spent every night on her knees at Arlene's bedside, repeating the Lord's prayer. She rarely attended church. Working six days a week didn't permit it, and on Sundays she did the washing, worked in her garden, and mended clothes.

"Do you think we were meant to meet, Stephen?" Liv asked, wishing she could keep the hopefulness from her voice.

His eyes flicked up, and at the look in her eyes, he stopped.

"Like destiny?"

"Sure," she shrugged.

"Does George believe in destiny?" he asked.

Liv glanced toward Stephen's bag and imagined the book inside.

"Yes, he does."

Stephen nodded.

"I saved your life, Liv. What could it be, except destiny?"

LIV HELD THE TORCH HIGH.

"Freya, Goddess of love, healer of the afflicted, giver of sensual pleasures and beauty,

Join us in this sacred place, the forest of our ancestors, as winter edges in, fierce and unforgiving,

Bless us with your bounty, your goodness, your magic,

Surround and fill us with your gifts, exalt us on our path ahead.

Freya, we invoke you."

Liv watched Stephen's face in the firelight. His eyes glowed like the delphinium that grew tall and wild in the summer.

He gazed at her with reverence, and Liv's voice shook as she spoke, her voice rising high, carried into the night on the smoke of their pyre.

CHAPTER 22

August 1945
Liv

LIV WATCHED her mother brush Arlene's hair. The brush made the girl's blonde curls light and fluffy.

Liv tried to remember the days when her mother, Polly, had brushed her own hair, but could not. Surely there had been some.

Yet Liv mostly remembered her mother curled in the bed, arms wrapped across her bony ribs, crying into the jacket that had belonged to her dead husband. Liv's brothers took care of the house. Danny had dropped out of school to drive a tractor for the Morrison Family Farm. Her second brother, five years her senior, had taken over the household duties.

Liv had been a wandering child who wasn't naturally inclined to women's duties. When Liv's mother remarried, both her brothers enlisted in the army and were gone within a year. They never returned to Michigan, but they'd survived the war. Letters from Germany and France still trickled in.

As a child, Liv had subsisted on George's love. He had visited often before Liv's mother married Roy. He took Liv to the Stoneroot Forest and told her stories of the five siblings he'd left in Norway. He described their winter nights and summer harvests.

What she loved most of all were stories of his mother, a short woman with blue-gray eyes who went to the sea every morning to divine the future. Not only the big things, George would tell her, but she would plan her dinner because in the waves, she saw the day's catch and which berries would be most ripe. She taught her children to forage with their eyes closed, learning the language of the plant so they could find it even when it went dormant in the winter.

Liv's mother loved her, but she looked at her differently than her other children. In Arlene, Liv's mother had found a kindred spirit. A beautiful little girl with soft curls who let you coddle her and dress her in pretty things.

Though Liv's family rarely had pretty things to provide. But when a little extra money was squirreled away, Liv's stepfather often took it prematurely and arrived with a doll for Arlene, or a new dress. Liv's mother would scold him, but she too delighted in her youngest's joy at the gifts. And though Liv might have resented her baby sister's special treatment, in truth, she too grew warm in the light of her sister's smile.

"Liv, I need you to go to town for bread," her mother said, not looking up from Arlene's head.

"I want to go," Arlene chirped, trying to pull away from her mother's hands.

"Oh no, you don't," Polly whispered, catching her daughter's shoulders and pulling her back. "You're due for a bath tonight. The water's already warming on the stove."

Arlene growled and frowned, but leaned back into her mother.

Liv knew Arlene loved her baths. Sitting in the basin as their mother poured pitchers of warm water over her hair. Afterward, she'd rub Arlene with the oil and lavender Liv had made. Arlene would be shiny and sweet-smelling, and everyone would be happy.

~

Liv stepped into the bakery but didn't make herself known. She heard the baker's wife and her friend talking in the kitchen.

For a few moments, she pressed herself against the wall and inhaled the scents of yeasty bread and apples simmering in sugar and butter.

"That Adele Kaiser is a trollop," the baker's wife snapped.

"Candace!" the second woman reprimanded, though her voice was filled with malicious glee.

"What?" the woman asked. "I don't care if you dress her in silks and paint her gold, it's a cryin' shame how she runs around with all those men. She thinks nobody knows because she lives in that big house in the woods. People know. I'd have half a mind to run her out'a town if she didn't have a boy to raise."

Liv turned to the glass window and saw Stephen's mother on the sidewalk outside the bread shop. She cast her head back and laughed at a man who'd stopped to talk with her. Liv studied the woman's red lips against her pale face. Her silky dark hair was short, and the curled wisps blew in the afternoon breeze.

"I heard they just about expelled her son from that fancy private school last year. Something about killing the headmaster's bird," the second woman continued.

"I believe it. The apple doesn't fall far from the tree. And if ever there was a tree bound to produce rotten apples, it's that one right there."

Stephen's mother gave the man a wave goodbye and climbed into her shiny black car.

Liv felt a little flare of anger at the woman's comment about Stephen, but she swallowed it. Her family depended on the bread shop's charity. She couldn't afford to anger the owner's wife.

Liv cleared her throat and stepped up to the little counter.

The second woman, small and thin with a pointed bird-like face, poked her head out.

A little shadow of distaste crossed her features before she slipped back, not bothering with a greeting.

"The Hart girl is here," the woman said.

Candace let out a huff and lumbered into the kitchen. She was perpetually red-faced, with a thick chin that hung over her neck like a rounded melon. She narrowed her brown eyes at Liv and left her mouth set in a line of disapproval.

Apparently, the woman hated the rich and poor alike.

"My mom sent me for a loaf of bread," Liv told her. "Please."

The woman made a show of pulling a little card from her files beneath the counter. She laboriously flipped though. The mere flicking of her fingers seemed to wind her. After she found their name, she added a tick mark next to a long line of tick marks for all the loaves of bread she'd given to the family. The shop owners could tally up the cards at the end of the month and receive reimbursement from the town.

Liv left the bakery with her face burning.

Adele Kaiser's black car was gone.

As Liv headed for home, she wondered about the women's conversation. Stephen held no great love for his mother. Liv could plainly see that, but were her relationships with other men the cause, or something deeper?

As she hurried down the sidewalk, she didn't see the group of girls on the corner. They drank from glass bottles of Coke. As Liv passed them, a familiar voice called out.

"Liv Hart!"

Liv looked up to find Veronica and her girlfriends watching her. They looked clean and pretty, hair curled and lips red. Veronica wore a red and white striped dress.

She extended her arm, and Liv gazed at the bottle of Coca-Cola she held out.

"Want one?" Veronica asked.

Liv clutched the warm bread to her chest, grossly aware of the pocket hanging loose from her worn shorts and her t-shirt stained from berries she'd picked that morning.

"It's for you," another girl beamed. Her name was Rosie, and she was short and slim with limp brown hair she tried to curl in the fashion of the day that ended up flat on the top and frizzy at the bottom. When she pulled her red lips back in a smile, she reminded Liv of a snarling raccoon.

"No thanks, I better not," she murmured, taking a step away.

"Oh, come on," Veronica begged. "We want to share."

Liv paused and turned back. She didn't want to take it, and yet she did want to. She wanted them to like her. She hated it, but the inclination sent her back a step and another, until she reached out and took the Coke.

They watched her, and she smiled.

"Thanks," she told them, taking a sip.

Rosie spurted laughter, almost choking on a swallow of her own pop.

The other girls snickered, but Veronica's smile had slipped away, replaced by a sneer.

"It's a pity to waste the spit at the bottom of the bottle. We combined it for you. How does it taste?"

Liv hadn't swallowed the sweet liquid. It sat in her mouth, and she wanted to spit it in Veronica's face.

Instead, she turned and spat in the gutter.

She walked away from the girls, listening to their laughter at her back.

CHAPTER 23

September 1965
Mack

MACK TRUDGED THROUGH A TORRENTIAL DOWNPOUR. His boots stuck in the mud, and each step made an audible slurp as he pulled his foot free. A few times he had to jerk one so hard, he feared the boot would come clear off.

It wasn't just rain either, but cold rain, icy rain that gnawed through your clothes in an instant and started working its way into your bones.

"Damn weather reporters, don't know their ass from a hole in the wall," he grumbled, pulling his ball cap further over his head. He'd checked the weather before he drove to the Stoneroot Forest that morning.

'Nothing but sunny skies,' the jovial weatherman had announced, donning a pair of sunglasses. 'Can anyone say Indian summer?'

Mack had parked at his cabin, packed his bag with a compass, water, dried beef, and the hag stones.

He stopped every few feet, lifted the pouch, and fumbled the stones from their leather sac. His large fingers, numb with cold, struggled to grasp each stone without dropping it.

He placed the stone to his eye and turned three-hundred and sixty degrees, gazing through the tiny hole at the blurry forest. He repeated the process with all six stones, and then returned them to the satchel and the satchel to his bag. It was a painstaking process, and by his fifth stop, he could barely feel the stones in his stiff fingers.

As he lifted one to his eye, it slipped from his hand and disappeared into a puddle of muddy water.

"Damn it!" he cursed, hunching over.

He sank his hands into the watery hole, digging into the mud, but couldn't find the rock. He brushed over sodden leaves and twigs.

The torrent of rain continued, casting leaves from the trees and sending branches plummeting to the earth.

Above him, a crow squawked.

He shielded his eyes from the rain and stared at the dark bird perched in an ancient-looking oak tree. The tree's limbs were fat and gnarled.

Mack studied the bird. Something white poked from its mouth, and after several seconds, he knew it was the white stone he'd dropped in the puddle.

"How the-" he started, but the bird took flight and disappeared into the forest.

"You've got to be kidding me," he grumbled as the bird vanished.

Lightning cracked the sky and a boom of thunder shook the trees. Mack half-expected to see a tree burst into flames.

"A forest fire," he grouched. "That'd just make my day."

Though no fire could take hold in the rain drenching the Stoneroot Forest. A spark would vanish before it ever lit orange.

As he trudged on, Mack missed his dog. He'd left her at the cabin, fearing she'd get lost or worse in the woods. But now, as the rain fell and the wind began to howl, he dreaded continuing alone.

He'd set off in the late morning when the sun had been high and the day promised blue skies. But now, evening approached. He had an hour before the sun would set.

"Just a little further," he decided. He checked the compass, continuing north.

The temperature had dropped, and Mack's teeth chattered as he walked. He flexed and released his toes, trying to drive the icy numbness out of his extremities.

He stopped again, fumbled through the stones, pressing each to his eye. Wilderness in every direction.

"This is a fool's mission," he mumbled, and turned back.

Diane had implied the same thing when he'd told her of his plan to trek into the woods and search for Corey's cabin with the hag stones. She insisted that finding George Corey's daughter would be a better use of his time, but he disagreed. Now he wished he'd listened to her.

He turned back toward his cabin, but the needle on the compass continued to point due north. He shifted in a circle. Every direction read north.

"Rain must have got it," he mumbled, needing to say the lie out loud. He tucked the compass in his pocket and shuffled in the direction he believed his cabin stood.

After several minutes, he pulled out the compass. Again, no matter which direction he aimed it, the little needle pointed north.

Another flash of lightning, followed almost immediately by a crash of thunder, split the sky, and Mack jumped, startled. He slipped on the wet leaves and went down on his butt.

He sat, stunned, gazing into the slowly darkening forest.

The shadows beneath the trees deepened and Mack realized with the night, the deeper cold would come. *The killing cold,* his Uncle Byron used to call it when they hunted the Stoneroot Forest in the winter.

Mack knew he could die in the forest.

In the spring, someone would find him much the same way as he had found George.

Mack, at least, would not have a knife in his ribs.

The cold earth seeped through his saturated pants, and he had the hysterical notion of lying down and taking a nap. He would drown.

He thought of Diane then, and the tilt of her eyes when she'd said goodbye to him the day before. He saw fear in her expression.

"Should 'a kissed her," he said. And had he known he might never get another chance; he would have done just that. "But I'm grateful," he told the sky, water running into his eyes and mouth. "I'm grateful for every second I had with you, Diane. Even the bad times were some of the best of my life."

He took out the stones and lifted one to his eye, but his numb fingers dropped the bag and he watched the flat, white stones disappear into the mucky earth.

He swore, but his curse had no heart.

Mack had grown tired, wet and heavy, and too exhausted to care if he ever made it out of the Stoneroot Forest.

He lifted the final stone to his eye and gaped at the scene beyond the hole.

A small cabin hunched in the forest before him. A curl of smoke floated from the chimney, mingling with the rain above.

When he took the stone from his eye, the cabin vanished and an endless, murky forest reappeared. He lifted it back up and squinted through the tiny hole at the cabin.

Struggling to his feet, the other stones forgotten, Mack walked toward the log house, not daring to remove the stone pressed to his eye for fear it would disappear.

Only when his hand closed upon the doorknob did he take the stone away. The cabin door remained before him, real and solid. He turned the handle and fell inside.

The cabin was rustic, but warm. A woven red rug lay in the center of a wood floor. A bed of straw covered in blankets, the frame fashioned from large knobby branches, stood against the wall. Two crude chairs sat near a crackling fire.

Mack found a basin of drinking water in the kitchen and dipped a copper ladle into the dark water, drinking several cups before stumbling to a chair and collapsing into it.

A sound startled him, and he turned to see the crow from the forest watching him from its single good eye. In the firelight, Mack could see the milky glaze over its other eye.

The bird stood on a branch inside the cabin.

As Mack watched, it dropped the stone from its mouth onto the table, where five other similar stones already lay. The small leather pouch rested beside them.

Mack blinked at the stones, his eyes growing heavy in the heat. He peeled off his soggy clothes, dropping them on the floor and glancing again at the bird. It shuddered, its wings slick from the rain dripping from its shining black feathers.

Pulling an itchy wool blanket from the bed, Mack leaned his head back and drifted into sleep.

He woke to find a tall man in the chair opposite him. A man with hair as black as the crow's feathers and eyes to match.

Mack knew he was the ghost, the dead man in the woods, and yet here the man sat, skin pink in the fire glow, watching Mack with his steady dark eyes.

"You're dead, though," Mack muttered drowsily.

George's eyes glanced up at him, and they were no longer dark holes in the man's face. They were kind eyes.

"What is death, my friend?" Corey asked.

"Dead, gone. I saw your bones in the ground," Mack murmured.

"And you believe you saw George Corey in the ground? All that George Corey was, in those raggedy bones? Could all of Mack Gallagher be contained therein?"

"You're confusing me," Mack sighed.

Warmth radiated from the hearth and cast George in shimmering light. The heat warped the edges. Nothing was sharp. It all seemed to flow and curve.

"Why do you think you found me, Mack?" George asked.

"Because my dog smelled your carcass," Mack drawled.

George chuckled.

"She did, yes. But what if I told you, you set her on that path? I called out to you, and you came."

"But you couldn't have because you were dead. You are dead..." he trailed off and let his head fall back.

"The living are so concerned with the dead," George said. "Mack, I called out to you and you answered the call. You are bound to my service, and I cannot set you free until you have fulfilled your purpose. A very long time ago, you and I made a deal. I saved your life. Now it is time to repay your debt."

Mack looked at the man again, his head lolling to the side.

"Huh? My life?"

George handed Mack a mug of something hot. Steam tendrils rose from the oily surface.

"Look deeply, my friend, and remember..."

As Mack gazed into the liquid, the shiny oil swirling and shifting, something tugged at his hair.

"Mackey? Mackey?" It was his mother's voice, and she was crying, pleading. "Please, wake up, Mack. Wake up."

Mack looked down at his body. He was young, around ten years old, and his face was gray, his lips were blue.

His mother beat against his chest and cried. He was near the water's edge at the little lake in the Stoneroot Forest.

He had been fishing, gotten hungry, and ran into the woods to eat a handful of berries. They were poisonous.

From the trees, the tall dark-haired man emerged. Wordlessly, George picked Mack up and carried him through the forest, his mother running behind, begging the man to help her and calling out for her son.

At the cabin, a young woman with messy blonde hair stood. She opened the door wide, and George and his mother pushed inside.

Corey and the girl began to play drums.

As Mack hovered over his body, he heard beautiful songs and whispers. The sounds wrapped him in warmth and light. He wanted to go with them, to leave the cold, stiff body on the ground.

But then hands, human hands, took hold of him and drew him toward his physical form.

He tried to resist, but the girl and her father soothed him, sang to him, and soon he had re-entered his body.

His abdomen seized, and he spewed a gelatinous mass of red berries onto the wood floor.

His mother's face shifted into focus. She clutched him, pressing her wet cheeks into his neck.

The memory started to fade, and he lurched forward in his chair, wanting to see his mother one last time.

The cup of broth pitched to the floor.

George Corey watched him.

"Why did I forget?" Mack asked, staring into the rug where the oils had disappeared.

"Because I asked you to," George told him.

"But why me? Couldn't you have called someone else here?"

"Not everyone can see through the stones, Mack. The magic is not in them, it's in you."

"You're sorely mistaken, Corey," Mack grumbled. "Magic is the last thing I've got going for me."

George smiled and held out his arm. The crow glided from its post to Corey's forearm.

"When we die, we step through the veil. Our memories of a thousand lives are restored. We *See,* truly *See*. When you die and return to the land of flesh, your eye remains open."

George touched a space on his forehead, near the center of his eyebrows.

"I chose you, Mack, because you can *See*."

"And if I refuse to do what you ask?" Mack wondered out loud.

"I will haunt you until you complete the task required of you. And my ghost — well he's a darker fellow altogether, isn't he?"

George leaned his head forward, and the crow rubbed its beak against Corey's ear.

"Am I dead too?" Mack asked suddenly. He wondered if he had drowned in the rainy woods after all. How disappointing that it was not his mother to greet him in the afterlife, but this stranger with the dark eyes.

"You are not dead, Mack Gallagher, but you have been living like a dead man. Fulfilling your debt to me is a new opportunity at life for you. I've given you this gift once before. I suggest you do not squander it a second time."

Mack waved his hand in front of his face. He stuck a finger in his mouth and bit down.

George watched him, an amused expression on his face.

"I can't be haunted, George," Mack told him, a gurgle of laughter following the statement. "Diane will never take me back if I have a ghost too."

George chuckled and stood. When he returned, he held a wooden box.

"I need you to save my daughter, Mack."

~

WHEN MACK WOKE in the morning, he shivered.

He sat up and regarded the cabin.

The fire in the hearth was long burned out. Not hours earlier, but months.

A layer of dust coated the surface of the table and the chairs. The chair George Corey had sat in contained a layer of undisturbed silt.

As Mack moved through the cottage, cobwebs clung to his beard and hair. He pulled them away, trying to make sense of the desolation before him.

The cabin had been warm and bright, filled with the smells of food and the air of life.

Mack spotted the satchel on the table, the leather strap tied tight. He knew all six stones sat inside. Next to the pouch lay the wooden box.

He picked them up and slid them into his bag.

Mack knew what he had to do.

~

"I DON'T UNDERSTAND," Diane told Mack when he appeared at her apartment the following day. "Why? You can't commit yourself, Mack. You're not insane. The… the figure," Diane stammered.

Mack gazed at her, hair loose and falling over her shoulders, her face clean of makeup, her feet bare.

"The ghost is real, Diane. I'm not committing myself because I fear for my sanity. It's the only way. George Corey told me. I found his cabin. I thought I had died. I was lost in the woods; I had given up."

He remembered the moment, his regret at not having kissed Diane, taken her in his arms, and now he stood before her again. Her face tilted up to his, her eyes searching.

"But, Mack, George is dead. You saw his body. You..."

He held up his hand.

"I can't explain it, Diane. Maybe someday I'll try. But today, right now, I have to go." He pulled a small package from his pocket, wrapped in gold foil. "Happy Birthday, Di." He handed her the gift, and she gazed at it and then back at him. He leaned down and kissed her cheek.

As he walked down the hall, he felt her watching him.

"Mack?" she called out.

He turned.

She had stepped into the hallway.

In three long strides he was back to her. He leaned down, pressed a hand into her back and kissed her. She did not push him away, but sank her fingers into his hair and kissed him back. He leaned his forehead against hers.

"I love you, Diane. I always have."

He turned and walked away.

CHAPTER 24

September 1965
Liv

LIV WASN'T sure when Stephen had begun to drug her food.

During the first days, she'd sniffed it, taken tiny bites and waited to ensure he'd put nothing into the tasteless mashed potatoes.

However, as she swallowed the last of the soupy oatmeal in her dish, she noticed flecks of white powder lining the metal bowl. She wiped her finger along the powder and sniffed it. The substance had no distinguishable smell.

"What did you give me?" she asked Stephen through the grate.

"A little something to keep you calm. I'd like to come in today, and I can't have you making a scene by running down the stairs like a mad woman." He chuckled.

Liv considered forcing herself to throw up, but knew it was useless. Stephen would only take more drastic measures the next time. She stood and walked to the little bed, sinking onto the flimsy mattress and lying down. She searched for the crow in the rafters, but he was nowhere in sight.

A short while later, Liv heard the key in the lock. The door swung in and Stephen took a hesitant step into the attic.

Her limbs lay heavy on the bed. She didn't bother lifting her head as he strode across the room, quickly securing straps to her arms and legs.

"For your own safety, Liv," he said, leaning over and peering into her face. "I want to tell you about this place," he continued. "This asylum is magnificent. When I started here, I longed to share the story with you. You were the only person in the world who would understand."

Liv bit her tongue against the cruel things she wanted to say. Her words were wasted on the man before her.

"I started my rounds at the Northern Michigan Asylum on a dreary day in September. It was a terribly, soggy day, and I remember how my shoes squished in the wet grass. By the time I stood at the desk of my adviser, Dr. Strickland, my socks and the hem of my pants were sodden."

Liv imagined him, dripping wet and likely looking like a lost boy as he stared up at the immense buildings. He did not look like a lost boy anymore. He stood above her, his eyes gleaming with excitement as he told his story.

"The day's activities did not surprise me," he continued. "I completed my psychiatric residency in New York at one of the most depraved and violent mental institutions in the country. They didn't appreciate me there, Liv. They loved lobotomies. Schizophrenia or hysteria, their favorite treatment was an ice pick to the frontal lobe."

He offered a derisive laugh, but Liv shuddered at the description. It terrified her that men like Stephen wielded such power over those least able to defend themselves.

"I saw the usual patients. Herbert was a paranoid schizophrenic. He gave me the evil eye when I passed. In the women's ward, I saw a young woman pulling her long red hairs out one by one. Another patient plucked them from the table and quickly braided them into her own thin, gray hair. Dr. Strickland watched me as if I might be shocked at these things, but they barely registered. Crazy was something I'd grown accustomed to by that time. I was looking for something more, and I knew I'd find it here." Stephen paced away, abruptly turning on his heel and striding back.

Liv thought back to her own intervening years. While Stephen played God with the mentally ill, she'd raised and nursed the future of the world. The little boys and girls who were bright-eyed and filled with hope, despite the dire circumstances that had brought them to the orphanage.

There were attendants who liked to control the children, even hurt them, but Liv drove them out. One by one, she revealed their dark nature, and they ran from the truth of their own corrupt hearts.

"They gave me a plain little apartment in the staff building," Stephen went on, "which suited me fine. In those days, I wanted nothing more than to live within these walls, to root out the secrets of this place." He paused for effect. "And then one afternoon, the mysteries revealed themselves. I overheard Dr. Green and Dr. Palmer speaking about a priestess who could raise the dead. She was coming to the asylum as a patient, to some sort of meeting. I knew I'd found it — my destiny, Liv."

"A priestess," Liv murmured, the word strangled in her throat. In her mind, she envisioned a wild woman with a headdress of feathers and bones. And then she imagined the woman's strong arms pinned against her body, the stiff confines of a straightjacket wrapped around her, flattening her bosom, hiding her heart, stifling her voice.

"I jimmied the lock on Palmer's door," Stephen lifted his hand and squinted his eyes as if reliving that long-ago break-in. "His apartment was identical to mine, with the bonus of the most hideous display of fruit bowl paintings you've ever seen. The man is plainer than the oatmeal I've been feeding you. Sorry, by the way. Truly, I've watched manic patients fall asleep in his office." Kaiser laughed and slapped the brass bed frame causing a jolt of surprise to invade Liv's thickened senses. "I found a letter imprinted with an odd wax seal. The letter spoke about a meeting of a brotherhood. More importantly, it described the priestess. I was floored. It was more than I envisioned when I first felt the power in this place."

Liv let her head fall to the side. She did not want to look on his face flushed and impassioned. She hated the way he gazed at her. Did he consider them old friends? She locked in an asylum attic, and he chattering away and practically bouncing out of his shoes?

"The letter wasn't enough. I had to know more. So, I broke in again, and you can imagine my surprise when I was greeted by Dr. Strickland, Dr. Green, and Dr. Palmer. They were sitting in the darkness waiting for me." Stephen's voice dropped low. "My heart plummeted right through the floor beneath me and splattered somewhere in the basement. I told Strickland, the mastermind of their group, that I wanted in. Palmer and Green looked like daft cows staring at me with their big dumb eyes, but not Strickland. My theory, Liv? He knew when he hired me that I would join the brotherhood. I was meant for the brotherhood."

Stephen sat with a sigh on the edge of Liv's bed and she cringed as he reached over and pushed her hair away from her eyes.

"Strickland sent those other two morons out and gave me a hard time for breaking into Palmer's apartment, but all the while I saw the intrigue in his eyes. He recognized something in me. He saw potential, something Green and Palmer didn't have an ounce of in their big toes. I made it clear that he'd be a fool to keep me on the outside."

"So, they let you in?" Liv asked, wishing the story would end and she could close her eyes and blot out the sound of his voice.

He laughed again, and now he was on his feet, pacing.

"Those bastards broke into my apartment in the middle of the night. I woke up to a rough canvas sack yanked over my head. Hands, six at least, maybe more, grabbed my arms and legs and lifted me from the bed. Had I gone too far? Were they carrying me to the furnace room to toss me into the fire and dispose of me for good? I panicked. I bit a man through the fabric. The man shrieked and jerked his arm away. I heard Palmer swear and relished the knowledge it was him I had bit. Before his fist hit me, I sensed it. The impact slammed into my nose and I saw a grotesque array of black stars. Blood was pouring out of my wrecked nose, and then I felt them haul me out of the building, into the cool night."

Liv imagined Stephen, blood seeping into a canvas sack pulled over his face. Why hadn't the men taken him to the forest and thrown him into a shallow grave?

Because they were like him.

The realization made her head pound.

Liv missed the children then. She missed their earnest faces and their warm, searching hands. She missed sitting in the rocking chair on the big front porch and rocking the babies while a breeze rippled in the mulberry tree that hung over the porch.

Children were not filled with secrets and dark desires. They wore their emotions plain on their lineless faces. George had always loved children. He sometimes told Liv *'their innocence balances the scales of good and evil in our world.'*

"We walked for ages, and then..." Stephen paused. "And then I heard it and felt it. The chamber, the eye. It seemed to call out to me. *Come in, Stephen. Come inside.*" His voice changed as he whispered the calls, as if he were singing an eerie, seductive song. "When they pulled the canvas sack from my head, I saw Dr. Strickland in a chair opposite me. I looked around at the chamber and I felt it watching us, holding us."

A tremor ran along Liv's spine and her arms and legs broke out in goosebumps. She too remembered the whispers from the chamber, the chilling call of something evil luring its prey.

Stephen moved around the bed, positioning himself in front of Liv's face once more. He squatted down and looked into her eyes.

"Strickland lifted a glass bottle of Sodium Pentothal. We used it often at the sanitarium in New York as a sleep-cure. But I knew why he'd brought it. It's a truth serum, a way of getting people to talk, though I soon learned he didn't need a truth serum for that," Stephen snorted.

"So, you were on the other side of the needle. How did that feel, Stephen?"

He didn't answer her, and though his eyes remained fixed on hers, they looked far away as if he stared right through her.

"Green injected me, and I felt that rush of cold fill my veins. It was in that moment I experienced fear. It had been a decade since I felt that way. The last time was twenty years ago in the cellar when you found me. When she locked me down there and probably would have left me to die."

"Maybe that would have been for the best," Liv murmured.

Stephen grew silent for several minutes, and Liv hoped he'd leave. Instead, he continued.

"I told him, *'if you think a dose of barbiturates will have me over here blubbering like a woman, you're sadly mistaken.'* Strickland laughed, and that's when I noticed the man in the corner. He wasn't a doctor at all, but a patient. His eyes were fluttering, and he was scribbling on a pad of paper. Dr. Palmer stood, ripped the top sheet from the notebook and scurried to Dr. Strickland, sliding the paper into his hands."

Kaiser's breath had grown fast and ragged.

"He knew, Liv - what I'd done, what we'd done. Strickland started to ask questions. He asked me about Gaylord, about my mother. I wanted to rip off the binds and hop a train like we did as kids. I never wanted to look on that patient with the sunken eyes and the scribbling hands ever again. *'Tell me about the witch, Stephen. The Norse witch,'* Strickland asked."

Liv wanted to cover her ears with her hands, but she couldn't. Even if Stephen had not bound her, her arms were like lead weights resting beside her.

"*'What is he?'* I demanded, nodding toward the patient, who again scribbled on the paper. Strickland did not respond. He looked down at the page. *'Tell me about the trunk, Dr. Kaiser,'* he asked me. I looked at the patient in the shadow. He had tilted his head as if he were waiting, listening for the next revelation, and that's when something in me exploded. I started rocking back and forth. I slammed the front of the chair down, and the front leg splintered and sent me to my knees. I wanted to scream. I wanted to kill the man in the corner, but then I heard it again. The voice of chamber. *Shhh...* it seemed to whisper. And I grew silent, my heart slowed, and the blood stopped pulsing in my head. It was helping me, Liv."

Stephen sighed and leaned forward into the side of the bed, clutching Liv's wrist in his clammy hands.

"The next morning, Strickland knocked on my door. '*Welcome to the Umbra Brotherhood, Dr. Kaiser. Burn these after reading them.*' He handed me a letter of introduction and a code of silence. I was in."

Liv held her breath as the story ended.

She waited for Stephen to go on and struggled with the delirious notion that he might crawl into bed beside her and fall asleep. Or worse he might stand in the room all night revealing the torture he'd inflicted on his patients in the last two decades. And she would listen and carry it, because she had helped to create the monster that was Stephen Kaiser.

He leaned down and Liv gasped as he planted a cold moist kiss on her forehead. Then he turned and left. She listened to the door close and the lock slide into place.

CHAPTER 25

September 1965
Jesse

JESSE PUSHED in the door to Quarry's Pub. The heat and the smell of spiced rum swirled up around him. He shrugged out of his coat, hung it on the rack by the door, and ambled over to the bar, where an older man sat sipping from a clear glass of golden liquid.

The man glanced at him as he sat down.

"Help ya?" the bartender asked. He was a short man, mostly bald, with a tuft of dark hair that rimmed his lower scalp. He planted his hands on the bar, and Jesse saw scabby knuckles. The man was a fighter, or he regularly threw drunks out of the bar, maybe both.

"I'll take an old-fashioned," Jesse told him, laying one of his newly acquired bills on the counter.

The man took it, made his drink, and dropped his change in front of him.

"Don't reckon I know ya," the man next to Jesse said. His voice was raspy and on the edge of slurring.

"Jesse Kaminski," Jesse told him honestly, offering his hand.

The man shook it.

"Bart Wynkoop," the man told him.

Jesse spotted a gold band on his ring finger. The man had the pouchy face of a regular drinker. Sacks of fleshy skin ballooned beneath his small, dark eyes.

"You new in town?" Bart asked.

Jesse sipped his drink and shook his head.

"I sell cars, and I'm planning on moving my family north. I heard about a gem of a house in these parts. My wife loves big, old antique places. Some friend of a friend told her something like that might be for sale around here. Figured I'd check it out on my way through town. They said it was a real big house tucked back in the woods, a Victorian style house," Jesse explained.

The man scratched his chin.

"Don't know nothin' about a Victorian. Half the houses in these parts are shacks, and the other half are these new ranch doohickies popping up every which way."

The bartender walked back toward them, cleaning a glass.

"Sounds like the old Kaiser place. But I ain't ever heard it went up for sale."

"The Kaiser place?" Jesse asked.

"Oh, yeah," the man beside him crooned before downing his glass. "Hit me with another, Punchie."

The bartender set the glass down and grabbed a bottle of scotch.

"Punchie?" Jesse asked.

"It's not what you think," the bartender told him dryly. "I played Punch in *Punch and Judy* a thousand years ago in the school play, and the nickname stuck like a fat woman's girdle."

"It fits in more ways than one," Bart murmured from the side of his mouth, winking at Jesse.

"Do people live in the Kaiser place?" Jesse asked.

"Nah," Punchie shook his head. "Not for twenty years, probably."

"The ma took off, and the son skedaddled not long after," Bart announced. "Boy, was she a tart, that Kaiser woman. Had quite a following in these parts, and from what I heard, not all those men were just admirers."

Punchie rolled his eyes.

"Bart, you think half the women in this town are floozies."

"I'd lean toward sixty percent," Bart corrected, leaning forward and giving Punchie a jeering smile.

This last drink had broken down the man's inhibitions. One more and he'd be singing like a rooster at dawn.

"I didn't know the Kaiser family," Punchie told Jesse. "Her boy went to some fancy private school. The mother was a socialite, but she sure didn't socialize with the townsfolk. I heard she threw big parties and people came from Chicago, New York." He shrugged. "But those are rumors."

"Rumors, my ass," Bart jeered. "Lawrence Rector was my best friend for forty years, and Adele Kaiser invited him to every one of those parties. He barely had a pot to piss in, but he was real smooth-like." Bart offered Jesse another exaggerated wink. "Looked like Clark Gable, too. The women got wet if he smiled at 'em. I can tell you, she did more than throw him a few bucks here and there. She bedded him whenever she didn't have a big fish on the line."

"She wasn't married?" Jesse asked, imagining the wedding picture of the pretty dark-haired woman.

"Her husband hung himself in the cellar," Punchie said, shaking his head. "A terrible thing for the son, I'm sure."

"I'll tell you this," Bart slurred. "Lawrence had a piece of her long before her husband took the noose's way out."

Punchie frowned at the man.

"Bart, even if that's true, I don't think you need to be telling half the town."

"Half the town?" Bart lurched from his stool and fell sideways into Jesse.

Jesse pushed him upright.

"Gotta piss," he muttered, and ambled toward a dark hallway in the back of the bar.

"So, if this Kaiser woman left town, what happened to her son?" Jesse asked.

Punchie shrugged.

"He was eighteen when she split. Far as I know, he went off to some big university. I hear he's a doctor, but I couldn't give ya a single name of a former friend of his. Well," he paused and pulled at the bit of hair on his chin. "There was a girl he chummed around with. But what was her name?" He wrinkled his brow. "I was older than the Kaiser kid, and the girl was new in town and only here for a year or so, and then she disappeared too."

"She disappeared?" Jesse tightened his grip on his glass.

"Liv," Punchie announced, nodding his head. "She lived in the shacks on the south end of town. The hillbilly ghetto, we called it as kids. Her ma died of the cancer a few years back. She had a few siblings, but they scattered. The sister is still around. Arlene Hester. Her husband works at the cigar factory. They live in one of the new neighborhoods on the west side of town."

"No one knows what happened to her sister, Liv?"

"Maybe she took off with the Kaiser boy. Hard to say. In those days, people came and went. The Depression, the war. Opportunities poppin' up and dryin' up all in the same day. A lot of people shifted. I was lucky, my dad owned this bar. Back then he served up a hot breakfast every morning and a barbecue every night. That kept us afloat during the prohibition. Course, he didn't go dry in those years. Nobody did, really, 'cept maybe the church. Though the church is usually the first to move operations into the back room and carry on business as usual."

A door slammed, and Jesse jumped.

He finished his drink and pushed the glass toward Punchie.

"One more, please."

The bartender refilled him.

"What do you want to move to a little hole in the wall like this for, anyway? Best we got around here is the picture show, and even they run movies that came out six months ago."

"Just an idea I'm kicking around. My wife's got her mind set on this house she heard about. I'd like to get in touch with the Kaiser family. Any idea how I might do that?"

Bart walked back to his stool, surprisingly steady on his feet. He sat down and gulped his glass empty.

Punchie frowned at the man but didn't cut him off.

"Talk to Mona Peters. She owns North Michigan Properties and handles the real estate here in town. If anyone knows how to find Adele or Stephen Kaiser, it's her."

Bart put an elbow on the bar and balanced his head on his hand.

"I'd put my money on finding that kid hanging in the basement in the old house, just like his old man."

Punchie grimaced and shook his head.

"Stop talkin' all that trash in my bar, Bart. I'm not lookin' to defend your dumb ass tonight if somebody overhears you."

Jesse sipped his drink and thought of the trunk on the third floor of the Kaiser house.

~

MONA PETERS' business and home occupied a white, two-story farmhouse with bright blue shutters and a little sign over the door that read, 'So Glad You're Here!'

When Jesse opened the door, a little bell tinkled.

A woman looked up from a long white counter. The counter tidily displayed real estate brochures. Crystal bowls of peppermint candies sat on either end.

The woman appeared to be in her seventies, though carefully applied makeup and recently dyed brown hair masked her age.

"Good day, young man. Welcome to North Michigan Properties. How can I be of service?" her voice was deep and jolly and reminded Jesse of Nell's mother. The woman could stop a kid dead in their tracks with the slightest shift in tone. He'd watched Gabriel freeze with a cookie halfway to his mouth when his Gram-Gram said *Gabe*, popping the B sound at the end and making it very clear he'd better put that cookie back.

Jesse grew self-conscious under the woman's gaze. If she shared other traits with Nell's mother, she'd be able to spot a lie from across a room.

He wished he'd worn his own clothes, tattered as they may be, rather than the young Kaiser's.

"Hi," he said, stepping up to the counter. He searched for a lie closer to the truth, but found nothing. "I'm interested in buying the Kaiser house out on Spellway Road."

The words tumbled out, and Mona Peters watched him silently. Her gaze made Jesse uncomfortable, but he plastered on his 'house hunting' face and prayed she wouldn't look too closely at his worn hands and stolen clothes.

"I'm Mona Peters," she told him, extending a manicured hand across the counter. Bracelets jangled on her thin wrists, her blue veins stark beneath her gauzy skin.

"Jesse Kaminski," he offered, shaking her hand.

"Polish," she said, eyeing him again. "My mother was Polish - her surname was Bartkiewicz. She loathed it. When she married my daddy, she said her favorite part was changing her name to Peters."

Jesse smiled politely.

"Polish names are a doozy," he agreed. "My wife wasn't crazy about Kaminski, but then her maiden name was Duckwitz, so she figured it was an improvement."

Mona laughed and shook her head.

"Enough about names. Tell me what on God's earth makes you think the Kaiser house is for sale?" she asked, walking through the little swinging gate and around the counter. "My office is just through here." She gestured toward a little hall.

He followed her into a round sitting room with sun filtering through a large bay window. She had arranged wicker furniture around a glass-topped table strewn with real estate pamphlets.

Jesse took a seat and crossed his legs.

"I don't think it's for sale," he admitted. "But my wife heard about the house through a friend, and I stopped by while passing through on business. It looked abandoned. I hoped to contact the owners..."

He noticed Mona's eyes lingering on his jacket. He wished he'd skipped the blazer that morning. It was too warm to wear one and probably the most recognizable piece of clothing from the young Kaiser's closet.

"A houndstooth jacket," she marveled, touching the lapel of the coat. "I haven't seen one of these ages. My Freddie, God rest his soul, loved his jacket so much he near-slept in it. When it finally got too small, he moped for weeks, complaining he had nothing to wear."

Jesse laughed and glanced down.

"My wife picks out my clothes. I'm not much for fashion myself."

"And you said you're passing through on business. What business is that?"

Jesse tried to embody the man he was claiming to be. He sat up tall and balanced his hands on his knees.

"I'm in the car business. I'm a salesman in Detroit."

"And that brought you to Gaylord?"

Jesse grinned. "My boss likes to size up the competition."

Mona smirked.

"Not much competition in these parts, but a man who devalues the underdog never stays at the top. Smart man, your boss. And he's fit to let you go?"

Jesse nodded, smiling, and then quickly shook his head.

"Well, no. I mean he's expanding. He wants a presence in the north, and I'm the man for the job."

Mona clasped her hands together at her narrow waist. She wore a blue dress in the almost exact color as the shutters, cinched at the waist with a fat white belt.

"And your wife is already dreaming of her new home." Mona tapped her pink fingernails on the arm of her chair. "There's a beautiful Colonial that came on the market not two weeks ago. Right downtown. You could walk to it from here. A little white gazebo in the backyard for entertaining your friends."

Jesse blinked at her.

"My wife is really fixed on the Kaiser house."

Mona pursed her lips and studied him.

Jesse wanted to wriggle out from under her stare and pressed his hands into his thighs to keep his leg from bouncing.

"The Kaisers haven't been around these parts in twenty years. Adele Kaiser and Stephen Kaiser. They're the only two, unless he's married and had a few baby Kaisers, though I doubt it. He always had an odd look in his eye, that boy."

Jesse feigned mild interest.

"Do you know how to reach them?"

Mona cocked her head.

"It's possible to reach them, but do I know how? No, I surely don't. Adele and I were not exactly friendly. She kept to herself, her and her boy. And not to be a terrible gossip, but the women who befriended Adele Kaiser soon saw their husbands visiting for tea more than themselves. She was a widow. And some might have reasoned, she grieved by…" Mona fluttered her hand, "having loose morals, but Adele's reputation developed long before her husband died. Some whispered her infidelities drove him to it."

Jesse sat back. Mona was repeating the same story he'd heard at the bar.

"I don't make a habit of speaking ill of others, Mr. Kaminski. I'm just telling you, finding Adele won't be an easy task. She didn't leave many friends in this town. I hate to say the same goes for her child, largely thanks to his mother."

~

JESSE BOUGHT a burger and fries at the Silver Spoon Diner, sliding onto a stool at the counter.

The diner was busy, most of the booths filled with teenagers sharing milkshakes and cheeseburgers.

He ate quietly, mulling over the stories offered by Mona and the men at the bar. Their revelations told him little about the body in the closet, but a picture of the family who'd occupied the house had begun to emerge.

As he stood to leave, a bulletin board by the door caught his eye.

He paused and gazed at listings for free kittens, furniture for sale, and piano lessons.

In the top right corner of the board, a missing poster hung. The image was in black and white and portrayed a young woman with bouncy dark curls and diamond-shaped eyes. She smiled with an easy confidence that Jesse remembered from the girls he went to high school with, the girls who knew they were pretty and expected you to notice.

Beneath the word Missing he read:

Veronica Ann Medawar.

Last seen: October 31, 1945

Age: 17 at time of disappearance.

Please help us find our missing daughter.

The waitress, a girl of no more than seventeen herself, saw him looking.

"That's my aunt," she told him.

"Your aunt?" Jesse glanced away from the poster. The waitress before him looked uncannily like the missing Veronica.

She bobbed her head up and down.

"I wasn't born when she went missing. Scary though, right? I've never been to a Halloween party. My dad forbids it."

"Did she disappear at a Halloween party?" Jesse asked.

"Just a sec," the girl told him, delivering the milkshake on her tray. The boy she handed it to reached out and tugged a strand of her long dark hair. She giggled and swatted his hand away.

Jesse felt self-conscious standing and staring at the board. He returned to the counter.

When the girl reappeared, he read her name tag: Katie.

"Katie, I think I'll have one of those milkshakes, too. Strawberry, please."

Gabriel hadn't lived long enough to have a favorite milkshake flavor, but Jesse liked to imagine he would have preferred strawberry. Wild strawberries grew behind their farmhouse, and Nell would spend hours picking the tiny fruit. Gabriel ate it faster than she could pick it and would immediately demand 'moe-beawwies.'

Katie delivered his milkshake.

"Have there ever been any leads?" He pointed back toward the corkboard.

Katie tucked her dark hair behind her ears and shook her head.

"No. My grandparents put up a reward and everything. Nobody's ever come forward. She just walked out the door and disappeared."

"Do they know where she went that night? You said a Halloween party?"

"My dad told me she was secretive about it. She said she was going to a costume party and put on the big fancy dress she'd worn to her sweetheart dance the year before. That was the last anyone saw her."

Jesse took a sip of his milkshake, remembering the flash of a girl running down the stairs. In the darkness, he'd barely made her out, and yet he thought she wore a dress, a fancy dress.

An image of the trunk immediately followed. He saw the dark coils of hair, and his stomach turned sour.

He pushed the milkshake away.

"You don't like it?" she asked.

"No, I do. Brain-freeze." He tapped his temple, and she grinned, gliding to the counter to grab a tray of food as the cook rang the little bell.

"We're busy, Katie. No time for yakking," the cook told her.

"Chill out, Dad," Katie replied, rolling her eyes.

Jesse gazed at the man through the little window. He could only see the top half of his head over the plates of burgers.

The man shifted his stare to Jesse, catching him with searching eyes.

Jesse looked quickly away. He took a final drink of his shake and pushed back from the counter.

He strode into the warm August day troubled by the image of the girl missing for twenty years.

CHAPTER 26

August 1945
Stephen

STEPHEN TRIED to slip by unnoticed.

He heard his mother's deep laughter reverberate from the parlor. Without seeing her, he knew her head would be thrown back, her delicate throat exposed to the man she entertained.

"Adele, you do surprise me," the man said, and Stephen recognized the tone. The flirtation, the seduction, eventually the rhythmic creaks from her bedroom.

He paused at the door, grinding his teeth as he twisted the knob. It groaned beneath his fingers.

"Stephen?" her voice called out, not in the usual shrill tone she spoke his name, but the soft, melodious venom she chose in the presence of others.

She stepped into the hall, her face flushed, and she narrowed her eyes at the open door.

"Mr. Hardwick and I have run out of wine. Run down to the cellar and fetch us another bottle."

Stephen clutched the door handle.

He wanted to run into the daylight. He hated the cellar. The damp, musty cellar with its stone walls and high beams. He could still see his father there, naked feet swaying back and forth over the dirt floor. A small pool of blood lay below the body. His father's nose had bled when he hung himself.

"I'd rather not, Mother."

Adele's bright lips pulled away from her teeth in a snarl.

She would punish him now whether he got the wine or not.

"Now," she hissed.

She reached out and snatched the collar of his shirt, her sharp nails digging deep into the flesh below his neck. He didn't cry out, but winced as she pulled him away from the door and shoved him in the direction of the cellar stairway.

He stumbled away, the warmth of his blood sticky beneath the collar of his shirt. He opened the cellar door and glanced back as his mother returned to the parlor. He left the door ajar and crept into the washroom.

Quietly, his heart thumping painfully, he hurried to the window. He moved fast, jerking the window up, jumping onto a chair and plummeting into the bushes that flanked the house.

He stood and ran for the trees, not daring to look back.

~

THAT NIGHT SOMETHING startled Stephen awake.

He lay frozen in his bed. A creak on the top stair had drawn him from sleep. He could not hear her pad down the hall, but a moment later, he heard the skeleton key slide into the lock. The door clicked open and swung in with a sigh.

Stephen did not open his eyes. He lay perfectly still, willing his breath to appear even and deep.

A weight settled on the edge of his bed, and he could smell her Shalimar perfume.

Her breath flitted over his ear as her fingernail dragged along his collarbone toward his neck.

"Wake up," she whispered.

But he didn't move.

"I said, wake up," she shrieked into his ear, jabbing her fingernail hard into his chin as she clutched his face and shook it.

Stephen opened his eyes.

His mother leaned over him, her hair set in curlers, her face a mass of white cream. Her dark eyes gazed furiously from her milky face.

"Mother. I didn't… I shouldn't have run off earlier."

"Get up," she growled, tearing off his blanket.

She grabbed his arm and wrenched him from the bed.

He lost his balance and landed hard on his knee on the wood floor. A ball of nausea coursed through him at the pain, but she'd already grabbed the collar of his shirt and wrenched him to his feet.

"Out," she barked, shoving him toward the door.

He limped out, stepping gingerly as each movement ignited pain in his knee, which triggered a woozy rolling in his stomach.

He walked to the stairs and clutched the rail as he descended. He didn't dare stop. She'd shove him down, and then his knee would be the least of his worries.

On the first floor, she shoved him toward the cellar door, striding passed him and yanking the door open.

The cellar lay beneath him. He wanted to press his hands on the doorframe and refuse to walk down, but his knee throbbed and when she poked him in the back, he stepped onto the stairs. He'd taken only a few steps when she closed the door behind him eliminating the bit of light that filtered in.

He listened as she slid the key into the lock and clicked it into place.

He drew in a deep, shaky breath and gritted his teeth for the last few steps into near total black.

The cold floor met his bare feet, and he shuffled to the wall, pressing his back against it.

Wincing, he slid along the wall, pushing his hands out. Somewhere in the cellar, the crates of wine were stacked. He could pull out the straw and make a little nest.

Something scurried over his foot, and he cried out, instinctively kicking a leg out and buckling his injured knee. He fell hard, landing again on the throbbing knee and plummeting forward onto his hands.

The pain rendered him senseless, and for a moment he thought he'd lose consciousness. Bright lights streaked behind his eyes. His arms shook as he tried to shift his weight off the leg and into his hands.

When he finally managed to stand, sweat poured down his face and his breath burst in loud, shuddering gulps. He hopped forward, barely touching his left toe to the floor from the pain in his knee.

Something struck his face. Something dangling from the ceiling. It scratched his cheek and swung away.

As he reached for it, he felt the bristly length of a noose hanging in the darkness.

"No," he whispered, and his voice sounded tiny and ripe with fear.

He batted the rope away, but it swung back around, scratching his face a second time.

"No," he screamed, and he shoved at the rope, losing his balance and falling backward.

His back hit first, and then his head. He lay, dazed, and listened to the creak of the rope above him.

~

Liv

Liv circled the house. Stephen's mother's car was gone, and Stephen had not arrived at the pond that day.

Had they gone somewhere together?

She didn't walk to the front door. Instead, she walked around the house, climbing a maple tree to peer in the kitchen window. It was empty.

She slipped behind the house, where she could see one of Stephen's bedroom windows. She picked up a handful of stones and lobbed one at the window. It soared high and missed the glass, thunking against the side of the house. She tried another and another, listening to the sharp ping against the glass, but his face did not appear.

Finally, convinced his mother wasn't home, she returned to the front door and knocked.

"Stephen?" she called when no one answered.

He didn't come to the door, and she started to retreat to the forest, but stopped and gazed back at the house.

She sensed him inside.

Walking back, she paused and stared into every window, looking for a face, a flick of a curtain.

"Stephen," she yelled again, feeling rather foolish. If he was in there and didn't want to come out, she should just leave, but... no. She couldn't leave.

As she rounded the house a second time, a thud startled her, and she jumped. It had come from the cellar doors.

She bent close to the door, which was padlocked shut.

"Liv!" Stephen's voice was muffled and weak.

"Stephen? Are you okay?"

"Liv, help me."

"Are you locked in?"

No reply, but she heard Stephen coughing behind the doors.

She ran from the house to the gardener's shed on the back of the property. Pruning shears hung from the wall. She grabbed them and raced back. She whacked at the deadbolt for several minutes, but it didn't break.

"Stephen, I can't break the lock," she yelled.

"Try."

Again, his voice sounded quiet, defeated even. Liv stared at the door, her pulse quickening. Something was very wrong.

She hurried back to the shed and crashed through the equipment and tools. Grabbing a hammer, she sprinted back to the doors. She shoved the hammer beneath the chain and stood on the nearly horizontal doors, yanking back as hard as she could. The chain strained, but did not break. She did it a second time and threw herself backwards. The chain held, but she felt it give. The third time it snapped, sending her sprawling onto her back in the yard. She unwound the chain through the door handles and pulled the doors open.

Stephen lay curled at the bottom of a short flight of cement stairs.

He looked up, shielding his eyes with his hand and squinting at her.

Liv jumped onto the stairs and nearly fell rushing down to him.

"Stephen." She didn't blurt the obvious. That he was hurt. She saw his swollen knee, a sickly blue-purple color. "Can you walk?"

She put her hands on his forearms. They were slick and hot. He had a fever.

He gazed at her with glassy, confused eyes.

"Hold on," she told him, settling him gently back on the floor.

She raced back to the shed a third time. A wheelbarrow stood in the corner. She backed it out and pushed it to the cellar doors.

The problem would be getting him up the steps.

She lifted his arm and draped it over her shoulders, in the shadowy darkness glimpsing a noose swinging from a wood beam. She frowned but said nothing as she hoisted him up, wrapping an arm around his waist.

"You have to help me, here," she whispered. "Just put a little weight on your good leg.

He grimaced, and she saw sweat slick on his pallid face.

Together they limped up the stairs.

Liv settled him into the wheelbarrow, trying to arrange his injured leg to reduce the pain as they bumped through the woods.

"Stephen, what happened?" she started to ask, pushing him away from the house, but he didn't respond. Stephen had slipped into unconsciousness.

Roots and brambles slowed their journey, but Liv made it to the road. Spellway Road was not exactly well travelled, but within five minutes, she spotted a truck. She threw a sprig of dill onto the dirt road and crossed her fingers behind her back. The man slowed and pulled over.

"That young man needs a doctor," the driver told Liv with a frown.

"I know. My dad's a doctor. We just need a ride."

George would have frowned at her use of the word doctor, but she didn't have time to explain the ancient power of Norse healing.

It took some convincing to get the man to drive her all the way to Kalkaska, but eventually he agreed, shaking his head and muttering under all his breath all the while.

The man helped her hoist Stephen into the passenger seat. She rode in the bed of the truck, clutching the wheelbarrow and watching Stephen's waxy profile. He'd woken several times, grumbled incoherent things about blood and bare feet before drifting back into sleep.

"I don't feel real good dropping you off here, Miss. There ain't a house for miles, far as I can see," the driver told her when he stopped at the edge of the Stoneroot Forest.

"There is," she assured him. "My father's place is in the woods. No road to get there, but I know the way."

The driver and Liv lifted Stephen into the wheelbarrow and with a final wave, she left the driver behind, his mouth drawn in a frown.

She'd barely slipped into the tree line when George appeared, as she knew he would.

"Liv," he said. "I told you not to bring him here." He spoke the words, but nudged her out of the way and took the handles of the wheelbarrow.

Liv practically walked on George's heels as they pushed Stephen back to the cabin. Stephen's face had grown paler, as if drained of blood completely.

Liv had seen dead people. Sometimes people appeared at George's cabin with their dead mother or child. In their desperation, they believed he could raise the dead. He could not. But still he brought the bodies in, laid them on the rug, and drummed for the spirits to guide the departed into the afterlife. The people left calmer, their fingers unfurled, the wild anguish in their eyes softened.

Stephen looked like the corpses Liv had seen.

"What happened?" George asked as the cabin came into sight.

"I don't know," Liv whispered. "He was locked in his cellar. I think his mother..." She trailed off as Stephen let out a little moan.

Liv opened the cabin door, and George carried Stephen inside. He laid him on the rug near the hearth.

Stephen blinked open his eyes, but did not seem to see George.

"Mother," he said in a tiny voice. "Daddy's in the basement."

George frowned, and Liv knelt beside her friend, wiping the sweat from his brow with a towel.

Gently, George started to extend Stephen's left leg.

Stephen's eyes flew open, and he cried out in pain.

"Volva, please get me two strips of linen."

Liv hurried to the chest near the bed, pulling out a long roll of fabric and cutting two lengths.

It took several minutes and a lot of coaxing, but George gradually pulled Stephen's leg straight. Stephen's knee was swollen and dark. George wrapped his knee, compressing the injury.

When George rolled him onto his side, the back of Stephen's head was matted with blood.

"Hold him in place, Volva," George whispered, mopping at the thick dark hair.

The gray rag grew darker, and Liv watched the tendrils of red swirl out and away as George dipped it in a basin of water.

"Should I get the drums?" Liv asked.

George pursed his lip and shook his head, no.

"We've treated his wounds. He will recover."

"But," Liv started, "his fever, and his words. He's plagued, George."

"That is not for us to decide, Volva. Our spirits cannot heal him."

CHAPTER 27

August 1945
Liv

"I GOT IT," Stephen announced, striding across the clearing to the decayed log where Liv lay long, allowing the sun to lull her into sleep. She sat up with a jolt when Stephen appeared. She hadn't seen him for the three days since she and George had delivered him to the big house in the woods.

His limp had lessened, and had she not known he was injured, she might have thought him perfectly fine.

"What happened with your mom, Stephen? When you got home?"

He looked at her as if she wasn't talking sense, and then waved a dismissive hand.

"Nothing. But look at this."

He thrust a box toward her. When he peeled open the lid, a foul smell filled the air between them.

"Ugh." She covered her nose with her hand. "What is that?"

Something dark and oily lay in the box. The sun's glare made it hard to make out, but as she studied it, she recognized a small black eye, the curve of a black nose.

"A cat?" she asked, horrified.

"A black cat," he said, closing the lid. "Just like in the book. Don't you see? We can do the spell now."

Liv frowned at Stephen. His hair, usually neatly combed, was unkempt and standing on end. His pale eyes looked darker, most of the blue obscured by the huge black pupil.

"Stephen, are you okay?"

"I'm fine," he shrilled, shaking the box at her. The dead cat thumped inside.

"We decided on the Night Haunts spell, Stephen. We don't need a dead cat for that. Where did you get it?"

He pulled the box away.

"Just in case," he muttered, placing it in the shade of an oak tree.

"I brought you this." Liv handed him a jar of cream for his leg. "Use it every day. You'll be healed in no time."

He took the cream and set it on the ground. When he peeled up his pant leg, Liv saw the mottled yellow bruise covering his shin and knee.

"Does it hurt?" she asked

He shook his head.

"Not much anymore. It feels better if I don't straighten it. I don't know if I thanked you, but thank you, Liv, and George too. I don't know what I would've done."

Liv didn't like to think of that either, and she wanted to probe Stephen. His mother must have said something, but she knew asking would only upset him.

Liv pulled several sprigs of grass and began to braid them together. It was hard to look at Stephen. Her throat had grown thick with tears she refused to shed.

"I'm dreading your being gone," she murmured.

"I'll still come home. I'll hop the trains. I am an expert stowaway now." He winked at her.

"Are you sure that's a good idea?" she asked. She wanted him to come home, but she thought again of him locked in the cellar, his knee swollen and dark.

"She's better when I'm not home. When I'm at boarding school, she gets lonely, so when I do come home, she's nicer."

"Has she always been like this, Stephen? Your mother?"

Stephen gazed out at the lake; his mouth turned down.

"I think so. Maybe not in the days before I came along. She never wanted children. My dad did, but not her."

"Did she tell you that?"

He chuckled and flicked a small green bug that had landed on his leg.

"Yep. On my thirteenth birthday. My birthdays were always hard for her. She talked about her labor and how painful it was. *'Your dad wanted you, he should have carried and given birth to you. Except he couldn't have, because he was weak. All of you men are weak,'* Stephen said her words in a shrill voice that made Liv's heart give a little throb. She wanted to hug him, and almost did, but he'd turned away and his body had grown as rigid as the trees beside them.

"My mother is throwing a costume party on Halloween. Will you come?" he asked.

Liv started at the abrupt change in subject.

"A costume party?"

Stephen nodded, some of the anger draining from his expression.

"She hosts one every year. I've never been allowed to go. I'm usually away at school. I want you to come. We'll wear costumes. She'll never know."

Liv had never been to a costume party. Once in a while, Liv heard her mother reading about dress-up parties in New York City, but such affairs seemed to happen in another world.

"I thought she didn't like people in the house?"

"She doesn't allow *me* to bring people into the house. She has people over all the time. She throws parties, hosts dinners, entertains men."

Liv blinked at him, trying to make sense of this mysterious mother who was throwing parties while the rest of the world ate cabbage and wore shoes that flapped when they walked. And abused her son, let's not forget that, she thought.

"We'll do the curse, too," Stephen added. "I'll invite Veronica. I mean, what better night than Halloween?"

Stephen's face lit at the suggestion, but Liv's heart sank.

"Sure, a costume party and a curse. This will be quite a Halloween."

CHAPTER 28

September 1965
Mack

MACK'S first morning in the Northern Michigan Asylum for the Insane dawned like many others, except his bed was narrow, his room cold, and a large man with a lazy eye and a habit of grinding his teeth woke him repeatedly in the night asking if he'd brought the sandwiches.

Mack had gotten loaded the night before and stumbled into the psychiatric hospital, crooning about his lost love and insisting he be committed.

They complied.

He'd woken once in the night to Corey's ghost hovering over his bed, glaring down at him from empty black eyes. Mack's roommate had howled like he was on fire, and an orderly had rushed in to calm the man. The patient continued to blubber and stare into the corner where Corey had been.

Mack wondered if he'd made a terrible mistake.

Each hour that had passed since his night in the dead man's cabin took him further from the clarity of those moments.

George Corey had told him what he must do, and yet… had the man really been there at all? Or was he merely a hallucination from the fear of being lost in the forest?

"Mack Gallagher?" an orderly with arms bulging beneath his white uniform called across the room. "It's time to meet with your doctor."

Mack followed the man out of the ward and down the hall. They stepped into an office as sterile and bland as Mack's own room.

A man with startling pale blue eyes looked up from his desk.

"Have a seat," the doctor told him.

He was tall and thin, with hair as black as coal and pale, unblemished skin. He reminded Mack, rather uneasily, of Dracula. He'd watched the film with his mother at the marquee as a boy. For weeks after, each time he stood before a mirror, he'd spin around expecting to see the Count standing behind him, clawed hands raised and pointed teeth bared.

Mack glanced at the small gold placard on the man's desk. It read *Dr. Stephen Kaiser, PhD.*

Mack sat in the chair. His head pulsed behind his eyes, and he wanted to crawl into a dark hole and sleep for three days.

"Mr. Gallagher, my name is Dr. Kaiser. I'll be your psychiatrist here at the Northern Michigan Asylum. Explain to me briefly why you committed yourself." Kaiser opened a folder and lifted his pen.

"I have a problem with drinking," Mack told him, pressing a finger hard into his right temple.

Kaiser arched an eyebrow but said nothing.

He asked several other questions, and then slid a series of ink-splattered pages to Mack.

"Tell me what you see on the first page."

"A bird."

"And this one?" Kaiser held up the second page.

"A man riding a bicycle."

"And this." Kaiser held up the third.

"A hag stone," Mack murmured, because that was what he saw in the dark blot with the hole in its center.

Kaiser looked up sharply and gazed at him for several long seconds.

"And this one?" Kaiser asked, pushing the next in front of Mack.

"A mountain."

"I'm curious about your third answer. What is a hag stone?" Kaiser asked, linking his fingers together on his desk.

Mack sighed, clenched his eyes shut against the pounding in his head. The lights were getting to him.

"It's a rock with a hole in the middle."

"That's it? A rock with a hole in it? Interesting. Tell me, where did you hear of such a thing?"

Mack glanced behind him, but the orderly had left. He considered the truth, but he was in an insane asylum. He didn't want the doctor to order electro-shock therapy if Mack suggested he was being haunted.

"My grandmother. She used to collect rocks by the river, and she called the ones with a hole in them hag stones."

Kaiser's eyes remained fixed on Mack.

"Are you in pain, Mack?" Kaiser asked.

"I had a few too many last night. Feels like a horse and buggy ran right across here." Mack drew a line across his forehead.

Kaiser shuffled the ink blots into a folder.

"You're here to dry out," Kaiser said finally. "I'll advise morphine and rest."

Mack studied the man's hands. They were long and slender, his fingernails so pale they almost looked purple.

Kaiser stood and opened the door, sticking his head out.

"Edmund, the patient is ready to return to Ward Six."

~

MACK SAT in a wooden chair near the window. His head throbbed and his guts felt as if someone had reached inside and twisted them in his fist.

Two days without a drink had him ready to keep the ghost, if he could walk into town and get a shot of whiskey.

A man beside him shuffled a deck. Each time he flipped the top card, the ace of spades appeared.

"Ace of spades," the man muttered.

In the corner of the room, a patient gently bumped his head against the wall. When Edmund, the orderly, attempted to steer the patient away, the man screamed as if Edmund had sliced him with a razorblade.

Mack closed his eyes. He needed to retrieve the wooden box and hag stones, which he'd hidden on the grounds before checking himself in to the world's most deranged hotel.

George Corey had been clear about Mack's need of the stones. Without them, he would be unable to recognize George's daughter — and more, the man who murdered him.

"I need some fresh air," Mack told another orderly, Marvin.

Marvin shook his head and gestured at one of the tall windows. Rain gusted against the glass, obscuring the world beyond.

Mack tried to read, attempted a game of checkers with a man who preferred to stack the black and red pieces into little towers and then flick them over yelling, *'Take that, Larry, you one-eyed son of a bitch!'*

Eventually Mack retired to his room.

As he lay on the bed, he noticed a dark figure from the corner of his eye. When he turned, the corner stood empty.

"Maybe I am losing it," he muttered before falling into a fitful sleep.

~

MACK CUPPED the stone in his hand, leaning his forehead against the side of his knuckles as if he had a headache — which, miraculously, he didn't.

Discreetly, he half-opened his hand and peered through the hag stone at the group of doctors gathered in the hallway. He didn't know what he was looking for.

He had asked Corey for names, descriptions, but the man had shaken his head.

"There are rules in death magic. The stones will be your guides."

The men looked ordinary, white coats and grim expressions as they took turns looking through the small viewing window into a newly admitted patient's room.

"Wake up!" a voice shrieked in his ear, and Mack stumbled, almost dropping the stone.

A small, wiry man with a thin black mustache stepped toward him.

"No sleeping in Nam, you stupid shit. You want a bullet in your back?" The man shook his head angrily and stormed past Mack.

Mack gritted his teeth and rested against the wall, stuffing the stone into the pocket of his jeans.

After three days, they'd given him his regular clothes and he'd been surprised how much it elated him to wear his own pants again. Primarily due to his size and the fact that the patient attire clung too tightly to his chest and barely fit over his thighs at all.

Still, most of the shakes had worn off, and the headaches had slowly vanished with the help of the morphine. For the first time in his adult life, Mack was three days sober.

~

MACK SHUFFLED into Dr. Kaiser's office and took a seat.

Kaiser glanced up from a form he'd been reading.

"How are you feeling, Mack? Edmund mentioned the night sweats have subsided?"

Mack nodded, touching the stone in his pocket.

"Today's been better." Mack held up his hand to show the doctor that the tremble in his fingers had calmed. "The truth is, Dr. Kaiser, physically I feel okay, but mentally," he tapped his head, "I want a drink like I've been trapped in the desert for a month. I think about it constantly. I thought maybe you had a book about head stuff, like how to change your mind."

Kaiser stood and turned to the bookshelf behind him, nodding.

"I do have some books about changing habits," Kaiser offered.

As his fingers brushed over the titles, Mack slipped a stone from his pocket and held it to his eye.

A black, swirling mist surrounded the doctor. It seeped out of him and leaked over the walls and floor. The darkness crawled like oozing black vines up the plaster and across the ceiling.

Mack sat frozen, the stone pressed against his eye.

The doctor selected a title and turned abruptly.

Mack jerked his hand from his face, and the stone skittered across the floor.

The doctor seemed not to have noticed.

Mack's hands shook as he took the book from Dr. Kaiser.

Kaiser held the book, studying Mack for a moment before releasing it.

"Guess that tremble is lingering on a bit," Kaiser murmured. "Benzodiazepine should do the trick."

"Sure, doc, whatever you think," Mack told him, forcing an evenness into his voice.

"The mind is very powerful, Mr. Gallagher. To control it takes continued effort, but most all, a desire to change."

Not taking his eyes from Mack, Kaiser sat back in his chair.

"You're free to go," he said.

Mack glanced at the rug where the stone had landed. He could not retrieve it without alerting Dr. Kaiser to its presence.

"Thanks," Mack grumbled and stood.

"WE HAVE A PROBLEM, MACK." The voice roused him from a deep sleep.

It was Kaiser's voice, low and accusatory. The doctor had found the stone and understood the implications. Mack was trapped in the asylum. The man could subject him to anything.

Mack sat up and swung his legs off the bed, ready to fight.

The room stood empty save for Rodney, Mack's roommate, snoring with every exhale.

Mack's own breath rushed out in a whoosh.

Kaiser was not in the room.

~

MACK STEPPED into the canteen and inhaled the rich, spicy smell of chili.

"Chili?" he asked the guy next to him.

"Yep, and they don't skimp on the garlic either." The man rubbed his belly and winked at Mack.

Rufus was on another floor at the asylum. He suffered from seizures and a disease that had him falling asleep at inconvenient times. Mack had first met him when the man slumped over while standing in line at the canteen.

"Out like a light," another patient had told him with a nudge.

On the opposite side of the room, squeezed between two orderlies, stood a small, fine-boned woman with long golden hair and slanted blue eyes. She looked like a grown porcelain doll, and Mack did a double-take when he saw her.

"Who is that?" Mack jostled Rufus, who glanced toward the woman.

"Sophia," Rufus mumbled from the corner of his mouth. Unlike many of the patients in the asylum, Rufus adhered to the same social expectations of the world beyond the asylum. You could talk about people, but you didn't make it obvious. "Sophia the Seer."

Mack looked at her again. The woman watched him. A small frown turned down her pretty mouth, and her forehead was creased with worry. She locked eyes with Mack for an instant and then looked quickly away.

Her expression unsettled him.

Mack got his cup of chili and followed Rufus into the sunny day. They walked back to their building, but Mack turned around again and again, looking for Sophia.

When she stepped from the canteen, the women orderlies stayed close, as if they didn't dare let her out of their sight.

"What's with the guard dogs?" Mack asked.

Rufus shrugged.

"Dr. Kaiser claims she's dangerous. I've only seen her at the canteen twice, and she's been here for years. She's in the high-risk women's ward."

Mack frowned.

"She doesn't look high risk to me."

"They never do," Rufus said matter-of-factly.

"What's with the name? Sophia the Seer?" Mack asked, watching the women orderlies hurry Sophia back to Building Fifty.

Rufus looked sidelong at Mack.

"People say she speaks with the dead."

CHAPTER 29

September 1965
Mack

A TWENTY-DOLLAR BRIBE bought him five minutes with Sophia.

A quickly arranged meeting set up by two orderlies in a seldom used hallway.

"Are you George Corey's daughter?" Mack asked her.

Sophia stood with her arms crossed over her chest. Her eyes looked red and swollen, as if she'd been crying.

"No," she told him.

"Are you okay?" he asked.

She pressed her lips together and gazed past him.

"What do you want?" She sounded weary, as if she barely had the energy to stand, let alone meet him secretly in a hallway.

"Can you see the… the ghost?"

Sophia's eyes stayed fixed beyond him, and then she blinked away. She nodded.

"Does he speak? I'm trying to find his daughter," Mack went on.

"He doesn't speak. He watches you. That is all."

Mack frowned.

"I've been doing what he says, but I need help. His daughter is here in the asylum."

Sophia's eyes brightened.

"There are rumors that a woman is being kept in the attic of the women's cottage."

"In the attic?" Mack grew excited.

A door banged open at the end of the hall, and the orderlies stopped talking.

The woman orderly grabbed Sophia's arm and pulled her roughly away.

"I'm sorry," Mack called out. "I'm sorry you're here."

Sophia offered him a nod; her mouth pressed grimly as they disappeared down the stairs.

~

MACK SAT in a rocking chair that creaked back and forth. The sound grated on him, but he couldn't seem to stop.

He tried to remember that night in Corey's cabin.

You must retrieve an item from the man who murdered me. You will find it near his heart, Corey had told him.

Dr. Kaiser was the murderer. He had to be, but why? The man gave him the creeps, sure, but he couldn't exactly picture him sinking a knife into George Corey's heart. Why had he done it?

Mack imagined Kaiser sitting across from him in his office. In the breast pocket of the doctor's coat, Mack had noticed a small bulge. Perhaps the item Corey meant for him to take was in there. But how could he get it?

Across the room, a man swept a broom over the same spot. Every few minutes he leaned down, brushed his finger along the area, grimaced with disgust, and returned to his sweeping.

At the end of the hall, a door opened and Dr. Kaiser, accompanied by two other doctors, stepped out.

Mack watched them; their heads bowed close together. He had the sense they did not speak of ordinary treatments and patients.

They carried a secret. Their eyes were guarded and their faces pinched when they talked.

Across the room, Frank the Foamer was standing at the wall, tracing circles with his fingers.

Mack had a sudden idea. An immediate pang of guilt rose at the thought, but if it worked...

Frank the Foamer, as other men on the ward called him, was a paranoid schizophrenic. He'd undergone so much electro-shock therapy that he regularly drooled, hence his nickname. He lived in perpetual terror that giant cockroaches were sneaking through the steam pipes into the asylum.

Mack stood and hurried across the room. He paused behind Frank and gently flicked his ear.

"Frank, there's a huge cockroach on your neck," he murmured.

On cue, Frank screamed a blood-curdling cry and spun away from the wall, slapping at his neck, spittle flying from his mouth. As he hyperventilated, his eyes rolled back in his head, and he collapsed to the floor.

The three doctors looked irritated at the disruption, but hurried to the man's aid.

As Frank lay on the ground sputtering and kicking his legs, one doctor leaned down and tried to still him.

"Hold his legs, man," the doctor shouted at Kaiser, who reluctantly dropped to one knee and grabbed one of Frank's legs as Mack held the other.

Mack waited until he felt the pressure building in Frank's calf, and then he let go. The man's leg flung up and kicked Kaiser in the chin.

The doctor cried out, his head jerking back as he fell over backwards.

Mack leaned over him, offering one hand while deftly slipping the other into the man's pocket and closing his fingers on what lay inside.

The doctor was dazed as he stood, tenderly touching the space on his jaw where he'd been struck. He shot a venomous look at the convulsing patient, jerked his hand from Mack's, and stalked down the hallway.

Several orderlies arrived and the other doctors stood, following Kaiser.

Mack shoved the item in his pocket and hurried for the bathroom.

He peeked under stalls but found the bathroom empty.

Closing himself in one of the toilets, Mack pulled out the item he'd stolen from Kaiser's jacket.

He gazed at an antique ring with layers of gold swirls and curves. A small, dark ruby rested in the high center like an eye. Mack tilted the ring, and then pried gently at a small ridge. The top opened to reveal a tiny chamber coated with a fine white powder.

"A poison ring," he whispered.

He knew of poison rings, because his mother used to love medieval history and showed him pictures of poison rings used by people in earlier times. The poison might have been intended for their enemies, or perhaps themselves.

Either way, Mack remembered grimacing at his mother's explanation and shouting 'gross,' before running outside to shoot squirrels with his slingshot.

He didn't understand the ring's purpose in banishing Corey's ghost and rescuing his daughter, but he knew it was the object Corey wanted him to find.

Now he had to find George's daughter.

Mack ate his burger in two bites, and then slipped away from the canteen.

When the orderlies were out of sight, he broke into a run. He ran into the woods, circling back around and gazing at the women's cottage from the trees.

When the lawn was clear, he raced across and plastered himself against the brick exterior.

The door to the cottage swung out, and a nurse hurried through it, tucking her gray hair beneath a white cap.

Mack slipped quickly to the door, sticking his foot in the crack before it closed.

The nurse paused, and Mack caught his breath, searching for the lie that would explain his sneaking into the women's cottage. She bent down, fixed her nylon, and then continued out of sight.

Mack edged through the door and quickly ducked into a dark stairwell. He ran up the stairs, trying to stay light on his feet, a challenge since his feet were huge and his body was anything but light.

The stairs ended at a heavy white door with a grate at the top and bottom.

He peered through the metal screen, but the attic space was filled with walls and angles, making it hard to see what lay deeper in the space.

"I'm looking for George Corey's daughter," he whispered.

No one responded.

As he started to back away, two brown eyes slid before him.

He recoiled, his heart skipping a beat.

"Who are you?" the woman asked.

"Are you George Corey's daughter?" he said.

She didn't answer, so he went on.

"Your father sent me."

Her eyes widened.

"He's alive? George is alive?"

Mack grimaced, wishing he'd not spoken the words.

"No. He's dead. I found his body."

A sharp intake of breath sounded behind the door and her face disappeared from the grate. Mack heard the woman slide down the door and land on the wood with a dull thump.

"I'm sorry," Mack said.

She didn't speak, so he went on.

"George told me to come here. To give you this."

Mack got on his hands and knees and shoved the folded parchment from the wood box beneath the door. He set the ring he'd stolen from Kaiser next to it and slid that in second. For a moment, he heard nothing.

"What's your name?" he asked.

She said nothing, and then: "Liv."

"Liv, I'm Mack. I think you helped save my life a long time ago. I'm here to repay the favor."

She let out a sound like a laugh merging into a sob.

"George wanted me to tell you it wasn't your fault. He said, it's time to make things right."

Something thudded softly against the door, likely her head.

"It's too late to make things right," she muttered.

Mack shook his head.

"It's not, Liv. Okay? Trust me."

"Okay," she said finally. "Thank you."

"Do you know what to do with those things?" Mack asked. "The ring and the stuff in the paper?"

"Yes."

Mack stood, put a hand to the door and wished he could say something more to ease her apparent grief.

"Goodbye, Liv," he whispered, and slipped back down the stairs.

CHAPTER 30

September 1965
Liv

LIV LAY CURLED on her side. She'd dreamed vividly the night before. Not prophetic dreams, but the textured dreams of childhood memory.

In her dreams, she and Stephen ran barefoot through the woods, laughter ringing out as they escaped from Murphy's orchard with armloads of apples. Liv had never stolen food. Despite her family's poverty, she understood the farmers needed every apple they grew.

But Ben Murphy was a mean man who threw the fruit and vegetables he grew away when the families he sold them to were short of money, or if he perceived one of them to be acting out of line. The month before, he'd taken a basket of apples meant for the Holtz's, a family with six kids who lived in a shack not far from Liv's, and dumped it in the river when their oldest boy mentioned he didn't want to go off to war.

Liv and Stephen had stolen enough apples to share with the Holtz kids, and a few for themselves too.

When Liv woke to the drab light of early morning, she could still smell the ripe apples she and Stephen had carried in their arms.

Across the room, the metal grate slid open.

Liv watched Stephen's slender hands push a tray of food into the attic.

"How are you sleeping, Liv? The bats aren't giving you trouble, are they?"

She could not tell if he meant the comment cruelly, but what difference did it make?

She stood and shuffled to the food, her back aching from the thin cot.

"Tell me how it works, Liv," Stephen continued.

He pushed something against the grate, and she saw the hag stone she wore around her neck. He must have taken it the night he abducted her.

He swung it back and forth like a pendulum.

Liv took a bite of soggy cereal, watching the white stone sway from side to side.

"I keep trying to see," he continued. "But there's nothing there. I mean, nothing extraordinary. Do you remember the first time I looked through the stone, Liv? The world shifted. I saw energy pouring out of everything, light and dark and a thousand colors I didn't know existed. Now, there's nothing. Not so much as a speck of dust drifting in the sun."

Liv did remember that day. Those memories felt like impostors. They appeared to portray a friendship, a growing love, when really, they were merely a foundation upon which to build a house of horror.

"You'll never be able to see, Stephen. You're weak. You've always been weak," she fumed, biting back tears.

Stephen said nothing, but the hag stone disappeared from the grate.

"Maybe I should just drop it on the floor and crush it beneath my shoe," he told her, tapping the stone against the cement floor.

Liv looked away. She didn't fear his threat. Stephen coveted magical items more than anything else in the world. He was a slave to his desire for such things.

"Go ahead," she muttered. "If I look through it, I only see darkness."

"You're lying to me, Liv. Lying is my pet peeve. You should know I'm not below making you talk. And these days — well, let's just say I have new instruments at my disposal."

"You're sick, Stephen. All those years ago it wasn't your fault, but now..." she trailed off.

His voice came again, closer, as if he'd pressed his mouth to the grate.

"You know what I think, Liv? I think you're angry that I did it. I became what George envisioned for you. I am the master of my universe. I have access to power you can't even dream of."

Liv sat up. She took the folded parchment Mack had slipped beneath the door. It contained a silty black powder.

"The nightmare has gone on long enough, Stephen. It's time to wake up," she said, and she poured the powder into her hand. Leaning down, she blew it through the grate.

She heard the sharp intake of his breath, and then his cough.

He scrambled away from the door and the cough continued.

He swore, and she imagined him brushing at the powder clinging to his eyelashes and coating the fine hairs in his nose.

"What was that? What did you do?" he hissed between coughs, but she didn't reply and after another minute, she heard the clap of his footfalls as he receded down the stairs.

~

Stephen

Stephen washed his face, leaning into the mirror and searching for the remaining particles of black dust.

His nose and throat burned from the silty powder. He'd breathed it deeply and knew he could not remove it from his bloodstream. It had traveled into his nose. But he'd stripped Liv before putting her in the straitjacket that first night. He'd emptied her pockets and taken the hag stone necklace.

She didn't have the powder, so where had it come from? Something she'd concocted in the attic. A mixture of dust and bat droppings, meant to unnerve him?

He glanced at his watch and swore under his breath.

He had to meet Dr. Strickland in twenty minutes.

The door swung open into the bathroom.

"Occupied," he snarled, but when he glanced behind him, no one stood in the doorway. The door was firmly closed.

Dabbing his face with a towel, he cast a final glance in the mirror and froze.

George Corey stood behind him in the bathroom. Bones poked through his yellowing flesh. His eyes blazed black and furious. The man snatched the knife embedded in his chest, reached back, and flung it at Stephen.

Stephen yelped and dove sideways, crashing into the little wooden table stacked with washcloths and soaps. He landed hard on his side, twisting around to face the man and holding up his hands to block the knife attack.

He wheezed; his breath painful beneath what were surely bruised ribs.

No knife fell upon him.

George Corey did not occupy the space at all.

Stephen held his aching side and climbed slowly to his feet.

Liv

THE CROW LANDED next to Liv, perching on the brass of her bed frame. She held out a sliver of bread, and he nipped it from her fingers.

Beside her on the white sheet sat the poison ring Mack had

retrieved. She slid her pinkie into the ring and lifted it up, tilting it to and fro in the light that filtered through the small windows near the floor of the attic.

The musty room grew thick and warm as she sat, but when she tried to walk to the window, her legs wobbled beneath her. She sagged onto the bed, and the crow took flight, soaring around the shadowy ceiling before landing on a wood beam above.

She lifted her hand and watched it weave and bob, blurring and refocusing.

"He drugged me," she croaked, looking toward the bowl of applesauce. She had not intended to eat it, but her stomach's rumblings had gotten the best of her.

The room grew fuzzy and indistinct.

The poison ring fell from her pinkie and clattered to the floor. She watched the dark ruby fade into darkness.

~

Stephen

Stephen sat impatiently in an overly soft chair in Dr. Strickland's sitting room.

The man watched him through clouded, yellow eyes.

"I'm hardly a young man anymore," Strickland wheezed, drawing an oxygen mask to his face and taking several raspy puffs of air. "But the other doctors in the brotherhood find you difficult to speak with, Stephen. You're bitter and cruel. They fear your retaliation if they speak up."

Stephen regarded Dr. Strickland.

The man who'd once towered over patients and doctors alike had shrunken. His scalp was a map of age spots, mottled with sparse gray hair.

He'd brought Stephen into the brotherhood, but his power had drained years earlier. He no longer attended meetings, but wasted the remaining years of his life being fawned over by his overbearing wife and grown children, all scrabbling for the inheritance he would leave in his wake.

"Have you ever watched ants, Dr. Kaiser?" Strickland hunched forward and seized a plastic box with his arthritic hands.

Stephen saw ants milling through the tiny channels encased in plastic.

"They kill their ill counterparts. They must, you see, in order to preserve the colony. If a diseased ant is allowed to spread his sickness, they all will die." Strickland shook the plastic frame before returning it to his table.

He reached a shaky hand to a half-cigar resting in a gold flecked ash tray. He lit the cigar and blew a plume of foul-smelling smoke in Stephen's direction.

Disgusted, Stephen waved the smoke away. The effort of breathing pained him, and he tried to hide his discomfort from the old man.

"Pity me, do you?" Strickland barked a laugh that betrayed his diseased lungs. "It is I who pities you, Stephen Kaiser. I've seen your secrets, after all."

Strickland cackled and took another pull on his cigar before blotting it out in a crystal ashtray shaped like a feather.

Stephen glared at the doctor, refusing to speak. The man had no control over him anymore.

"You've got a woman locked in the attic of the women's cottage," Strickland huffed, leaning his head back against his reclining chair. "Get her out, and soon, or the brotherhood will dispose of her for you. And Stephen, do not doubt their swift justice. If they sense weakness in the colony, they will root it out and destroy it."

~

STEPHEN BROODED over the doctor's words as he drove back to the asylum.

He parked and walked to the women's cottage, nodding at nurses and orderlies, but grimly ignoring anyone who spoke to him.

His nurse, Alice, waited by the door, the medical supplies he'd requested clutched in her bony hands.

"Dr. Kaiser," she said, tilting her head toward him.

"Alice," he responded, gesturing to her as he took the stairs to the attic.

She struggled to keep up as he ascended. Alice was a large-boned woman with a penchant for sweets and a hard, almost hateful opinion of the patients at the Northern Michigan Asylum. She believed wholly in Dr. Kaiser's work and never questioned his authority. She was the kind of nurse who took her doctor's secrets to the grave.

Kaiser also suspected that Alice was in love with him, whatever strange series of emotions love included for a woman who spent her days filling her belly with chocolate and delighting in administering cold baths and electro-shock therapy to her patients.

Stephen peered through the grate to ensure that Liv slept before turning the key and pushing open the door.

Liv

LIV WOKE to find Stephen had bound her to the bed. Leather straps cut into the skin on her forearms and shins.

She dug her fingernails into the mattress and strained upward. The leather straps did not budge.

"You've really come into yourself, Liv. I keep marveling at how grown up you are," Stephen said as he moved around her bed, smiling as if he'd popped in to visit an old friend.

"Stephen. What happened to George?"

The words tumbled out.

The night before, the question had rolled in her head like a marble caught in a sieve. And she didn't need to ask the question. She knew. She'd known before she left Boston. She'd known the moment the little boy said *the man in the hole*. George had called her home because he was dead. The curse had come full circle. A life for a life.

Stephen shook his head.

"George? I haven't seen him in ages."

"Is that how you do it, Stephen? Block what you've done? Do you lock it in a trunk and throw away the key?"

Stephen stiffened, and the nurse, Alice, touched his arm tenderly.

Liv did not like the nurse. Her hands were cruel. She did not touch, but poked, and did so to cause pain.

"Livvy," he started.

"Don't call me that," she snarled.

"Don't make this harder than it has to be."

She laughed.

"And to think I wanted to protect you. I sacrificed everything for you, Stephen. Everything."

Stephen shook his head sadly.

"I did hear about your mother, Liv. I was sorry to hear. Cancer, of all things. And she was hardly in a position to afford treatment."

Liv's stomach dropped, and her lungs seemed to deflate within her body.

"My mother?" she whispered.

Stephen widened his eyes in mock surprise.

"You didn't know?" He slapped a palm against his forehead. "I'm sorry, Liv. That was callous of me."

The fight seemed to drain from her body. She let her arms relax against the restraints. When the nurse held up a syringe and lightly depressed it, sending a squirt of clear liquid into the air, Liv concentrated on the needle.

"Sedate her, Doctor?"

"Yes." Stephen put a hand on her forehead. "Poor dear needs a rest." He turned his attention to Liv. "We're transporting you today, Liv. You'll get much better treatment once we've committed you."

CHAPTER 31

September 1965
Jesse

JESSE CLOSED the closet door in Stephen Kaiser's room, unwilling to look at the trunk as he searched the boy's room.

He opened drawers, sifting through pants and socks. He peeked between books and flipped open their covers, searching for some evidence that might reveal who lay inside the trunk.

When he lifted the boy's mattress, he spotted a faded leather folder.

He opened it, and a single page drifted out and landed on the floor.

At the top in bold cursive, he read: *Curse of the Night Haunts.*

Beneath the title, someone had written a series of materials including bat guano, valerian, two feathers from the tail of a hawk, a piece of birch bark, and an item belonging to the accursed.

Instructions followed:

The stave must be written in blood from the left thumb of the caster of the curse, on a night when the moon is between three-quarters and full. To draw the stave, the caster must dip the hawk's feather into the blood, and print the symbol on the birch bark. Both feathers must be used. Dip the bloodied thumb in a mixture of the guano and valerian, and place three thumb prints beneath the stave. Wrap the stave with a personal item, which belongs to the accursed and contains their scent. The stave must be handed to the recipient from the castor's left hand, the blood hand, and the gift must be accepted freely.

In the bottom corner of the paper, Jesse's eyes flicked over a name, and he froze.

Veronica, it said in small, dark cursive.

He noted two different styles of handwriting. One was dark, deep cursive - the writing of an educated person. The writer seemed to press hard, leaving indents beneath his words.

The second set of writing was hardly legible. Big awkward letters with arrows and symbols. This was the person who knew the spell. They were offering deeper insights into how to perform it.

Jesse returned to the boy's bureau and dug through his undergarments. He pulled out the picture he'd found days earlier.

The boy, he assumed was Stephen Kaiser, stood next to a young woman with tangled blonde hair. She held a tall walking stick in her hand. They were at odds, these two, an unlikely friendship, and yet he could see they were friends. They leaned into each other as they stood, a warmth, even an intimacy jumping off the page.

On the back of the photo written in black cursive he read: Stephen and Liv, August 1945.

A leather bag hung over the girl's shoulder with feathers sticking out. They were not hawk's feathers, more like a crow's. They were long and black.

Still, he felt sure the spell contained the writing of these two young people.

A noise from within the closet startled him, and he dropped the photograph. It drifted down, seemed to catch a breeze and slipped beneath the closet door.

He had no reason to retrieve it. No further clues could be discovered in the young faces of Stephen and Liv, but he shuffled forward just the same.

With a deep breath that he hoped might still the turmoil within him, he pulled open the closet door.

The trunk sat unmoving, the lid ajar, revealing only a crevice of darkness. A dry rustling seemed to come from within the chest.

Something pale reached from the dark opening.

"Dear God, no…" he breathed as a slender hand slid from the truck and clutched the edge, as if the person inside intended to push herself up and step from the chest.

Jesse blundered backwards. His legs hit the bed, and he leapt away as if the wood frame might burn him. He started for the door, made it as far as the hallway, and then stopped.

"She's dead," he whispered, and the thickness - the stifling warmth that left him struggling for breath — loosened and scattered.

He walked back into the room and stared at the chest exposed in the closet. The lid was closed, and no cadaverous hand reached out. A skeleton lay in the chest, not a flesh-and-blood woman with a solid hand adorned with glittering rings.

He did not know what lay between the realms of God and man, but something existed, something that could conjure a solid hand from the emptiness. Something that wanted him, Jesse Kaminski, to take notice.

JESSE HAD NOT INTENDED to take the money, but the woman in the trunk had invaded his brain like a cancer, and it seemed to be spreading fast.

For the first time since his wife and son died, he had a purpose, and if he was going to follow it to its conclusion, he needed wheels. He'd also spent the better part of the night convincing himself that the woman wanted him to take the money. Could it have been sheer chance that it had been left behind? No, he decided, some series of events put the money in that drawer, so that someday justice could be delivered for the dead woman.

He bought a used Chevy for two hundred dollars from a car lot decorated with bright red flags.

Afterward, he pulled into Quarry's Pub.

Jesse slid onto a barstool and offered a half-wave to the bartender.

"Back for more, eh?" the bartender asked, wiping spilled beer from the counter in front of Jesse.

Jesse nodded.

"Old-fashioned?" the bartender asked.

"Yeah, thanks."

The same drunk Jesse had encountered days earlier sat two stools away. He offered Jesse a bleary look and a grin.

"Still fixin' to buy that ol' house in the woods?" the man asked.

Jesse shrugged, shook the ice cubes in his glass and took a sip.

"Maybe. Course, I'd have to track down the owners first, and that's working out to be a mighty pain in the backside."

The bartender refilled Bart's glass.

"I was asking around about the Kaisers and heard a strange tale about another girl who went missing around the same time. Veronica Medawar?" Jesse asked.

The bartender frowned and shook his head.

"Terrible tragedy right there. She up and disappeared on Halloween night, her senior year of high school. I was a few years graduated by then, but the town was abuzz over that girl's disappearance."

"No one knows what happened to her?"

"The family insisted somebody took her, but the police speculated she ended up in the Dead Stream. It's fast-moving and if you fall in, especially at night, you're a goner."

"But they never found her body?"

"She wouldn't be the first to go into that river and disappear," Punchie admitted.

The drunk leaned over.

"Lost two cousins to that river ma 'self. Brothers by the names of Charlie and Grady. Went fishin' one day and never came back.

They found Charlie's body tangled in a tree about three miles from where the boys went in, but never a trace of Grady."

Jesse thought of the Dead Stream. He hadn't swam in it, but he found it hard to believe the current could have taken so many lives.

"Why would the girl be near the river on Halloween?" he asked.

The bartender spoke with his back turned.

"Kids followed the river all the time. It was faster than the road. Bonfires in the woods, that kind of thing. She was all dressed up like she was going to a fancy party. Some people suspect she was meeting a boy. That's just talk, though. Nobody knows."

"Is it still an open case?" Jesse asked.

Bart spurted beer and guffawed.

"What do you think this is, New York City? We don't have no detectives in Gaylord. And ain't no big city hotshots comin' in here to dig a river for a girl disappeared twenty years ago. No sir, it ain't an open case."

The bartender rolled his eyes at the man.

"I'd guess they'll call it open until that girl's body shows up. If it ever does."

"But the Kaiser boy and his friend disappeared then, too?"

The bartender gave him a funny look and shook his head.

"The Kaiser kid was already off to college by then. His little girlfriend probably run off with him. I've got to wonder at your interest in all this?"

Jesse smiled and finished his drink.

"I told ya before, I'm a curious guy."

"How curious is ya?" Bart asked, leaning heavily toward Jesse and giving him a wink. "That right there is the Medawar girl's big brother." He hooked a thumb toward a man sitting alone at a small table.

Jesse recognized the cook from The Silver Spoon Diner.

"What's he drinking?" he asked the bartender.

"Bud," Punchie told him, "but I don't advise goin' over and diggin' all this up 'cause you're curious. That's a tormented man, right there. He's liable to give ya a fist in the mouth for your troubles."

"I'll take a Bud and another old-fashioned," Jesse said, standing up.

He took the drinks and ambled over to the man who sat half-watching a baseball game on a television perched in the corner.

"Buy ya a drink?" Jesse asked, offering the beer.

The man looked at it suspiciously, shooting a glance toward Punchie, who nodded at him.

"Sure," he grumbled and downed the rest of his own beer before accepting the one in Jesse's hand.

"Mind if I sit?" Jesse asked, pulling back a chair.

The man sighed and shrugged.

"I don't own the place."

"I'm Jesse Kaminski," Jesse told him, offering a hand which the man didn't shake. "I'm in town on business."

"I seen you around," the man told him, continuing to watch the game.

"I noticed the missing poster for your sister, Veronica at your diner."

The man's eyes swiveled back around to Jesse, and Jesse knew he was the kind of guy who might punch a man in the face. His eyes looked stormy and unforgiving.

Jesse chose his next words carefully.

"My dad was a private eye. He's dead and gone now, but I caught the same bug, so to speak. It's not my occupation. No, I'm a car man, but when I hear about certain cases, the need to look deeper starts gnawing away at me."

Jesse's dad was not a private detective, but his dad's best friend had been. The man used to regale Jesse and his dad with stories of spying on men's wives or tracking drug dealers around town. And once, just once, the man helped solve a murder case. An old woman had been robbed and beaten in a Detroit alley. The woman's son hired the private investigator when the police couldn't turn up a suspect. The P.I. had spent a month getting close to the street kids, until one day they finally blurted out that one of the kid's fathers had done the deed.

The man at the table scowled at Jesse, holding his glass of beer in both hands. His jaw was set, and Jesse could see the throb of a vein pulsing in the man's forehead.

"Veronica's been gone twenty years. You think you're gonna blow into town, an outsider, and know somethin' we don't? See somethin' we can't? What are you after, chump? Money? Piss off."

The man turned back to the game.

Jesse was not afraid of taking a pounding. His dad died when Jesse was twelve. He'd learned to be scrappy in the orphanages, and later on the street. He could hold his own. Not that he wanted to fight the man. He didn't, but he wasn't afraid to. Sometimes a knock to the head was the only way a man heard sense.

Jesse drained his glass and slammed it on the table. He laughed and shook his head.

"Typical small-town bullshit," he chided. "If you'd rather go to your grave not knowing, that's your choice."

Jesse stood and walked from the bar. He felt the man's eyes on him as he pushed through the swinging door into the cool September night.

He turned and started down the road, slowing when he heard the door to the bar shove open and the slap of footsteps on the concrete.

He braced to get hit from behind, but the man didn't shove him.

"Wait a sec," the man said. He put a hand on Jesse's shoulder. Jesse didn't flinch.

"Like I said before," Jesse told him, extending a hand. "I'm Jesse Kaminski."

The man nodded and took Jesse's hand.

"Tony Medawar. I shouldn't have cold-shouldered you. I had a long day at the diner, and..." He tensed and looked at the starry sky. "This time of year is fucked for me. Twenty years, and I'm still..." He didn't finish, couldn't finish, Jesse thought as he heard the thickness enter Tony's voice.

"I get it, man," Jesse told him. "It's okay."

"Can I make ya a burger?" Tony gestured to the Silver Spoon Diner a few blocks in the other direction.

"Yeah, sure."

"So how do we do this?" Tony asked. "My parents talked to a private dick back in the '40s, but he never found a thing and they paid through the nose for him."

"For starters, I'm not interested in money. Like I said, I'm a car man. This is something I'm interested in because... well, it's the right thing, is all. Your sister's picture has stuck with me. But I need to know the facts. Everything you can tell me about the night Veronica disappeared."

Jesse took a bite of his burger as Tony sat on a barstool, squinting at the tiny red and gold flecks on the countertop.

"It was Halloween 1945. I graduated the year before, and I was working for my old man. He owned a shoe store. I didn't buy this place until '55. I was still living at home, saving for a place and what-not. I remember getting home from work that afternoon, and I could hear the record player on in Veronica's room. My ma told me she'd been in there for an hour doing God knows what. She had 'Chattanooga Choo-Choo' playing on the record player, and now and then you'd hear her stomping like she was up there dancing." Tony laughed and slapped the counter. "Damn, she could dance. She really could. Swing, jive, jitterbug, you name it and Veronica could do it."

Tony took a sip of the root beer float he'd made. "These take me back," he said. "Root beer floats after high school dances. But Veronica is frozen there, you know? She's trapped in 1945. She never got married, had kids. My Katie looks a lot like her." Tony inclined his head toward the missing poster pinned to the corkboard.

Jesse looked at the girl's dark curls and thought again of the spirals of hair in the trunk.

"I didn't see her leave," Tony admitted. "She was actin' sneaky that night. Usually, she came down and pranced around, showed off her outfit, had my ma fussing with her hair and makeup. My dad spotted her as she went down the walk. She was wearing a big purple dress. The formal kind. Not a Halloween costume, but he thought maybe the theme was princesses or some such thing."

"And no one knew where she was going? Not your parents?"

"Not a soul," Tony answered. "No one in our family and none of her friends, and that was the really strange thing. She told her friends everything. She had a tight little group of girls. Typical teen girls - bossy and gossipy, but Veronica was a good girl. She was real pretty and popular. She was the girl everyone wanted to be. But she didn't use a bathroom without her girlfriends. When we started calling the next day, none of them knew where Veronica went on Halloween. It was a big secret. She told them they'd know soon enough. Her girlfriends all went to a costume party at this kid Brandon Maloney's house. Half the senior class was there, but not Veronica. She had told them the day before Halloween that she had other plans, but she couldn't tell them about it until after."

Jesse frowned, listening closely and thinking about the spell. Had something gone wrong that night? Had Stephen Kaiser and Liv lured Veronica to the house to curse her and somehow, she ended up dead?

"Tony, was Veronica friends with a boy named Stephen Kaiser?"

Tony scrunched his brow, and then shook his head.

"Nah. I remember him vaguely. The rich kid whose father hung himself. His mom was a real Betty, but I only saw her around town a few times. He went to boarding school, so he didn't exactly chum around with the local kids."

"Except I heard he was friends with a girl named Liv."

Tony scratched his chin.

"Yeah, Liv Hart. I might have seen them around town a time or two. She was a ragamuffin, that one. I think Veronica and her friends gave her a hard time, but it was just kids' stuff."

"Gave her a hard time?"

Tony shrugged.

"Oh, you know, teased her because she was poor, probably said stuff about never brushing her hair. I mean, come on, you should have seen the girl. She looked like wolves had raised her. Her sister lives in town, though, and she's as sweet as ice cream. Arlene Hester. But I'm not sure what this has to do with Veronica?"

Jesse shook his head.

"It probably doesn't, but someone mentioned Stephen Kaiser left town around the same time, so I wanted to ask."

"You think they ran off together?" Tony asked, a hopeful tinge in his voice. "I'd have a half a mind to slap her upside the head if that were true, but man, I wish it were. We had a funeral for her in 1955, on the ten-year anniversary. My parents have burial plots at Pine Grove Cemetery, and they wanted their daughter beside them when the time came. We buried a casket with her favorite dress and a stuffed bear she'd had since she was a baby. One of the worst days of my life," he muttered, and the bit of hope in his voice had soured.

"Are your parents still alive?" Jesse asked.

"My mom is," Tony said. "My dad died three years ago, heart attack. He knows now. Sometimes I think about that. One way or another, he knows."

CHAPTER 32

September 1945
Liv

GEORGE SET a plate in front of her. A bloody organ lay in the center of the tin plate.

"The boar's heart. Eat it, Volva. You will need his courage."

Liv shook her head.

She had eaten the hearts of many things. George had been feeding her the organs of animals since she was a child, but usually he prepared a soup or made it palatable in some way. This one was raw and cold.

"I've been having dreams, child."

George faced her across the table.

She'd returned his book to the hollow beneath the floor, but it seemed to pulse with energy. Could George sense it?

"What kind of dreams?" she asked, pushing the heart around on the plate. Her stomach gurgled at the sight.

"Dark spirits are courting you, Volva. Eat the heart."

"No, I can't. I'll get sick."

George pushed the plate closer.

"There are trials ahead for you, my child. Eat the heart."

She saw the set of his jaw, the hard-flinty edge in his eyes. Holding her breath, she lifted the heart and took a bite. Blood squirted into her mouth and she gagged, dropping the heart and pushing away from the table.

"No, I can't. I'm not going to."

She grabbed a rag from the basin and wiped at her face.

The heart lay in the center of the table.

"How will you have the strength to perform a curse without courage, Volva? Hmm…?"

He watched her impassively.

Liv glanced toward his bed, where the book of spells lay beneath the floorboards.

"Did you think I wouldn't know? Did you think I didn't know days before you took it?"

"Stephen wanted to see it. That's all. We're not going to curse anyone, George. I swear. I-"

He held up a hand, but it was the expression of disappointment in his face that silenced her.

George shook his head.

"The old ways will protect you, Volva. But if you turn away from them, if you cannot prostrate yourself at the feet of the wise ones…" He trailed off. He took her seat at the table and pulled the plate over, cutting a bite from the organ and putting it into his mouth.

They did not speak as he ate. When he finished, Liv cleaned his plate and returned it to the cupboard.

"We will celebrate the winter nights next week."

Liv nodded, gazing through the window toward trees shifting from green to gold.

Stephen would leave for school soon. Her gut ached at the thought. She imagined the spells in George's book. There were ways to make him stay, but she'd never dare.

LIV STUMBLED when she saw them - Stephen and Veronica sitting together at the Silver Spoon Diner.

The toe of her worn shoe caught on the edge of the sidewalk and she plunged forward, landing on her hands and knees. Pain streaked through her limbs, and she climbed gingerly to her feet. Her knees were scraped and bloody; her hands matched. She brushed the tiny stones embedded in her palms back to the ground, and then looked again at the window.

Stephen and Veronica watched her, their half-empty cream sodas sitting before them on the table.

Veronica's face melted with delight. Liv could see the bob of her dark head as she laughed. Stephen did not smile, his expression pitying, but he did not come to her aid.

Stephen had left for school two weeks before.

And now, here he sat with Veronica.

Liv's face grew hot, and she wanted to turn and run back the way she'd come, but she didn't. Tilting her chin up, the abrasions on her knees throbbing each time she bent her legs, she walked down the street. Tears threatened, but she held them back.

She imagined sitting with George in the peaceful quiet of the Stoneroot Forest. He often spoke of emotion as a spirit who crept into the body and stole reason. The spirit rejoiced in chaos. If Liv cried, the spirit would celebrate and return again to steal her power.

She stopped at the little schoolhouse Arlene attended.

Her sister squealed and jumped from the circle of children when she saw Liv. She raced across the yard and crashed into her legs.

"Whoa," Liv said, wincing. "How was your day, peanut?" She patted her sister's blonde curls.

"Are you hurt, Livvy?' Arlene asked, touching a finger to Liv's bloody knee.

"Just a scratch," Liv assured her, though the pain in her heart felt much deeper.

She steered the little girl toward home.

"Did you know that Mrs. Bartleby's son lost his leg in France in the War to End All Wars?" Arlene chirped. "He's a hero. All the kids think so. And he has twin sons that are only a year younger than me. Funny they called it the War to End all Wars because we're at war again."

Arlene prattled on as they took the dusty two-mile walk home.

Liv only half-listened. She couldn't erase the image of Stephen and Veronica together at the diner. Each time she pictured them, her stomach grew tight.

~

"HEY!" Liv heard Stephen's call as he stripped off his clothes and ran down the dock.

He dove into the lake and barely rippled the water.

Liv swam away. She reached the weedy shore and climbed out. By the time his head broke the surface, she'd shuffled into her clothes and shoved her wet feet into her shoes.

"Hey! Where are you going?" he asked.

She didn't answer, but turned and walked into the woods. She fanned her shirt away from her clammy skin. It wouldn't dry anytime soon. She hadn't even shaken off before putting her clothes on.

"Liv! Wait up." Stephen ran up beside her, barefoot and wearing only his Jockey shorts.

Liv didn't look at him. The tears she'd felt at the cafe the day before struggled up from her belly. They wanted to pour forth. She stuffed them deeper.

"Liv, stop!" He grabbed her arm and tugged her to face him.

She saw hurt and confusion in his pale blue eyes. She wondered what he saw in her own.

"Why are you upset, Liv?"

She swallowed and jerked her shoulder back, pulling her arm out of his grasp.

She opened her mouth, and a little sob fell out. It seemed to flop on the forest floor between them, limp and strange.

She closed her eyes and tried again.

"You were with her. With Veronica."

When she opened her eyes, Stephen had a funny little smile on his face.

"Of course I was, Liv," he said. "It's all part of the plan. How are we going to kill her if we don't befriend her first?"

"Damn it, Stephen!" she cried. "We're not killing her. It's all a joke. I saw her. She was laughing at me."

Liv turned, but Stephen grabbed her again. His hand was hot and slick in her own. Liv's heart pummeled against her rib cage. There was something different in the touch, something softer.

When he pulled her to face him, she saw a flush in his cheeks.

"Liv," he murmured. "I invited Veronica to the diner to ask her to the Halloween party. I would never go out with her. I hate her. I hate her for you."

He stepped closer to Liv. His breath pushed hot against her cheek. His hand slid from her wrist to her upper arm. If he moved any closer, her breasts would press against him.

His eyes were so pale now, a blue that reminded her of stones in the river, polished nearly white but still holding a remnant of their original color.

He leaned in, his mouth parted, and she jerked back, stumbling. She tripped over a root and landed hard on her butt.

Without a word, she jumped up and ran away from him into the forest.

She didn't stop running until she reached the railroad tracks near the shacks.

Only then did she pause and bend over. Her stomach cramped, and she thought she might throw up. After a few breaths, the feeling passed.

Her body buzzed with the sensation of his touch, and too with the shame of her reaction. She'd run away. She'd never kissed a boy.

Well, twice little Henry Pools, who lived in a house near hers as a child, had kissed her, but both times she's slugged him in the arm and told him if he ever did it again, he'd have a black eye to show for it.

But Stephen was different. He was eighteen, on the cusp of being a man, and she was seventeen, almost a woman.

Liv's mother had tried to tell her as much more than once. She'd fussed with her hair or looked at Liv's shabby clothes and insisted she'd make her new ones as soon as they could afford it. They never could, and Liv had never cared. Except now as she looked down at the frayed men's shirt, her nipples poking through the fabric, she felt horribly plain. Worse than plain.

Veronica was the kind of girl Stephen was meant to go steady with. Veronica with her coiffed chocolate curls and her pouty red lips.

Liv's only defining trait was George, and he was a secret. The volva existed in the Stoneroot Forest. Only there did Liv feel special.

~

THE NEXT DAY, Stephen found her at the pond.

He sat heavily on the dock.

Liv's feet dangled in the water and she watched a school of minnows nipping at her toes.

"Have you forgiven me yet?" he asked, holding out a piece of chocolate.

She took the chocolate and ate it in one bite, ignoring the flicker in her belly as his hand grazed hers.

"Now I have," she laughed.

He nudged her with an elbow.

"I've missed you, Liv. It's been weird not seeing you every day."

"For me too. How's college?" She hated that Stephen had left for school. She hated returning to her own school and trudging through the halls each day feeling more alone than ever, but she said none of those things.

"It's great. My roommate is a total cold fish, but I'm swamped with studies, so I'm not exactly looking for a pal. Plus, I've been working on our curse. Halloween can't come soon enough."

Liv looked at him sideways.

"Working on it?"

Yeah, practicing. We don't want to screw it up and give her sweet dreams by accident."

Liv forced a laugh but felt no humor as she envisioned Veronica. The girl had been watching her since school started. Every time Liv passed her, Veronica whispered to one of her girlfriends, and they broke into peals of laughter.

"I won't see you the weekend before Halloween," Liv told him. We're celebrating Vetrnaetr, winter nights."

"Vetra-nater?" he asked, sounding it out slowly.

"It's an old Norse holiday. We give thanks for summer, prepare for winter, that kind of thing."

"So, tell me about it."

Stephen reclined on the dock, bending his knees. Liv laid beside him, noticing the warmth of his arm pressed against hers.

She gazed into the blue sky thick with wooly clouds and sighed, feeling happier than she had in weeks.

"We feast on winter nights," Liv murmured, putting a hand on her belly. "George prepares roast deer and hog, sweet apples, and mashed yams. We drink honey mead. It's the only night all year that George drinks alcohol. And then we stay up late and tell stories by the fire. Our holiday is small compared to the winter nights in Norway. His entire village came together in a big mead hall. There was barely room to rest your hands, the tables were so filled with food. In George's little village, everyone practiced seidr, or Norse magic, but Amma was their primary Volva. She was the mother of the mountain on their island. She spoke during winter nights and then chose the storytellers. They feasted until dawn, and then slept the following day."

Stephen rolled to his side.

"Why did George leave Norway? It seems like he was happy there. Why would he come here?" Stephen wondered.

Liv watched the clouds and thought of George's explanation for why he'd left.

"He was called," Liv murmured. "One morning he went to the

ocean to fetch crabs, and the ocean told him he would sail to America."

Stephen cocked an eyebrow.

"For what, though? To live in a cabin in the woods?"

Liv traced the outline of a cloud shaped like an arrow with her finger.

"To create me," she whispered.

CHAPTER 33

September 1965
Liv

"I've decided what I have to do, Liv. I have to keep you alive, but I can't risk your destroying all that I've created."

Liv listened, chin resting on her chest, a line of saliva dripping from the corner of her mouth.

Her brain drifted somewhere in the space above her neck. A big cottony thing, unable to follow complex sentences.

"Meet me at the pond?" she asked, trying to lift her gaze, but her head, despite its lightness, stayed put. She tried again, but managed only to crane her eyes upward and find Stephen sitting on a wooden chair beneath a too-bright light.

He studied her; his mouth turned down.

"Shall I read your fortune, Stephen?" she asked, flopping her head to the side and resting her bleary eyes on his face.

He narrowed his eyes.

"I don't have time for children's games."

She laughed and her eyes rolled back in her head.

"You're going to lose her, Stephen."

Who?" he asked, a mixture of irritation and curiosity in his voice.

"The woman who speaks with ghosts."

Stephen stiffened.

"And then," Liv babbled, "you're going to lose yourself."

She laughed a loud, shocking laugh that made Stephen drop the vial of medicine clutched in his hand.

It shattered on the floor, but he didn't pick it up.

The door cracked open behind him.

"Dr. Kaiser?" A man spoke, and Liv tried to focus on the figure who stepped into the room.

"Is this your-"

But Stephen cut him off.

"Get out, get out!" he screeched and shoved the doctor back out the door.

He fumbled across the metal table, sending bottles and vials skidding to the floor. He plunged a syringe into a glass tube and then stuck it into Liv's neck.

"I can make you sleep forever if I want, Liv. How would you like that?" He put a hand to his temple.

Liv saw the red blood vessels running through the whites of his eyes, the deep creases in his forehead.

She struggled to keep her eyes open, to watch his unraveling, but his drugs worked quickly. She drifted down.

~

MACK

"CAN I get a pass to go outdoors?" Mack tapped Edmund, the regular orderly in his ward, on the shoulder. The man jumped up and swung around as if he meant to strike Mack.

Mack stepped back and held up his hands.

Edmund, big and burly and hardly the type to scare, looked at him apologetically.

"Sorry, Mack. Everyone's on edge today. No grounds passes until further notice."

Mack frowned and wandered over to two men whispering by the game table. One man, a newcomer named Riley, was talking fervently and gesturing with his hands. The second man, a little guy named Travis, with pointed features and a diagnosis of manic disorder, gave Mack a significant look when he approached.

"What's got everyone so hot and bothered?" Mack asked.

"Riley here," Travis forked his thumb at the new guy, "was just telling me there was an escape last night, and a murder."

"Say what?" Mack's stomach dropped, and he thought of Liv.

Riley nodded in big, sweeping motions that sent his long silky hair flinging back and forth dramatically. He was a kid, no more than twenty, but he commanded a room. Ward Six had been abuzz since he'd arrived two days earlier.

He leaned into Mack, elated to share the inside scoop.

"The blonde fox from Ward Five split, man. She escaped!"

Mack shook his head, puzzled.

"The blonde who?"

"Sophia!" Travis told him, as if it were obvious.

Riley did another outlandish nod.

"But that ain't the half of it," Travis cut in. "Tell him."

"Let me take a breath, old-timer," Riley told him, adding an extra-long pause into his story. "They found Kent dead in her room. Murdered!"

Now both men watched Mack in anticipation.

Mack plastered on the appropriate look of dismay, and he was dismayed. He liked Kent, the orderly who generally worked the womens' ward but always had a kind word for everyone. He also knew, without any of the facts, that Sophia didn't kill him, though from the looks on Travis and Riley's faces, the rumor mill was saying otherwise.

"And something else to wet your whistle," Riley added, a conspiratorial gleam in his eye. "I saw Kaiser and his nurse Alice smuggle a woman into the operations corridor last night. They locked her in there."

"What did she look like?" Mack asked, his legs and hands growing jittery.

Riley waved at the top of his head. "Blonde hair all pinned on her head. And she was in a straightjacket! So much for their no-straightjacket policy, huh?"

"Better never put me in a straightjacket," Travis hissed, flexing his tiny fists.

"How do I find her?" Mack asked, surprising Riley and Travis both.

"Oh, she's long gone, brother. She's probably on a bus to Texas," Riley told him.

"That or hidin' in the woods, waitin' to kill the doctors off one by one. Wouldn't that be a trip?" Travis asked. "A crazy woman livin' in those woods."

"Somethin' lives in 'em," Riley grumbled. "Those woods give me some serious vibes, and they ain't the good kind."

Mack shook his head.

"Not Sophia. How do I find the woman in the operations corridor?"

Riley cocked an eyebrow.

"Thinkin' of doin' a little explorin'? They'll throw ya in solitary if they catch you."

"I'll take the risk," Mack insisted.

Riley appraised him with new respect.

"Best to wait until lights out. Edmund can't stay awake to save his life, and he's in the chair that leads to the side stairs. Slip past him and go down two floors. It's all offices in the first hall. Follow that to the end and turn right. Those are the operating rooms."

"How do you know all this?" Mack asked. "You've been here two days."

Riley grinned.

"I've been here three-hundred and forty-four days. But I don't stay for long. Gotta keep movin'. I like to think of this place as my home away from home. I've been getting prodded by these doctors since I was eleven years old. I could escape blind-folded walkin' backwards. But why bother? The food's not so bad."

Travis roared as if Riley had just offered the most hilarious joke he'd ever heard.

Riley winked at Mack, and Mack saw something troubling in the kid's gaze, an emptiness in his hazel eyes.

"Thanks," Mack told him before turning and heading for his room.

~

RILEY HAD BEEN RIGHT; Edmund could barely keep his eyes open once the sun set.

Long shadows from the lights at either end of the corridor provided plenty of cover for Mack as he slipped down the hall to the stairs. He counted the steps as he walked, sensing George Corey in the surrounding space.

He checked each door as he hurried down the operations hallway. He found the third door locked.

"Liv," he called through the door. "Liv, are you in there?"

He felt a puff of cold breath against his ear and spun around.

No one stood behind him, but footsteps sounded from the end of the corridor. Mack ducked into the room across the hall.

A table sat in the center of the room.

As Mack crept closer, his breath caught in his throat. Something large and lumpy lay beneath the white sheet on the steel table.

His hand trembled as he reached out, fearing he'd find Liv beneath the sheet.

He peeled back the cover to find a young man, a dark red burn around his neck, his eyes half-open and staring sightlessly into the void.

Kent did not look peaceful in death. His skin was mottled and yellowing. His tongue, large and gray, poked from the corner of his mouth.

Mack stumbled back, halting when he heard the door to the room opposite him swing open.

He listened to muffled voices and watched through a slit in the door as Dr. Kaiser slipped out. In the room behind him, he glimpsed Liv.

After Kaiser disappeared down the hallway, Mack hurried to Liv's door and dropped to his hands and knees.

"Liv," he whispered. "Liv?"

"I'm here," she said.

"Something happened," Mack told her, relieved at the sound of her voice. "The patient who speaks to the dead escaped.

"It's starting," Liv said.

He had to strain to hear her.

"What do you mean?"

"The wheel of fate, Mack. It started turning when he murdered George. And now he has killed again. He will try for three."

"What do you mean three? Did he kill Kent, the orderly? Who's number three? You?" Mack considered beating the door down. He could do it. A few swift kicks and he'd be inside, but the orderlies and the nurses would come running. They'd be armed with needles and straitjackets and padded rooms. By the time Mack woke up, Liv would likely be dead.

"Yes, and then will come his undoing," Liv told him, "but only if that bone is in the woods. I have to work tonight."

"You're locked in there. How can you possibly do anything? And what do you mean, bone? One of George's bones?"

"Be ready tomorrow, Mack. Tomorrow Stephen Kaiser will try again to take a life."

CHAPTER 34

September 1965
Jesse

A PETITE WOMAN with short curls that clung to her head walked out the door of the little yellow Cape Cod on Palmetto Avenue. She carried a watering can.

Two girls followed, one larger than the other, nearly as tall as her mother with long wavy blond hair. The smaller girl had her mother's curls and small features.

Jesse brushed off his coat and stepped from his car.

The woman looked up as he approached. She offered a hesitant smile.

"Arlene Hester?" he asked.

"Yes?" her voice was as small as her frame, but her eyes were big and bright.

"My name's Jesse Kaminski. I'm trying to find your sister, Liv."

The woman's eyes opened wider, and she dropped the watering can. It clanked on the stone pathway in front of her flowers.

"You know Liv?" she asked.

The older girl picked up the watering can and watched Jesse suspiciously.

"Well, no," he admitted. "Her name came up recently and-"

"Where? Where did her name come up?" the woman asked eagerly.

"I've been looking into buying the Kaiser house, but can't seem to find the woman who owns it, or her son. Someone mentioned that Liv and Stephen Kaiser were close friends."

"For a summer," Arlene murmured. She looked at her older daughter sadly. "Honey, can you take Penny in the house and play?"

"Sure." The older girl took her little sister's hand, and the girl followed without complaint.

"Liv left after that summer. That was twenty years ago," Arlene said, holding the water can tight to her stomach.

"And then what? She moved away, or..."

"Mr. Kaminski, I don't know what happened to my sister. I never saw her again. I never spoke with her again. My mother told us she moved out west. That was it."

Jesse frowned.

"Why did she leave, Mrs. Hester?"

Arlene stared at him.

"I wonder why you'd like to know, sir. Clearly, she won't be able to help you purchase a home in a state she hasn't lived in for two decades."

"I'm a curious man. I apologize for the intrusion."

Jesse turned and started away.

"No, wait," Arlene called.

Jesse turned back.

"I was hurt when she left. I was only seven, but I remember her. I miss her even now. Our mother died three years ago." Arlene picked a wilted pink rose from the bush.

"And your father?" Jesse asked.

Arlene looked away from him, and then into the flower.

"My oldest girl looks like Liv - Melanie. She's tall and strong and has the same wild hair. Interesting, because we'd always believed it came from Liv's father. Maybe it did. And somehow my daughter received it anyway." Arlene laughed and shrugged. "Liv and I did not share a father. Her father was a secret in our family. Even our brothers didn't know she had a different father than them. I mean, everyone knew that I did because my mother's first husband, Mark, died in 1927. But she slept with a man after Mark died. His name was George Corey, and he lived in the Stoneroot Forest. He was Liv's biological father."

Arlene put a startled hand to her mouth as if surprised at all she'd just shared.

"Why was he a secret?"

Arlene plucked one of the wrinkled petals and dropped it to the stone path beneath her.

"I shouldn't be telling you this," she said, glancing back toward her house. My mother…"

"Is gone," Jesse reminded her. "I'm very sorry for your loss, but perhaps I can help you find your sister."

"George was a secret because women did not have sex with strange men when they were newly widowed in those days." She laughed and blushed. "I'd imagine they don't do it now-a-days either, though the world has certainly changed. George was also… a strange man. He lived in a little cabin deep in the woods. He didn't drive a car or use a telephone. He taught Liv about plants and…" She fluttered her fingers, as if she didn't have words for the things George taught Liv.

"If he was a secret, how did you know about him?"

"It wasn't a secret that he existed, but Liv referred to him as an uncle. My mom said that he'd been a close friend of Mark's and he'd taken Liv under his wing. After Liv left, my mom told me the truth. She grieved her missing daughter for many years. She started to go visit George every few months, hoping for word. He would tell her things, though he claimed Liv never communicated with him."

"I don't understand."

Arlene chuckled.

"Neither did I. Or do I, for that matter. George called Liv 'Volva'. He came to America from Norway when he was a young man. In

Norway, he lived on a secluded island and he practiced a kind of witchcraft, I guess." She frowned as she tried to explain. "I can't believe I'm telling you these things. I've never spoken of them to anyone. My mother forbade it. But you're right, she's gone now. George told us that Liv took care of children and lived on the east coast. He never mentioned happiness, but he spoke a lot about purpose and cleansing the past through service. He was a strange man, and most of what he said went over my head. Over my mother's head too, but she found comfort in his reassurances that Liv was okay."

"But you never had evidence from Liv that she was okay?"

"My mother received a few blank postcards over the years – usually on her birthday. Years would lapse between them, and then one day, a postcard with an ocean sunset would arrive. My mom believed they came from Liv."

Jesse nodded.

"Did you know Liv's friend, Stephen Kaiser?"

Arlene nodded.

"Not well, but he saved my life."

"He saved your life?"

"I jumped into the Dead Stream and nearly drowned. He went in after me, though he wasn't much of a swimmer himself. If he hadn't, I wouldn't be here today. The moment I stepped off the bank, the riptide took me. I've never been so scared in my life. I could swim. I loved to swim, but I was no match for that river."

"Do you think Stephen and Liv left together?"

Arlene shook her head.

"My mother asked George the same thing, and he insisted that she did not. He also told my mother to stay away from Stephen Kaiser."

"Why is that?"

"I wish I knew."

"Arlene, could you direct me to George? Maybe he could-" Jesse started.

But she was already shaking her head.

"I never went to his home. He lived in the Stoneroot Forest down near Kalkaska, but that was twenty years ago."

"The Stoneroot Forest," Jesse repeated, committing the name to memory. "Thanks for talking to me, Arlene."

She smiled.

"If you find Liv, tell her Arlene misses her."

He nodded, offered her a salute and walked backwards down her driveway. He spotted the older daughter in the window watching him curiously.

CHAPTER 35

October 30, 1945
Liv

"Boo!"

Liv felt hands on her shoulders and she jumped, sending the leather bag filled with bloodroot to the forest floor.

Stephen stepped in front of her.

"You're back!" she exclaimed, grabbing his hands and nearly jumping up and down with glee.

"Look who's happy to see me." He grinned and knelt, gathering the roots back into her bag. "What are these?" He lifted a root, caked in dirt, and sniffed it.

"Bloodroot. We can use it to treat croup, but it's also poisonous, so don't take a bite."

He dropped the root back into the bag and handed it to her.

"I thought you weren't coming home until tomorrow for Halloween. Didn't you have class today?" she asked.

"I skipped out, jumped on a train this morning. My mother went to Chicago to buy overpriced champagne for the masquerade ball and no doubt visit a friend. She's gone for the night."

The way he said 'friend' revealed Stephen's opinion of his mother's friends.

"A man friend?" Liv asked.

Stephen took Liv's hand.

"It doesn't matter. Come home with me. I have a present for you."

~

STEPHEN LED Liv to the third floor, and then pushed open the door to the attic. They walked up the narrow staircase.

The rafters were low. The room smelled sweet, as if the fine layer of dust that coated the boxes was actually sugar.

As they walked deeper, Liv saw flickering lights. In the back of the attic, Stephen had arranged candles in a circle around a red blanket. A silver tray of chocolate pumpkins sat in the center.

"You know," he told her, picking up a chocolate and handing it to her, "some people call the night before Halloween, Mischief Night. A few guys at school were going out to soap windows and throw eggs. Kid's stuff. I couldn't imagine anyone I'd want to do mischief with more than you."

Liv took the chocolate but couldn't put it in her mouth. Her legs trembled and her stomach did little flips. The candles and the warmth of the room made her dizzy, and she put a hand up to a rafter to steady herself.

"This is for you," he said, sitting on the blanket and putting his hand on a black gift box. A red bow sat in the center.

Liv sank to her knees and pulled the box toward her. She lifted the lid. Nestled in a sheath of tissue paper, she found an olive-colored satin gown. On top of the gown rested a jewel-encrusted mask in the shape of a cat's face.

"I bought it in Detroit," he told her, just over her shoulder now. She felt his breath on her neck, and when she turned, Liv saw the candlelight dancing in his pale eyes.

When he leaned forward, she drew in a breath, but did not pull away.

He kissed her.

His lips were soft, and warm.

She kissed back, yielding into him as he eased her back onto the blanket. Helplessness spiraled her down and down.

She went willingly, thinking of winter nights with George only days before. She had sung in the spirit of Freya, the goddess not only of battle, but also of love.

As she wrapped her arms around Stephen's neck, she imagined the images of Freya in George's books, a woman with wild hair and blazing eyes.

Stephen's kissing grew more urgent, and Liv's own desire grew to a crescendo to meet his. He pulled at her clothes and she shrugged out of her pants, laughing when one foot got stuck. Her fingers shook as she unbuckled his suspenders and then loosened his trousers.

Her thoughts lured her away, wanted to criticize her awkwardness, remind her of the frayed elastic in her panties or her breasts loose beneath her shirt.

"I am here," she whispered.

Stephen paused and gazed at her for a long moment.

"Destiny," he breathed, and then lowered his mouth to hers.

~

LIV SLEPT next to Stephen all night. Curled beneath his satin covers, she felt the achy wetness between her legs.

She had not only kissed a boy that night; she had gone all the way. There were people who would whisper about women who did such things out of wedlock, but Liv had not been raised in such families. George spoke of Viking women as free, their bodies not bound by the close-minded ideas of men. Her own mother had created Liv from a night of grief mingled with yearning.

As Stephen slept beside her, his breath soft and lilting, Liv's mind wandered to the future. What would become of their love? Of this night?

The following night was Halloween, and the Masquerade Ball. They had planned to play their trick on Veronica, inviting her to the party and then handing her the Night Haunts curse.

Suddenly none of it mattered. Not the kids who'd teased Liv, not Veronica and her friends, not the poverty she'd grown up in, not even George and the old ways. Liv wanted only to lie in bed with Stephen forever.

~

SHE WALKED HOME in the chill of early morning. Stephen had kissed her goodbye, his lips warm in the cold October dawn. Icy dew clung to Liv's shoes and the hem of her pants. She held the gift box tucked under one arm.

The night before drove her deep into her thoughts. As she walked, she did not see the trees or the road edge, but only Stephen leaning over her in the firelight.

A longing to return to him sat heavy in her limbs, but a sense of wanting to run lingered there too. Because what would become of their friendship now that they'd crossed that invisible threshold?

Snores filled her ramshackle home when she crept in.

Her mother sat at the kitchen table, already awake for the day at five a.m., sipping her chicory coffee and looking haggard.

When Liv walked in, her mother's eyes widened.

"You're home," she gasped. "I had the most terrible dream that you'd gone away."

She stood and walked to Liv, pulling her close.

"I'm sorry, Mom. I didn't mean to worry you."

Liv's mother didn't speak and did not acknowledge the gift box other than with a flick of her eye. She pulled away from her daughter and studied her. Liv felt as if the night before was plain on her face.

Her mother did not ask.

"There's warm water in the basin. Best wash your face and go to bed."

Liv did as she was told.

When she crawled into bed next to her sister, she watched the rise and fall of the little girl's chest as she breathed. She wanted to curl around her and inhale the scent of her tangled hair.

Instead, she lay in the early light beginning to filter through the window and thought of Stephen.

CHAPTER 36

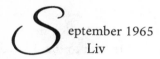

September 1965
Liv

LIV SAT on the stiff white hospital bed. She wrapped a sheet over the bowl Kaiser had delivered her stew in that evening. She'd dumped the meal into her bedpan, knowing if she ate it, she'd be unable to perform the tasks that lay ahead. She cinched the fabric beneath the bowl, knotting and pulling it tight.

She rested the bowl in her lap, closed her eyes and began to lightly drum on the fabric. The sound was soft, muffled, nothing like the drums from her childhood with George, but she knew what mattered most of all when calling in the spirits - a clear intention, a voice so filled with purpose it could cross the barriers between the living and the dead.

Though it was not the spirits of the dead she sought that night, but the spirit of a cat.

She hummed low, and beat her makeshift drum.

Rhythmically she began to rock back and forth. Eyes half-closed, Liv watched the room slide in and out of focus, until finally it slipped away like water cascading over a cliff.

On the fringes of a trance, Liv gazed into the moonlit forest that surrounded Stephen Kaiser's childhood home.

The house filled her with dread, but she slid by the windows, like accusing eyes, and followed the scent of the animal she sought. She found her crouched in a bush, watching a field mouse who shivered in a crevice within the bark of a fallen tree.

"Kǫttr," she called to the cat.

The cat's ears pricked and a shiver ran along her spine. Her silken black fur rose in a sinewy spike from nape to tail.

The spirit of the cat listened, and when Liv moved into the animal, the spirit shifted and made room for her.

They ran through the cold high grass, the wet flicking against her whiskers. Up the porch, a swift, smooth jump carried her to the first eave. They scampered to the highest roof and there beneath an overhang, the cat squirmed into a hole in the abandoned house. On the pads of her hardened feet, she landed in the attic, nudged open the door with her nose and trotted to the floor below.

Stephen's door stood ajar, and the cat slipped inside.

~

Jesse

JESSE SAT in the dark kitchen, hands wrapped around a mug of tea. Overhead, a door creaked. He held the drink tighter, willing the sound away.

He didn't want to follow the sound and see what apparition waited for him upstairs.

When another door creaked, he forced himself out of his chair.

He took the steps two at a time to the third floor, not bothering to hide his presence. If he crept slowly, the fear would have crippled him.

The door to the closet stood open, and a shaft of moonlight lit the open trunk.

A movement startled him and he jumped back, bumping the bedside table. He waited for the hand to reach out.

Instead, a coal-black cat bounded from the trunk.

In its mouth, Jesse saw a small bone.

"No," he muttered, taking a step toward the cat. But he stopped as the cat lifted its gaze to his.

Its eyes were uncannily human. He almost expected the cat to open its mouth and speak.

It didn't, but darted passed him and out the door.

He did not chase it, but followed it into the hallway.

He thought he heard the patter its feet overhead, but couldn't be sure.

When he returned to the room, he gazed at the trunk, guilt-ridden that he hadn't done better to protect the body inside it.

"I've done a lot wrong in my life," he said. "But maybe I can do right by you, Veronica. Maybe I can bring you home to your momma and brother."

He closed the bedroom door and walked down the stairs, calmer than he'd been in days.

He had options. If he called the police, they'd find the body, check the teeth or whatever they did to match her to the missing girl. Veronica's family could bury their daughter in the plot next to her father. It was the right thing to do, but once he'd done that, it was over. His search, the house, his purpose.

He wanted to follow it first, see if he could give them more than the body. Maybe he could give them the killer, too.

He believed Liv was his key, the daughter of the man from the Stoneroot Forest.

If anyone could find her, it was George Corey.

Liv

Liv stayed with the cat as she darted through the forest, leaping over decayed logs and scampering up trees if something rustled close by.

When she reached Spellway Road, Liv urged the cat to slow and wait. The better part of the night had passed and dawn crested the horizon before a pick-up truck headed for Traverse City slid into view. Liv felt the cat's pace quicken as the truck slowed at a stop sign. The cat ran and sprang into the bed of the truck, slithering between two barrels. She laid down, panting, and rested the bone on her forelegs.

Liv pulled her spirit from the animal.

Slowly, as if she drifted on a wave, she rolled back into her own body. The bowl rested beneath her fingers and she slid it aside, reclining on the bed. Though she hadn't so much as taken a step, she was exhausted. Sweat ran along her brow and the rapid beat of the cat's heart seemed to flutter beneath her ribs.

She closed her eyes and willed her body to sleep.

CHAPTER 37

September 1965
Liv

THE DAY PASSED in quiet anticipation.

Liv heard the hospital abuzz with patients and doctors, nurses and orderlies rushing about. She imagined plucking off the roof and watching them scurrying up and down the hallways.

The room contained no windows.

Stephen had left a lamp lit by the door. It cast streaks of light on the white plaster walls.

In the tile floor, she saw a drain and noticed a clump of something dark — hair, she thought, cringing.

When Stephen finally lumbered into the room, Liv knew the sun had set over the dense asylum forest.

Sweat rolled down his face and soaked his collar. His black hair was mussed, his face unshaven, and she smelled him from across the room. It was not merely that he'd skipped his shower that morning. His body knew what his mind refused to accept: he was in danger, fight or flight was at hand. But Stephen forged on, refusing, or perhaps incapable, of knowing when to stop.

"You don't look well, Stephen," Liv murmured, but he seemed not to hear her.

He dug a photo from a leather bag, and then picked up a strait-jacket with his free hand.

"Look," he commanded, thrusting the photo in Liv's face.

Liv gazed at a young woman and two small girls — sisters, she thought, based on their matching Christmas dresses.

"Who are…" but she didn't finish. As she gazed at the girl's mother with her soft blonde curls framing her heart-shaped face, she knew. Arlene. Her own baby sister, now grown into a woman and a mother.

"That's right," Stephen nodded. "Take a good look. You fight me," he held up the straightjacket, "and I'm going for them next, Liv. Understand? You know I'll do it."

Liv pressed her lips together and nodded.

She had not intended to fight him.

His demise would come from within.

~

Mack

Mack slipped from the behind the willow, stealthily avoiding twigs and dried leaves as he crept behind Stephen Kaiser.

Liv had spotted him. He saw her eyes widen slightly.

As Dr. Kaiser fumbled with a wall of brush, she mouthed the words 'not yet' at Mack.

He nodded and hung back, watching curiously as a dark hole opened in the foliage. A secret door lay within the bushes.

As Kaiser pushed Liv, bound by the straightjacket, ahead of him into a dark hallway, Mack sprang to the doorway and shoved a stick in the opening before it closed.

The heavy door slid shut, and for a moment Mack though the stick would snap and Liv would disappear into the darkness. Somehow it held.

Liv

"I THOUGHT I had to keep you alive. All this time," Stephen laughed. "But if you're... if you're gone, Liv. The nightmares will be gone and the voices and the... the..." He stopped, hands braced on the table, breathing hard.

She could see the outline of his ribs through his sweat-stained shirt.

"Shut up," he screamed suddenly, head jerking up as he spun around and flung a hand out as if to grab something that wasn't there.

"Who haunts you, Stephen?"

He continued to gaze feverishly at the emptiness before him, and then he turned and glared at her.

"You," he hissed.

Stephen took a while to gather himself, but soon he bustled around the room, focused. Liv watched him open a plastic crate.

He lifted out the corpse of a large muskrat. The rotted body released a noxious stench, and Liv closed her eyes and looked away.

"The spell called for an otter, but this is close. It's close enough," he mumbled to himself.

He laid the carcass on a wooden table he'd arranged with other things: candles, feathers, a series of stones, and a jar of blood.

"And let's not forget this," he uttered.

He turned to face Liv and lifted the poison ring. She knew he'd taken it. She'd left it for him to find.

"She used to threaten me with this," he said, turning the ring back and forth. The ruby glittered in the firelight. "Open your mouth, she'd scream, and I did it. A hundred times I must have opened my mouth and waited for her to dump the poison in. After a time, I wanted her to. Once, I even dared her." A hollow, angry laugh erupted from him. "She left the room and came back a moment later. Told me again to open my mouth. I did, and she poured the powder in."

Stephen lowered the ring, glaring at it.

"What happened?" Liv asked, unable to forget that long-ago boy she had loved, unable to cut off her pity for the man he'd become.

"It was borax," he whispered. A look of disgust pressed his features ugly, and he licked his lips as if something bitter coated his tongue. "She'd taken the poison out and replaced it with laundry soap. I spit it out, and she slapped me. Told me to clean the carpet where I'd spit. And then I spent two nights in the cellar."

As he spoke, his back curved, his shoulders hunching forward as if trying to protect the heart within his chest. Though it was too late for that now. All the good had gone from him.

As she gazed at Stephen's crude altar, the blood of his animal sacrifice splashed across the rough-hewn wood, she understood his intention. She would be his final sacrifice. He mistakenly believed he'd access the power of the chamber by taking her life.

Sweat rolled down his face as he worked, muttering under his breath, dabbing his fingers into the blood and wiping it across his forehead and then pressing it to his lips.

She watched him with detached awe, and she hardly felt her feet pressed into the cold stone floor or her arms secured to her body by the straightjacket.

The energy in the chamber shifted with Stephen and she thought, yes, it yearned for the sacrifice as well. Whatever the spirit of the place had once been, it had become a mouth hungry for suffering and death.

George had told her of such places, places where ancient people went to satisfy the spirits with sacrificial offerings. Places that later grew overgrown and derelict after the people realized that feeding it only made it hungrier and more powerful.

"Stephen, what happened to George?" she asked.

He intended to kill her. He no longer had to keep his silence.

He blinked down at the altar, lifting a stone and then shaking his head and replacing it. When he looked up, his expression was flat and cold.

"George," he said stretching the syllable out long. "George died. Your precious George," he muttered. "He hated me; you know?"

Liv did know.

"Is that why you killed him?"

"Ha," Stephen laughed and looked at her, incredulous. "I'm not an animal, Liv."

He flipped through a book. It was not one of George's spell books, but Liv could see the symbols within it were surprisingly similar.

"Where did you get that, Stephen?"

"I didn't take it from George," Stephen snapped. "Though if you want the truth, I intended to. I intended to take the stones and the books, all the magic he withheld from me, and you. He kept it from you too, Liv. This," he slapped a bloody palm on the book. "I bought from a man in Iceland. I went there a year ago. I was dreaming these symbols, Liv. Your and George's staves, or whatever you called them. But even after I got the book, I couldn't stop thinking of the hag stones. I needed them. To do this magic, I needed the stones."

"So, you killed George for a pile of stones you could have found on the bank of a river?"

He glared at her and spat on the floor.

He looked at the spit, horrified.

"My tooth," he shrieked, dropping to the ground.

Liv gazed at the clear spittle. There was no tooth.

Stephen picked up a stone and held it out, accusingly.

"You did this! You and your black powder and your black magic!"

He threw the stone across the room and climbed to his feet.

"I went to the Stoneroot Forest and George tricked me. *'Come with me, Stephen. I'll take you to my cabin,'* he said. But he didn't. He led me deeper and deeper into the woods until I was lost, and then he… he disappeared." Stephen clutched his head, as if the thoughts were trying to escape. "He appeared and then disappeared over and over until I didn't know if I was dreaming, imagining him. And then I was holding a knife. I don't even know where it came from, and the next time he appeared, I plunged it into his heart."

Liv listened to the story numbly. George had lured Stephen to the cabin. He'd intended for Stephen to kill him.

"Damn you, George," she mumbled.

Stephen looked up at her sharply.

His eyes watered and ran. He was not crying tears of sadness, but tears of desperation.

He touched a finger to his cheek and howled, rubbing at his cheeks with both hands.

"Blood, there's blood coming from my eyes."

But there was no blood.

In the darkened corridor, Liv saw Mack. He held a large rock in his hand.

He waited until Stephen turned back to the altar.

Liv nodded, and he raced into the room.

Stephen barely had time to straighten when Mack crashed the rock into the back of his head. Stephen went down on his knees and fell forward, thumping against the table and falling to the floor.

Mack stared dumbfounded at the crumpled doctor.

"Release me," she commanded Mack. "Don't worry, I can feel him. He's still alive."

Mack undid her straps.

Liv grabbed the poison ring from the altar and followed Mack down the tunnel.

Around her, the whispers called her back.

Stay, they seemed to say. *Stay for a little while longer.*

She slowed and stopped, bracing a hand against the damp stone wall.

Mack turned.

"What are you doing?" he asked, and then as if seeing something in her face, he grabbed her hand and pulled her forward into the cool night.

Once out of the chamber, her legs seemed to function again. Some of the fog in her mind abated.

"There," Liv exclaimed, pointing at the black cat who stood at the base of the willow, watching them. She took the bone sitting near the cat's paws and slipped the poison ring over it.

Digging quickly, she stuffed the finger and ring into a shallow hole and threw dirt upon it.

"Liv," Mack yelled, and she looked up as Stephen raced from the chamber, a knife clutched in his hand.

Mack dove in front of her, and Liv screamed as the blade sank into his chest.

The cat screeched and jumped onto Stephen's back. He shrieked and tried to wrench it free, but its claws were lodged deep in his shoulder.

"*Volva*," George's voice floated across the forest. The sound had emerged from dark grove of leafy trees.

Liv helped Mack, limping and clutching his bleeding chest, toward the trees.

A thick mist began to rise from the ground. Soon their feet and ankles were obscured, and then their legs.

Liv heard Stephen searching for them, cursing and tearing at the brambles.

They slipped deeper into the woods and soon Stephen's shouts were drowned by the forest.

"My truck's in the parking lot," Mack wheezed gesturing forward.

Somehow they made it to the blue pick-up truck with a partially peeled bumper sticker on the rear fender that read 'I've got Detroit Tiger Fever,' next to a goofy cartoon tiger. Mack struggled into the passenger seat.

"Keys are under the rug," he muttered, gesturing at the floor.

Liv pulled the keys out, stuffed them in the ignition and roared from the parking lot. The truck fishtailed as they turned onto the road that led them away from the asylum. Liv did not have a driver's license.

Mack glanced at her, his face slick and pale.

"You okay?" he mumbled.

Liv gritted her teeth and nodded. She wasn't a good driver. She'd only driven a handful of times in her life mostly with her mother on the rare occasion they borrowed someone's vehicle.

She sped away from Traverse City, knowing the hospital could not save Mack from Stephen's knife. If he were to survive, she had to get him to the Stoneroot Forest.

CHAPTER 38

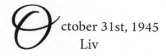

October 31st, 1945
Liv

LIV PAUSED at the edge of the wilderness, breathless as she took in the house blazing in the violet dusk. Light flickered in the windows and poured forth from the first-floor windows and the door that opened to reveal dozens of costumed strangers. People milled on the porch. The sounds of a string band floated a haunted melody across the lawn.

Liv clutched the cat mask and tried to slow her pounding heart.

Her body tingled with the anticipation of seeing Stephen, but also with dread. Had everything changed in a single night? Yes, and she had wanted it to. She had wanted to give herself to Stephen, had been dreaming of such things since that very first day at the river, though the thought only struck her now.

"Freya, come with me," she whispered, gazing at the first stars breaking through the darkening sky.

Liv held up her long skirt and hurried across the grass, following a couple up the wide porch stairs. Music and laughter drifted from the house.

She walked through the door, and the warmth and the scents of roasted meat and sugary confections took her breath away.

A man in a black tuxedo played a violin. Liv could not see his face. A long-nosed black mask with a sloped forehead and budding brows covered it.

Tall candelabras stood in every corner and cast the masked faces in golden light. Every surface held black vases overflowing with purple dahlias.

For several seconds, Liv stood in the threshold of the door, her heart pounding, her feet frozen. When soft, warm fingers grazed her elbow, she startled and cast her eyes up to see a man in a black tuxedo, pale blue eyes sparkling beneath a horned goat mask.

Stephen smiled, a secretive smile, and slipped into a group of people deeper in the foyer.

Liv did not follow him. Instead she lifted a glass of champagne from a tray when a black-clad waiter paused in front of her. The champagne was sweet and bubbly, and giddiness lit her from toes to scalp.

Hidden beneath her mask, Liv drifted into the parlor, where dozens of people stood in silk and satin gowns and black tuxedos - all mysterious in their masks.

Liv saw Stephen's mother standing near the windows, her black hair in ringlets on her head. She wore a sparkling navy dress with a neckline that revealed her voluptuous pale breasts. The top half of her face was hidden beneath a glittering wolf mask.

Near the stairway, Liv saw Stephen watching her.

When she saw him break from the crowd and slip up the stairs, she followed him.

"I've thought of nothing but you all day," he told her, wrapping his hands around her waist and pulling her close. He tasted of champagne and smoke, as if he'd been inhaling the cigars of the men tucked into the parlor downstairs.

"Me too," Liv whispered, inclining her forehead against his.

They stood that way until a girl's voice broke their silence.

"Stephen?"

Liv cringed at the sound of Veronica's voice.

Stephen's eyes lit up mischievously.

"Shh..." He put a finger to Liv's lips and guided her into the shadows.

When Veronica appeared at the top of the stairs, Liv bristled. The girl wore a long, satiny lavender dress sheathed in sparkling chiffon. Her dark curls rose from the purple peacock mask she held coyly over her eyes. She took the mask away and flashed a huge, uncertain smile at Stephen.

"You made it," he said, sweeping into the hallway and twirling Veronica around.

She laughed and put a hand to her neck, as if woozy from his adoration.

Liv glared at her and felt a terrible desire to push the girl down the stairs.

She watched as Stephen took her hand and led her to the third-floor stairwell. As he guided Veronica up the stairs, he glanced back at Liv, stretching out his free hand and beckoning for her to follow.

CHAPTER 39

September 1965
Jesse

Jesse drove down the road that edged the dense woods of the Stoneroot Forest eventually pulling onto the shoulder and turning off the engine.

He didn't know where Corey's cabin was. He could easily spend days scouring the woods and never find it.

"But I'm here now," he reminded himself, tucking his keys into the pocket of his coat and stepping from the car.

He walked through the trees, propping up branches every few feet to mark his passage back out.

As he moved deeper, he heard the crunching of twigs underfoot and ducked behind a wide oak tree. As he gazed into the Stoneroot forest, he saw a dark, cloaked figure dragging something through the woods. Whatever the man carried, it must have been heavy, for he stopped frequently, hunching over.

Jesse slipped out from behind the tree and crept closer.

The hooded figure's head popped up, and Jesse slipped behind another tree.

This time when the figure bent over the object at his feet, Jesse saw that a man lay there. The figure held the man by his arms and dragged him through the dried leaves.

Was he witnessing a murder?

Jesse thought of shouting and running at the cloaked figure to scare him away, but as the figure bent over the man, the hood fell down, revealing wavy blonde hair.

Liv.

Her name was in his mind without warning. He didn't know her and had no reason to suspect it was her, and yet…

"Liv," he said, his voice ringing across the divide between them.

The woman's head shot up, and she dropped the man's arms.

She gazed at him, her brown eyes watchful and alert, like an animal considering if it should run or attack.

He held up his hands.

"I won't hurt you," he said, though the man laying at her feet implied it was she who might hurt him.

"Who are you?" she asked, standing up tall. She was taller than she'd initially appeared, likely only a few inches shorter than his six feet.

"My name's Jesse. I know about you. About George and Arlene and Stephen…"

Liv frowned, looked beyond him as if searching for his accomplice.

"I'm alone," he said.

She lifted something from her chest. Jesse watched as she gazed at him through a small white stone. When she let it drop, it caught on a leather loop around her neck.

"Help me," she said, reaching down for the man's arms.

Jesse hesitated for only a second, and then he ran to where she stood. She was flushed, her breath short and quick, as if she'd pulled the man a long way.

When Jesse looked down at the man, he cringed. A red flower bloomed on the man's chest. The blood was thick, and it pooled in the little hollow of the man's breastbone.

"He's been stabbed. I need to get him to the cabin," she huffed, beginning to drag him.

"George Corey's cabin?" Jesse asked.

Liv paused, a little furrow knotting her brow, and then she nodded.

"Shouldn't he go to a hospital?" Jesse asked, thinking they should be dragging him out of the forest, not into it.

"They can't bring him back," Liv murmured. "He's gone too far into the veil."

~

Liv

When Liv saw George's cabin, she gasped with relief and held tighter to Mack's arms.

"Stay with me, Mack. Stay with me," she murmured. "Get the door," she told Jesse.

Jesse looked at her, confused.

"But there's nothing," he started, before growing silent.

Liv knew he hadn't seen the cabin only seconds before.

He went to the cottage and pushed in the door before returning to Mack.

"Can you lift him?" she asked.

He nodded, though his face drained of color when he looked again at the wound in the man's chest.

Liv hurried into the cabin, her stomach dropping at the dust-coated surfaces, the empty crow's perch, the hearth as cold as a grave. She gathered twigs and leaves, building the fire quickly, breathing huge billows of oxygen into the budding flames as George had taught her so long ago.

Jesse struggled through the doorway with Mack, who was large and heavy and had been unconscious for more than an hour. When he tried to lay him near the fireplace, his arms seemed to give out and he mostly dropped him.

Mack's head hit the wood floor with a thud, and Jesse looked horrified.

"It's okay. He can't feel it," she muttered. She pulled Mack onto the rug and stuffed a straw pillow beneath his head. "I have to stop the bleeding," she murmured.

The fire grew hungry, burning through the sticks and catching hold of the larger logs she'd place on top. The cold in the room backed away.

She stood and handed Jesse a rag. "Put it on the wound and press down. He's already lost too much blood."

As Jesse pressed his hand over the spreading red blur on Mack's chest, Liv went to the little counter. George's cabin was unchanged, the jars of herbs set in their same locations, dried herbs hanging from a string in front of the window, though they'd hung for so long that some had crumbled away and left piles of brown dust on the wood counter below. In the corner of the room she saw George's staff, and her own next to it.

She started to drift back to the day he'd given it to her, immediately swallowed by her shame at having left it — and him — behind.

"I can't find his pulse," Jesse called.

Liv looked up, knowing she'd wasted precious seconds getting caught in the web of memories. Tearing a piece of linen from a swath of fabric George had hung near the water drum, she filled it with ground yarrow. A spicy cabbage smell drifted up from the dried herb as she hurried it across the room.

"Move your hands," she told Jesse, kneeling.

As he slid his hands back, more blood gurgled up from the wound. Liv pushed the sack of yarrow onto Mack's chest. His face looked pale and gaunt, his lips turning blue.

"Hold this," she said, her hands trembling as she pulled them away.

She went to George's bed, trying not to look at the indentation there, the space where his body laid for so many years, and grabbed a drum from the floor.

Jesse looked at her strangely when she returned.

"You're going to play music?"

"I need you to be quiet, okay? Not a word. I don't know if I can do this, but I have to try."

She sat down and started beating her hands against the drum. The motion felt awkward; she could not find a rhythm, and the strangeness tore at her. She wanted to cry, to hang her head and give up, but she couldn't.

Her hands continued their pounding, her mind insisting the spirits had abandoned her, but the room had begun to fade. The crackling fire gave way to another sound: water rushing down a river, carrying away rocks and twigs and sand. The Dead Stream rushed above and below her. Liv struggled against it, the current pushing her lower, holding her captive as she thrashed against the branches snaking around her ankle.

"He's dying." Jesse's voice broke through her dream, and she hurtled across the veil back into the cabin.

Smoke billowed from the fire, as if someone had thrown water over the flames.

Jesse held the yarrow pouch over Mack's wounds, but blood gushed through his fingers, turning his pale hands red.

He looked at Liv desperately, but she could do nothing but watch as the man who had tried to save her faded, his lips opening to release a bubble of blood that popped and trailed down his cheek.

Mack's eyes fluttered open and locked on Liv's.

"Tell Diane…" Mack choked on the words. Another spurt of blood exploded from his mouth and splattered Liv in the face. "Tell Diane I love her."

His eyes closed.

Liv rocked away from him, a sob and snarl combining in her belly and tearing across the silent room. She howled and ripped the hag stone from her chest, flinging it into the smoky hearth.

As she opened her mouth wider, a flood of water rushed in. The river surrounded her once more, pushing, ravaging her. Her hair was pulled and wrenched, forcing her head forward, deeper. She saw the watery green death down there, shadows darting, but then voices from above drew her back. The spirits called, begging that she turn and look into the light.

She twisted around and looked up through the clear, watery void. She expected to see Stephen there, as she must have twenty years before, but it was not his face that peered down.

George's strong hands reached into the river. She felt their fingers intertwine; their palms meet.

George pulled her from the river and held her close. She rocked and sobbed against him.

Further down the stream, a trunk floated, half-open, a dark dress billowing out.

The steady beat of her drum brought her back into the cabin.

When she opened her eyes, fire still blazed in the hearth, and Jesse sat perfectly still, his hands pressed against Mack's wound.

"I think he's waking up," he whispered when he saw Liv watching him.

Liv looked down.

Jesse's hands were clean.

Mack, too, was clear of blood. He had not spit up. He had not died.

Mack blinked, his face contorting with pain.

"Ugh, fuck-all. That bastard stabbed me," he groaned.

Liv's hands slowed, her breath catching.

"Mack?" she whispered.

He turned his head, offered her a weak smile.

"I saw George, Liv. He said you'd come through."

CHAPTER 40

Halloween
October 31, 1945
Liv

SHE STOOD in the doorway watching Stephen and Veronica in his room.

He winked at her.

"I have a gift for you," he told Veronica, carefully holding the curse in his left hand. "But you can't open it until you get home."

Veronica giggled and took the folded present, unaware that she was holding her own yellow scarf wrapped around a curse that would bring her nightmares for months.

"I've been wondering when you were going to ask me out, Stephen Kaiser," she flirted. "Pity you waited until you went off to college."

Liv rolled her eyes, tempted to dash Veronica's fun, but footsteps sounded in the hall behind her.

"What are you doing?" a woman hissed, and Liv recognized the voice of Adele Kaiser.

When Liv turned, Adele stood in the hall, her mask clutched in her hands, her eyes dark and furious.

"Umm… I…" Liv ducked into Stephen's room, barely aware of Veronica's look of surprise.

"Liv!" Stephen laughed, but the sound was cut off as Adele stormed in behind her.

The color drained from Stephen's face.

Veronica looked confused, her eyes shifting to Liv and then to Adele.

"You sneaky, disgusting little bastard," Adele seethed. She lifted an accusatory finger at Stephen, her hand shaking with rage.

Stephen walked to the bureau beside his bed.

No one spoke. The very air seemed sucked from the room.

He reached down, and when his hand emerged, Liv tried to make sense of the leathery thing he clutched.

"I curse you," he spat, lifting a silver candlestick from his table and slamming it into his mother's temple.

His mask had fallen away. In one hand he clutched the flap of cat's skin, the blood writing blurred in the dim light.

His mother's face sagged, and she collapsed to the floor.

Liv stared in frozen horror at the gaping wound, blood pouring down the woman's pale cheek.

Veronica shrieked and fled through the bedroom door.

Liv tried to follow, but Stephen reached out and grabbed her wrist as she turned for the door. His grip felt hot and slick. She could pull her arm away. She had to, but her brain couldn't seem to send the signal.

His mother put a hand to her head. Rings glittered there. The gold poison ring Stephen had told her about came away with a smear of blood. She stared at her pale hand in confusion. A dark red gash lay across the white of her flesh, as if she'd been cut, but it was the blood spilling from her head. She teetered forward, attempted to push out her other hand to catch herself, but her arm nearly splayed to the side as she landed face-down on the wood floor.

Liv wrenched away.

Stephen's bloodless face gazed down. His mother lay unmoving.

Liv pushed open the bedroom door and pounded down the stairs. Her shoes fell off, and she left them, running barefoot into the chilly night.

CHAPTER 41

September 1965
Liv

LIV AND JESSE did not sleep that night. Mack drifted in and out of consciousness, sometimes alert and feverish, laughing and telling stories only to quickly slip into oblivion.

When Liv finished the story of Halloween night, Jesse frowned.

"Adele is in the trunk? Stephen's mother?"

Liv nodded.

He sighed and rested his head heavily against his chair.

"Then what happened to Veronica?"

"I killed Veronica," Liv confessed.

Jesse sat up and scooted to the edge of his chair, shaking his head as if he couldn't believe it.

"You didn't kill her," he said. "You couldn't have, wouldn't have."

Liv's face was pale and gaunt, her brown eyes haunted.

"You don't know me, Jesse. How can you say that?"

He looked at her earnestly.

"Because I know people, Liv. You're not a killer."

"After I left Stephen's house, I was..." Liv put her face in her hands, "gone, like a *draugar*."

"A draugar?" Jesse asked.

"An undead thing. A person who has died, but their body has not. I walked in a trance, and then..." Liv shut her eyes against the memory, but there etched in the darkness was Veronica, in her bloodstained dress. "She screamed at me. *'You're a murderer.'* Her scream was so loud, it shook me to my core." Liv wrapped her arms around herself. "She told me she would tell her father. That I would rot in prison for the rest of my life. I lost it."

She paused and lifted a black feather from the rug, smoothing it across her closed eyes.

"George used to say emotion is a spirit — let it in, and it will possess you. You will do unimaginable things to appease it. That spirit took hold of me, and I flew at her with this rage and grief and fear. She ran away, but I was fast and I knew the woods. And then suddenly she was falling. I realized we'd come upon the Dead Stream. I called out for her, but she'd plunged right over a ledge on the bank of the river and into that icy water."

Liv let the feather go, and it slowly spiraled back to the rug.

"I tried to climb down, but the water was high and it was so dark. I left her, Jesse. I didn't go for help. I should have gotten help." She choked on the words.

"You're right," he murmured. "You should have, but that's then and this is now. You're not a murderer, Liv. You made a mistake."

Liv wiped away her tears.

"I ran home, snuck into my house and packed a bag. I never went back. I fled like a coward."

Jesse moved from his seat and knelt on the floor near Liv's chair.

"My wife and son died. They drowned in a lake. After they were in the ground, I gave up. I didn't want to live. Something in us, something that protects us, I think, tells us to run away. If we stayed, the past would haunt us. We would live there forever, locked in our despair."

~

"WHAT HAPPENS NOW?" Mack asked.

They'd driven Jesse's car to a hospital in Grayling.

"You go inside and ask them to put a fresh bandage on that wound, and get some painkillers," Jesse told him.

"And we're going to go see my sister," Liv added.

"So, what? I'm chopped liver? What if George shows up at my bedside tonight because I left you on your own?" Mack demanded, trying to hide a smile.

"You didn't leave me on my own," Liv assured him, nodding her head at Jesse. "And we'll see you soon. Call Diane."

"Huh?" He gave her a questioning look.

"Diane," Jesse repeated. "You were mumbling her name all night. When you weren't snoring, that is."

Mack laughed and hung his head.

"I think I'll do that."

~

WHEN THEY PARKED in front of Arlene's house, Liv saw her sister in an upstairs window. She was brushing her daughter's long blonde hair. The girl tilted her head back, smiling.

"I can take a walk," Jesse told her. "Give you a minute to gather yourself?"

She smiled at the man beside her and shook her head.

"I've had twenty years to gather myself."

She stepped from the car and made it halfway up the driveway when Arlene's face was suddenly pressed close to the second-floor window. Moments later, she burst through her front door.

"Livvy," Arlene shouted, not bothering with formalities. She rushed into Liv's arms as if she were still a scrawny seven-year-old greeting her big sister at the schoolhouse.

"Peanut," Liv murmured, dissolving into her sister's arms. They hugged until Arlene's daughters walked onto the lawn, their curios eyes studying Liv.

Arlene pulled away, her cheeks red and wet.

"Girls, come here," she called. "I want you to meet your aunt, Liv."

~

AFTER THREE HOURS, crying and talking with Arlene, Liv and Jesse drove to the Northern Michigan Asylum for the Insane.

They emerged from the long drive that wound through the trees. The asylum loomed over the sloping lawns.

"I've heard of this place, but..." Jesse released a low whistle.

"Yeah, it's something," Liv whispered under her breath.

"What if he sees you?" Jesse coasted the car to a halt and glanced at Liv.

"He won't. I'm out of his reach now." If Jesse had insisted she explain, she would have been unable. But he didn't.

They watched people clad in white shuffling between the buildings.

Beneath a maple tree, the leaves beginning to spot gold, Liv watched a group of children play Ring Around the Rosie. They danced in a circle and then fell into a heap on the ground.

Jesse watched them as well, grief-stricken.

He glanced at her and their eyes met, and she understood. Not all of what had propelled Jesse Kaminski to walk away from his life, but enough.

When she turned back to the asylum, she saw Stephen.

He stood outside the largest building, the one topped with sharp points, staring up at it as if he couldn't figure out how to get inside.

"That's him," Liv said, pointing.

Jesse leaned forward in his seat, squinting.

"He looks fine," Jesse murmured.

"He's not," Liv told him.

She handed Jesse a hag stone from George's little bag.

Jesse lifted it and recoiled, dropping the stones.

"He's black! He looked dead, like a charred skeleton."

Liv nodded.

"He may have years left to live, but the darkness has taken him."

~

Two Weeks Later

Liv

"Norway? Are you two sure about this?" Mack asked.

Liv, Jesse and Mack stood on the deck at the train station in Traverse City. She'd bought a trunk, and she and Jesse had put their combined meager belongings inside.

Liv nodded, watching smoke puff from the stack as the long passenger train pulled into the station. A deafening whistle split the morning quiet.

"I've been waiting to take this trip my entire life," she said. She touched the hag stone hanging around her neck.

"And you?" Mack shifted his gaze to Jesse.

Jesse studied Mack for a moment before reaching into his coat and extracting a photograph.

"This is Nell and Gabriel. My wife and son, who drowned last year. My life, our life," he nodded at the photo, "ended with them. There's a new life waiting for me across the Atlantic."

Mack rocked back on his heels.

"Couple of beauties right there," Mack said, looking at the photo.

Liv had already seen the photograph. Her heart ached for her new friend, but she knew his path had been brought to her for reasons that reason could not explain.

Jesse returned the picture to his pocket and reached into the leather briefcase he'd bought the day before.

He took out several sealed envelopes.

"This one is for the police," Jesse told Mack, pressing the envelope into the man's enormous hands. "It tells them where to find the body of Adele Kaiser, and also who killed her. They might not take our word for it, but hopefully they can manage to put the pieces together." He took out a second envelope.

"Tony Medawar," Mack read out loud.

"He's the brother of Veronica, the girl who drowned in the Dead Stream. Liv wrote the story of the night she died — leaving out her name, of course. Hopefully it brings them some peace."

Mack slapped the envelopes against his hand.

"I hope they nail that bastard," he mumbled, taking a hand gingerly to the wound hidden beneath his shirt.

Liv didn't respond. It had already ended for Stephen. A torment far worse than prison awaited him.

"All aboard," the conductor yelled.

The wave of people shifted forward on the platform.

Liv hugged Mack goodbye. As he pulled away, she slid one of George's hag stones into his palm.

"Thank you, Mack," she whispered.

EPILOGUE

Five Years Later
Norway

Liv

LIV LOOKED up from the rocky mountainside. Far below, frothy waves crashed against the shore. A boat was moored there.

"Mack," she murmured, walking down the rocks slowly.

Mack grinned, his bristly red beard revealing two rows of huge white teeth. He picked Liv up and spun her around. Liv laughed and clapped him on the back.

Behind Mack stood a petite woman with black hair tucked beneath a sky-blue knit cap.

"Diane," Liv said, taking the woman's gloved hands in her own.

"I've heard so much about you," Diane said. "Your hands must be freezing."

Liv glanced at her bare hands, red and chapped from foraging without gloves.

She shook her head.

"I don't even notice it anymore. Apparently, I was made for this place. My body knows how to handle it."

"And this is George," Mack announced, grabbing a small boy who'd run up behind him, his cheeks rosy and his hair as red and wild as his father's.

Liv's eyes lit up at the sight of the boy. He would be big like his father, but he had his mother's dark eyes.

"Daddy says you're magic!" George breathed, stepping to Liv and reaching for the hag stone dangling around her neck. "Daddy has one of these too."

Liv knelt and watched George lift the stone, pulling her close so he could peer through it, and then dropping it when he spotted a fuzzy white mountain goat on an outcropping of rocks. He took off up the hill.

"Slow down, George," Diane called hurrying after him.

"Where's Jesse?" Mack asked, gazing up the mountain at the scattering of cabins.

"He's with Ingrid, our daughter."

Mack's mouth dropped open.

"A daughter. You and Jesse?"

Liv smiled.

"Yes, a gift from the Gods. Come meet her."

They picked their way up the rocky hillside.

Liv pushed into a warm little cabin. The walls hung with woven rugs to block out the chill from the ocean. Jesse sat in a rocking chair, Ingrid in his lap. They read from a storybook, *The Marsh King's Daughter*.

"Modir," the little girl called, holding out her chubby pink arms.

Liv leaned down and kissed Jesse's cheek before lifting the girl and holding her out to Mack.

"Mack," Jesse smiled, standing and giving the man a one-armed hug. "You made it."

"And quite the journey, too," Mack grinned. "Diane, George, come here," he called out the cabin door. He reached into his bag and drew out a paper. "I thought you might want to see this." Mack handed Liv a copy of a newspaper from Gaylord, Michigan.

"Highly esteemed psychiatrist arrested for the murder of his mother and a local girl who vanished twenty years ago," Liv read out loud.

"They arrested him?" Jesse asked.

"Last year. It took them a while to build their case, but they got him," Mack explained.

"I don't understand," Liv said. "Why would they name Veronica as well?"

"They found her in the cellar, Liv, with a noose around her neck — or what was left of her, I guess," Mack told her.

"But she drowned," Liv muttered, the memory still a regular visitor on restless nights.

Mack shook his head.

"Doesn't look that way."

Liv shuddered, realizing Stephen must have followed her that night. Had he pulled Veronica from the river, only to take her back to his house and murder her?

She'd never know.

Liv studied the grainy photograph of Stephen, a constriction holding her heart hostage for a moment.

"After Stephen went nuts, getting a story out of him was difficult. He's not going to trial," Mack continued. "He's already been institutionalized. He's been deemed incompetent to stand trial, but he's locked up. It's over."

Liv walked to the door and stepped out. The cold wind rushed in from the sea and swirled up around her, lifting her hair.

For a moment, she saw George standing on an outcropping of rock, a little smile on his lips. He tilted his head toward her, and then he was gone.

READ MORE BY J.R. ERICKSON

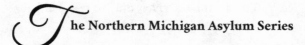

The Northern Michigan Asylum Series

- Some Can See
- Calling Back the Dead
- Ashes Beneath Her
- Dead Stream Curse

The Born of Shadows Series

- Ula
- Sorcière
- Kanti
- Sky Mothers
- Snake Island

ACKNOWLEDGMENTS

Endless gratitude to everyone who helped bring this book to life. Special thanks to my family and friends who support me on this journey. Thank you to my editor Sonya Bateman, to my cover designer Rena Hoberman, to my amazing beta and advanced readers. Thank you to the lovers of spooky fiction who keep this series going.

ABOUT THE AUTHOR

J.R. Erickson, also known as Jacki Riegle, writes stories that weave together the threads of fantasy and reality. She is the author of the Northern Michigan Asylum Series as well the urban fantasy series: Born of Shadows.

These days, Jacki passes her time in the Traverse City area with her excavator husband, her wild little boy, and her three kitties: Floki, Beast and Mamoo.

To find out more about J.R. Erickson, visit her website at www.jr-ericksonauthor.com.

Printed in the USA
CPSIA information can be obtained
at www.ICGtesting.com
LVHW042036181024
794197LV00002B/225

9 781734 302844